FRIENDS & FOES

This Large Print Book carries the
Seal of Approval of N.A.V.H.

FRIENDS & FOES

ReShonda Tate Billingsley
and
Victoria Christopher Murray

THORNDIKE PRESS
A part of Gale, Cengage Learning

GALE
CENGAGE Learning·

Detroit • New York • San Francisco • New Haven, Conn • Waterville, Maine • London

GALE
CENGAGE Learning

LIBRARY OF CONGRESS CATALOGING-IN-PUBLICATION DATA

Billingsley, ReShonda Tate.
    Friends & foes / by ReShonda Tate Billingsley and Victoria Christopher Murray. — Large Print edition.
        pages cm. — (Thorndike Press Large Print African-American)
    ISBN-13: 978-1-4104-5808-7 (hardcover)
    ISBN-10: 1-4104-5808-3 (hardcover)
    1. African Americans—Fiction. 2. Murder—Investigation—Fiction. 3. Large type books. I. Murray, Victoria Christopher. II. Title. III. Title: Friends and foes.
PS3602.I445F75 2013
813'.6—dc23   2013002447

Published in 2013 by arrangement with Gallery Books, a division of Simon & Schuster, Inc.

Printed in Mexico
3 4 5 6 7 17 16 15 14 13

A NOTE FROM RESHONDA

It's amazing that when I sat down to read over this book — months after we turned it in — I found myself going, "Okay, who wrote that? Me or Victoria?" That's how seamless this story was to me. When you lose track of your own writing, you know you're writing a cohesive story.

I always tease Victoria that she's the writing yin to my yang. But I think it's because we both are committed to bringing the reader the best story ever. Plus, I know Jasmine, just like she knows Rachel. So when we're writing, we just let the characters take over. Sometimes that means Jasmine will one-up Rachel (not often, but every now and then ☺) . . . and other times Rachel will come out on top. I have to say it again: This is the most fun I've ever had writing a book. It also challenged me creatively. I'm not sure if readers know, but I don't change one single word that Victoria writes. She doesn't change any of mine. She writes a chapter, sends it to me, I feed off it to craft my own . . . and so it goes. It's a talent, I know, but your girl's got skills! (That was such a Rachel comment, wasn't it?)

I've said all that to say a big thanks to my writing partner for helping me step up my game to bring the readers what I hope will be yet another enjoyable story.

There are so many other people I have to thank as well who have made the entire literary journey possible — my family (my ever-supportive husband and my three wonderful children), my mom, my sister, extended family and friends, my sister circle, my colleagues, and all of the book clubs, libraries, and readers. And to my agent, editor, publicist, and everyone else at Simon & Schuster/Gallery Books — a thousand thanks! To Reina King and Regina King: We did it! Thank you for your commitment to giving Rachel life on the screen. To Crystal Garrett, Shelby Stone, Queen Latifah, Shakim Compere and Flava Unit, Roger Bobb and your crew, everyone at BET, and the fabulous cast and crew of *Let the Church Say Amen*. I could go on and on thanking all of you who worked so hard to make my movie dream come true. I can't wait for the world to see it!

That's it for now. I didn't call names, so I should be safe in the I-can't-believe-you-left-me-out argument! Until next time, enjoy!

Join me on Twitter @ReShondaT and on Facebook

A NOTE FROM VICTORIA

I have procrastinated enough. I have to write this note and I can't come up with any more excuses not to do this. So, I guess I'll get started. It's not that I don't want to thank everyone. My heart is filled with gratitude because I could never do what I do without the help of so many. It's just that I know because I'm a woman of a certain age, I'll forget someone, and that brings along a whole lot of drama. (Sometimes, even more drama than Jasmine and Rachel can conjure up.) So since I prefer my drama on the pages of my novels, I'll just say a short prayer and then get to typing. . . .

First, once again, I have to say how much fun I had writing this novel with ReShonda. She keeps me laughing and on my toes writing because I have to work so hard to save poor Rachel from every kind of situation. I love writing with ReShonda, and I wish this blessing of a great friendship and partnership on everyone.

I have been part of the Simon & Schuster team since 2004, and for a couple of those years I've had the opportunity to work with the team at Gallery Books. And this has been another great experience. Thank you, Brigitte Smith, for believing in this partnership and for being our champion. Looking forward to a few more stories with Rachel and Jasmine. Melissa Gramstad, you have worked so hard on our tour. Thank you so much for that.

And of course, what can we say about our readers? TeamJasmine or TeamRachel, it doesn't matter. You have been in our corner. Thank each and every one of you for always being excited about what we do.

Finally, I have to end where this all begins for me. I feel so blessed that God uses my fingers to do this. I would never be able to write a word without Him. The stories, the discipline, the inspiration all comes from Him and I'm so grateful to God for this gift, this life.

Before she was First Lady Jasmine Cox Larson Bush, before she had children, before she met Hosea, Jasmine was . . . *Scandalous.* This is the story of Jasmine

before *Temptation* and how Jasmine became Jasmine. In ebook format — $4.99

Join me on Twitter @VictoriaECM and on Facebook — Fans of Victoria Christopher Murray

CHAPTER ONE

God has a great sense of humor.

Rachel Jackson Adams could remember her mother's words as if she'd just uttered them yesterday. When Rachel was growing up, it was one of the sayings Loretta Jackson loved most.

Well, God must be some kind of comedian because this had to be the biggest joke of all.

"Why are you sitting there with your mouth wide open?"

Rachel jumped at the sound of Lester's voice. She'd been so engrossed in the email she'd just read, she hadn't even heard her husband come in the house.

Rachel didn't bother to speak as she shook her head in disbelief. "This is unbelievable," she muttered, more to herself than to him as she leaned back in the leather office chair.

Lester set down his briefcase, walked over, and kissed his wife on the head. "What's unbelievable? Macy's is having a going-out-of-business sale? Dillard's is closing early?" he joked.

The evil eye she flashed at him wiped the smile right off his face. After nine years of marriage, Lester knew when his wife was about to lose it and she was definitely on the verge right now.

"Okay, babe, what's going on? You look like you're about to explode," Lester asked, all traces of laughter gone.

"I am," Rachel snapped. She spun her laptop around to face him. "Look at this mess."

Lester peered at the screen. "Okay, it's an email."

"No kidding." She jabbed a manicured nail at the screen. "It's an email from Yvette."

"Who is Yvette?"

She huffed and rolled her eyes. "Good grief, Lester, the publicist for the American Baptist Coalition. You know, the woman we hired."

"Okay, calm down," Lester said as he continued reading. "I just didn't immediately realize who you were talking about." When he got to the end of the email, a huge grin spread across Lester's face. "That is phenomenal."

Rachel popped her husband upside the back of his head.

"Wow, what did you do that for?"

"What do you mean, it's phenomenal?"

He looked at her, confused. "*Oprah* isn't phenomenal?" She didn't answer, just kept glaring at him like he'd done something wrong. "Sweetheart, I don't understand," he continued. "The American Baptist Coalition is about to be represented on *Oprah* and you're upset about that?"

"You doggone right, I'm upset," Rachel said, slamming the laptop shut. "Why in the world is *she* going on *Oprah*?"

"Lady Jasmine?" he asked, still bewildered.

"Her name ain't no damn *Lady* Jasmine!" Rachel yelled. "I told you to stop calling her that. Call her *Shady* Jasmine, Jas, Jazzy, shoot, call her Pepper Pulaski after the name she used to use when she was a stripper for all I care, but stop calling her that like she's some type of royalty!"

Lester took a deep breath, trying to stay calm in order to keep her calm. "Okay, let's back up because I really don't understand your anger."

Her husband really and truly could work her nerves sometimes. He could be so naïve. Granted, over the years he'd gotten a little

15

backbone and since he'd become a popular preacher, his confidence had soared. It had gone to even new heights when he'd won the election for the presidency of the American Baptist Coalition six months ago. That had been a brutal fight — not between Lester and the man he was running against, Pastor Hosea Bush, but between Rachel and Pastor Bush's wife, Jasmine. Things had gotten downright ugly between the two of them, but at the end of the day, Rachel had emerged victorious. Just like she knew she would.

And for the first four months, Rachel had been the shining star of the ABC. She'd increased their visibility, convinced them to hire the publicist, streamlined some of their programs, introduced a few others, and had worked around the clock to make the ABC even more powerful than it already was.

So why in the world was *Jasmine* the one going on *Oprah*?

"*I'm* the first lady of the American Baptist Coalition," Rachel slowly said. "If O is gonna be talking to anybody, she needs to be talking to *me.*"

Lester pointed at the email. "But Yvette said Jasmine will be talking about the new community center she's starting, Jacqueline's Hope."

"I don't care what she's talking about. It's. *Oprah.* The only person that should be talking to Oprah on behalf of the ABC is me! I'm in the driver's seat. Jasmine is back in the bed of the pickup truck. So why is it that every time I turn around, Jasmine don't-nobody-wanna-say-all-them-dang-last-names is getting all the attention?"

That brought a small smile to Lester's face. "Bush. Her name is Jasmine Bush." He chuckled. "As if you didn't know."

Rachel waved him off. "She's been married thirty times so I can't keep up. Why are you taking up for her, anyway?" The disdain Rachel held for Jasmine was no secret. The bourgie, over-the-top troll had caused her enough headaches to last a lifetime.

"Rachel, you get your fair share of press, too," he said, soothingly. "You just did a TV appearance last week."

"Yeah, on Fox 26 News. That's local. I'm a global type of woman and I'm resigned to local press? That's unacceptable."

"Oh, you're global now." He laughed.

Rachel stood, her hands plastered on her hips. Sure, this type of thing didn't used to be her forte, particularly since she had been a reluctant first lady. But after some rough patches, she'd come to like the power that came along with being an esteemed first

17

lady. "Lester Eugene Adams, I don't see anything funny."

He immediately wiped the smile off his face. "Sweetheart," he said gently, "this really is good news."

Rachel relaxed a bit, even though her anger didn't subside. "Why is she always trying to steal my thunder? We won this election fair and square, yet she has been the bane of my existence for the past few months. She thinks because she has Moses' mama on her side, she can just take over."

Lester sighed. "You promised to stop talking about Mae Frances like that."

Rachel didn't even want to get into a debate with Lester about that crazy old woman who walked around in a matted full-length mink coat that she probably got at an estate sale in 1967. The Bushes claimed that Mae Frances was just a family friend, but something about that old woman turned Rachel's stomach.

"Lester, I don't care about that old hag — or Mae Frances," Rachel quipped.

"I thought you and Jasmine were getting along," Lester replied.

"No, Jasmine recognized that she lost the election fair and square. And I thought not hearing from her for four months meant that she was gracious in defeat. But she was just plotting to see how she could steal my shine."

After the election, Jasmine had all but disappeared — thankfully. She'd hadn't even bothered to reply to the email Rachel sent asking if Jasmine wanted to be her assistant. Then last month, out of the blue, she'd sent the board a press release talking about the center she was opening in honor of her little girl who'd been kidnapped. As a mother, Rachel could sympathize with not knowing where your child was. But they'd found the little girl, and still Jasmine milked sympathy every chance she could.

Rachel felt disrespected because Jasmine hadn't even bothered to talk to her about the center. Then, she'd gone over Rachel's head and contacted the ABC ladies' auxiliary about hosting a fund-raiser. Now, she thought she was about to give the ultimate disrespect and go on *Oprah*? By herself? Oh, hell no. Not if Rachel had anything to say about it!

"You do realize this is not the first time they've done something like this," Rachel replied. "Do I need to remind you of the article about Hosea on Essence.com last week?"

"That was about his TV show getting syndicated."

"And did they or did they not mention his role in the ABC? Yet, they didn't bother to mention *your* name, Mr. President, at all."

"Honey, this isn't about me. Or you. This is about the ABC. One of the things we promised to do was bring more positive coverage. I think it's wonderful that Jasmine is helping us do that."

He stepped toward her and tried to take her hand. Rachel snatched it away. Sometimes she wished she could jump into her husband's body and take it over. He could be so doggone passive-aggressive. But that was okay, she thought to herself. That's why he had her. Because she was anything but passive.

"Fine, Lester. I'm going to start dinner. My dad will be back with the kids any minute now."

Lester grabbed her hand and stopped her. "Are you good?"

"I'm great," she said, feigning a smile. Rachel left the room and instead of going right into their oversized kitchen, she went left, up the spiral staircase and into her bedroom. She grabbed her purse, pulled her credit card out of her wallet, and snatched her cell phone off the nightstand. She punched in the number she knew by heart.

"United Airlines, may I help you?" the voice said.

"Yes . . . I need a ticket to Chicago . . ." Rachel smiled as she leaned back against her headboard. She thought Jasmine had learned that she wasn't the one to be played with, but it looked like ol' Jazzy needed to be reminded of that. So, let the games begin!

CHAPTER TWO

Jasmine swung her bare legs out of the Escalade SUV and right away, she felt the sting of the October air. New York may have been setting record temperatures with an Indian summer heat wave, but it was clear that Chicago knew what was up. The chill of the Windy City reminded everyone that it was closer to winter than summer, and even though Jasmine stood in the indoor parking lot of Harpo Studios, that reminder made her tug on the collar of her leather coat, wrapping it a bit more snugly around her neck.

"Are you ready for this?" Yvette Holloway, the PR representative for the American Baptist Coalition, whispered as she jumped out of the SUV behind Jasmine.

Jasmine couldn't hide her grin from the woman who was responsible for getting her this gig on *Oprah.* Yvette may have been hired by Lester and the board of the ABC, but from the moment she came on, Jasmine felt as if the public relations guru had been working for her.

It had started three months ago when, at Lester's suggestion, Yvette had flown to New York to meet the runner-up. According to Lester, he may have won the election to become president of the ABC, but he was sure that there was much the esteemed Pastor Hosea Bush could bring to the Coalition. He wanted Yvette to spend a little time with Pastor and First Lady Bush to see how the two might be able to assist in the organization's growth.

After sitting down with Jasmine and Hosea for three days, Yvette agreed that indeed, the Bushes had much to offer. During lunch on Yvette's final day in town, she'd confided in Jasmine.

"Can I tell you something?" Yvette had asked when Hosea had stepped away from their table in the five-star restaurant of the Four Seasons hotel.

"Sure."

"I've had a great time with you and Pastor."

"We've enjoyed you, too."

After a moment, Yvette had inhaled, then said, "I have a lot of contacts, but up till this point, I haven't really taken the ABC onto the national stage."

Jasmine shrugged. "From what you've told us, I think you've been doing a great job so far."

"Thank you." She paused. "I hope you won't think I'm conceited, but I'm capable of doing a whole lot more. I can get the ABC all over television; I have contacts that will get us on major network shows."

"If you can get them on TV," Jasmine had chuckled, "do it."

"I can, and I will, but . . . I'm not quite sure *how* to do it." When Jasmine frowned, Yvette gently placed her fork on her plate, and looked straight at Jasmine. "There are lots of things I have to consider."

"Like?"

Yvette didn't even blink when she said, "Like are the right people in front of the camera?"

It only took Jasmine a second to figure out the sentiment behind Yvette's words.

"Oh!" Jasmine had said. "The *right* people, the *best* people."

"Exactly!" Yvette exclaimed, surprised and relieved that she didn't have to put it all the way out there for Jasmine to understand. "I'd actually thought about calling Cecelia and asking her to step in."

"Cecelia?"

"Cecelia King."

"You know her?" Jasmine had asked, her forehead creased with a deep frown.

"Yeah." Yvette had shrugged as if it was no big deal.

Jasmine had shaken her head, patted Yvette on the hand, and told her not to worry. "You don't have to call Cecelia. She and her husband may be de facto members of the board, but technically, she's not part of the ABC anymore." Jasmine hadn't bothered to mention that she couldn't stand that woman. She really wanted to warn Yvette to stay away from anyone in the King family. But all Jasmine said was, "No worries at all. Hosea and I will be available for any appearances for you — television or otherwise."

With a loud exhale, Yvette said, "I hope you don't think I'm unprofessional. I really like Rachel. . . ."

Stop lyin'. But aloud, Jasmine only said, "You're just doing your job; you need someone who's articulate, someone who's knowledgeable about not only the Coalition, but about world events, as well. Rachel cannot be the face of the ABC. You can't put a trollop on TV and expect anyone to let you come back. You'll lose all your credibility and contacts that way."

Jasmine almost laughed now as she re-membered the pure shock on Yvette's face when she'd referred to Rachel as a trollop.

But it was true and Yvette knew it. Jasmine wasn't talking about the girl's looks; Rachel was attractive in a Flava-Flav-reality-show-contestant sort of way. But that was where her assets ended. There was no telling what Rachel would do if she was on camera. She wasn't intelligent enough to speak coherently. She had no poise, no class, it was a wonder she was even able to handle her responsibilities as a wife and a mother, though if those ghetto-brats she was raising were any indication of her skills, Jasmine needed to help the county find those children a new home.

So since Rachel was clearly not the one, it was Jasmine's pleasure to save the Coalition.

And save the Coalition she did. From that point, Yvette had set up all kinds of appearances for her and Hosea: on the local morning talk shows and even a segment on *Good Morning America*. But what was about to go down now — sitting down with Lady O — was on a whole other level.

Rachel and Lester may have been the first couple of the American Baptist Coalition, but she and Hosea were clearly the king and queen, and royalty always trumped peasants.

"Jasmine, are you okay?"

Her eyelids fluttered, bringing her back to the present. Jasmine had to take a quick look around the parking lot to remind herself where she was. "Yes," she said to Yvette. "I'm more than ready for this."

Before Yvette could respond, a freckle-faced woman who was more round than curvy rushed to the car.

"I'm so sorry, Mrs. Bush," she said, sounding as if she was out of breath. "I'm Jane, one of Oprah's producers. I should've been here to meet you."

"That's all right," Jasmine said, smiling. In the past, she would've had a major problem waiting for anyone. But this was *Oprah;* if she'd been left outside in the garage for an hour, it would've been all right with her.

Jane shook hands with Yvette, then led the two women into the building. "Will there be anyone else joining you?" she asked.

"No." Jasmine shook her head. "It's just me and Yvette."

"Actually," Yvette interrupted, "we will have two other people joining us. Pastor Earl Griffith and Cecelia King should be here any moment. They'll probably be coming together."

Jasmine spun her head around so quickly, she was sure she'd end up with whiplash. Why in the world were they coming?

"Great!" Jane said before Jasmine could ask a question. "I'll have someone on the lookout for them, but in the meantime, we're so excited to have you here." Jane chatted as she led Jasmine and Yvette down a hallway lined with photographs of the famous and infamous who'd spent an hour or two with Oprah on her couch. Oprah and John Travolta. Oprah and Will Smith. Oprah and Julia Roberts. Jasmine shuddered as she imagined the new picture that would be gracing this wall soon — Jasmine and Oprah!

Jane's high-pitched tone knocked through Jasmine's thoughts. "When we told Oprah your story, she cried."

"Really?"

"Uh-huh. To have your little girl kidnapped like that and then to turn it into something so positive. We're excited about what you're doing with Jacqueline's Hope. This was just the kind of project Oprah was looking for when she had her Angel Network and that's why she wanted you to be a part of her final season."

There weren't too many times when Jasmine was rendered speechless, but she couldn't think of a thing to say. The fact that her name had been part of Oprah's conversation took every thought out of her head and every word out of her mouth.

"Okay, here we are," Jane said as she stopped. "Please make yourself comfortable."

The moment Jasmine took the first step into the greenroom, she sank into the plushness of the salmon-colored carpet. The room seemed like it had been set up for a small celebration, with a spread of bagels, fruit, and yogurt laid out on a lace cloth–covered table against one wall. There were seven carafes with a variety of juices and a coffee machine next to that.

The rest of the room was all mirrors, reflecting the whitewashed furniture that looked like each piece had been designed just for this space. This may have been where many of the guests waited for the start of the show, but the room could have been a featured layout in *Architectural Digest*.

Jane glanced at her watch. "We have an hour before we go live. You did remember that today is a live show, right?"

"Yes," Jasmine and Yvette said together.

"Great, because that means we have to start right on time. We'll send the makeup

29

artist in here in just a bit, okay?"

Jasmine and Yvette nodded.

"This is so wonderful," Jane said with such cheer that Jasmine was sure she was about to break out in a song and dance. "If you need anything," Jane continued, "just let me know. No matter what it is."

"We will."

"I'm going to let Oprah know that you're here."

"Will Mrs. Bush be meeting Oprah before the show?" Yvette asked.

"No. She's read up on everything and is very well prepared. But she likes to meet her guests at the same time as the audience. Is that okay?"

"Definitely," Jasmine and Yvette said together.

When Jane left them alone, Jasmine wanted to jump up and down and do a happy-dance. But that was just the kind of thing that Rachel would do, so she certainly couldn't do that in front of Yvette.

"Isn't this something?" Yvette asked, spinning around slowly, taking in all four corners of the greenroom.

I guess she's as impressed as I am. "Yeah."

"Listen," Yvette said as she grabbed a banana from the table. "I have to make a few calls before the show."

"Wait, before you go, I have a question."

"Sure. What's up?"

"Cecelia King and Pastor Griffith — why are they coming?"

"Oh." Yvette waved her hand as if it was no big deal. "You know how Oprah likes to do things. She wanted me to invite a few other people from the Coalition."

"Well, I can understand Pastor Griffith," Jasmine said, almost gritting her teeth as she said that man's name. "But I told you before, Cecelia is not part of the Coalition."

Yvette's eyes darkened as the smile fell from her face. "Let me handle my business, Jasmine."

Jasmine stepped back, crossed her arms and let her eyes roam over Yvette from top to bottom and then back up again. Who did this young girl think she was talking to? And what was up with her defense of Cecelia King?

"Look," Yvette said, softening her eyes and stance as if she wanted to squelch the conflict before it got started. "I know what I'm doing. Mrs. King and Pastor Griffith are just in the audience; you are the star."

The star. Well, at least Yvette had that part right. Up to now, she had always allowed Jasmine to be the star. And when Jasmine thought about it, it made sense that Pastor

31

Griffith was invited since he lived in Chicago, and reluctantly she admitted that even Cecelia might be able to add a little something to the show.

"All right," Jasmine said. "I just want to make sure that we do everything right for not only the Coalition, but for Jacqueline's Hope, too."

"I promise you this will work," Yvette said. And then she chuckled. "Pastor Griffith being here is strategic. When those women get a look at that fine man, they'll be throwing money *your* way for *your* center."

Jasmine had to take a deep breath. Yvette was telling the stone-cold truth. Pastor Griffith was a looker, but with all she knew about him, she didn't want him, nor his poison, nor his money anywhere near her, Hosea, and Jacqueline's Hope.

"So, are we cool?" Yvette said.

It took Jasmine a second to respond as she wondered what Yvette would think if she knew what was really going on with Pastor Griffith. "Yeah," Jasmine replied. Maybe one day, she'd sit down with Yvette and school her on the truth behind that crooked pastor. But for now, Jasmine would just let this play out. Like Yvette said, she was the star.

Yvette's cell vibrated and when she

glanced down at the screen, she frowned. "Look, I really have to take this call," she said before she rushed out of the room.

Jasmine stared at the door for a moment and played over the conversation she'd just had. Then she inhaled deeply before she exhaled slowly. "Calm down," she whispered to herself. There was no need to get worked up before her big moment. The truth of it all was she was about to go onstage with Oprah to talk about the charity that was dearest to her heart.

As she took another glance around the room, Jasmine's lips slowly curled into a grin. She was actually in Chicago, at Harpo Studios, in the greenroom, about to meet the Queen herself.

Jasmine kicked up her heels and did a happy-dance. She swung her arms in the air, then broke into a little jig that looked something like the old-school running man. She didn't stop until her knees began to ache and then she fell onto the sofa that perfectly matched the carpet.

"I cannot believe this." Jasmine laughed. "Rachel Adams, eat your heart out!"

While Jasmine was absolutely thrilled to be meeting Oprah, part of the satisfaction was that she was doing this and Rachel was not.

When Jasmine and Rachel had been forced to work together during the presidential election for the Coalition, Jasmine had actually almost, just a little bit, kinda started to care for the girl. Yes, she wasn't very bright, but it wasn't her fault that she was country and ghetto. That had to be a hard load to carry. At one point, Jasmine had thought that she might even help Rachel, be her mentor, give her some class through osmosis.

But then, she'd received that email from Rachel just a week after the election. Even now, Jasmine seethed every time she remembered what Rachel had written:

Jasmine: Thank you and Hosea for being gracious in your loss and my victory. I want to offer you the position of being my executive assistant. Please call me so that we can discuss your salary. Best wishes and sincerely, Rachel Adams, First Lady, American Baptist Coalition.

Jasmine had read the email again; surely, there was something missing. Maybe Rachel knew another Jasmine who was married to a man named Hosea, because that mud-duck could not have seriously sent her that ridiculous request.

Jasmine had grabbed her iPad and before she had her keyboard in hand, she already knew exactly what she was going to say to remind Rachel Jackson Adams of her place and put her right back in it. That fool needed to know that her broke-down husband hadn't even won the ABC election. She needed to understand that Jasmine had rigged the vote because she didn't want Hosea caught up with a major drug cartel. And Jasmine wanted to tell Rachel that she hoped Rachel and Lester would be very happy in their matching jail cells when what was truly going on in the Coalition finally came to light.

But though she'd written it, of course she didn't send it. She wanted to, but there was no way she could let Pastor Griffith (who worked double duty as one of the leaders of the American Baptist Coalition *and* of the drug cartel) know that she was aware of his business dealings.

So Jasmine just deleted the email, never responded to Rachel, and had kept her mouth closed and her family safe. She ignored the fact that Rachel even existed and turned her focus to building Jacqueline's Hope. By doing that, she would be putting herself and Hosea in the position to take over the Coalition once the dealings of Pastor Griffith and his band of bandits with the ABC were exposed. According to Jasmine's best friend, Mae Frances, that was going to happen soon and if all of her prayers were answered, she'd get to see Rachel on national TV being dragged away in handcuffs.

Jasmine pushed herself off the sofa and grabbed her cell phone from her purse. She didn't need to concern herself with Rachel at all; that child was nothing more than a bookmark, holding Jasmine's place until God was ready for the Bushes to take over.

She pressed the speed dial number on her cell and smiled the moment Hosea answered the phone.

"What's up, darlin'?"

"I'm here!" she shouted, then lowered her voice. "You will never guess where I am."

Hosea chuckled. "You just said, 'I'm here,' so I'm guessing you're at the studio."

"Not just the studio, Hosea. I'm in the greenroom that is set up just for me!" Jasmine strolled as she spoke, taking in every inch of the room that was large enough to hold a small party. "You should see this place, babe. Nothing but class."

"Well, it is *Oprah.*"

"Yup, *Oprah.* I'm actually going to be on *Oprah,*" she screeched. "Remember to set the DVR."

"Already done."

"Are you getting ready to head over to the church?" Jasmine asked.

"Yup! I spoke to Pops just a few minutes ago and he said the sanctuary was filling up so much, he was gonna need to send someone out there to save me a seat."

He laughed, and Jasmine laughed with him. She was filled with glee. She was about to be even bigger than she already was as the first lady of City of Lights at Riverside Church. Probably all ten thousand members would come out this morning to watch the live satellite feed that was going to be set up on several large screens in the sanctuary.

"I wish you were here with me, babe," Jasmine said.

"Me, too, but you know how much I've wanted to get Michael Vick on my show and this afternoon is the time that Mae Frances arranged."

Jasmine shook her head. "You know you need to be paying her, right? With all the people she's hooked you up with for the show."

Hosea laughed, but Jasmine didn't. Mae Frances knew everyone — black and white, young and old. Forget about six degrees of separation. All you needed was Mae Frances's number and she would hook you up.

Jasmine said, "I still wish you were here."

"Well, you tell Oprah I said hey," he joked as if he and the talk-show star were friends. "Tell her to save a seat on her couch for me for next time."

"Oh, I'm sure she will. After today, she'll definitely want me back; we'll probably end up being great friends."

"Gayle King, watch out." Hosea laughed again and Jasmine wondered what did he find so funny? Becoming good friends with Oprah was part of her plan.

A knock on the door stopped her from explaining that to her husband, and a young woman with long, auburn braids that hung down her back peeked in. "Mrs. Bush, I'm here to do your makeup. Is that okay?"

Jasmine nodded and waved for the woman to enter. "Babe, I gotta go," she whispered. "I gotta get ready for my close-up."

"Okay, I love you, darlin'. Have a great time."

She clicked off her phone, then turned to the young African-American woman.

The girl introduced herself, "I'm Cherise," and then she motioned for Jasmine to sit in the chair in front of the mirror. "This won't take long at all," she said. "You're already fabulous." She smiled.

"Well, I want to look better than fabulous,

so see what you can do."

Cherise giggled. "All right!"

Jasmine leaned back in the chair, closed her eyes, and imagined what life was going to be like now — now that Oprah was about to become her best friend.

Oh yeah, Rachel could have the position of first lady of the ABC — for now. Jasmine was about to be far bigger than that.

CHAPTER THREE

Ahhh, the wonders of the Wonderbra. Rachel smiled as she adjusted her now 38 DDs, compliments of the most fabulous bra in the world. She hadn't known for sure if the bra would come in handy, but she'd worn it just in case. And judging by the sight of the overweight, six-foot-four security guard salivating at the mouth, she'd made the right choice.

Rachel cleared her throat.

"I'm s-sorry," the guard stuttered, his eyes drifting back up to Rachel's face. He adjusted his shirt, trying to loosen the buttons that seemed to be screaming for release, then fumbled with his clipboard. "Wh-what did you say your name was?"

"Jasmine. Jasmine Bush," Rachel said with an innocent smile. She knew she looked stunning in a royal blue wrap dress that accentuated her size eight frame. The bra had the twins sitting at attention and she'd allowed the slit in the dress to fall slightly, just enough to provide a peek at her thigh as she sat back in the driver's seat of the rental car.

The guard studied the clipboard, a perplexed expression crossing his face. "But we show you've already checked in."

Rachel stuck out her bottom lip in a sexy, playful pout as she toyed with her honey-brown curls. "Now how in the world would that be possible when I'm here?"

"I'm sorry," he replied, flustered. "Do you have ID?"

"I don't," Rachel said casually and began digging in her purse. This part, she had already worked out. "I actually just flew in and lost my license at the airport. I do have some literature. This is what I'm coming on the show to talk about." She handed the guard a flyer on the Jacqueline's Hope foundation she'd printed. "I know it's not what you need, but seriously, do I look like a terrorist?" She leaned forward seductively, making sure her cleavage was in full view.

The guard smiled, then licked his lips as his eyes wandered back down to her chest. "Hardly," he muttered, his voice coarse. He caught himself, cleared his throat.

"Look, what's your name, handsome?" Rachel purred.

"It's Eugene, Mrs. Bush."

She wiggled her ring finger, which was minus the three-carat rock she normally sported. "It's *Miss* Bush, Eugene."

His eyes lit up.

"You see my name on the list, so obviously I'm supposed to be here. Why don't you just call Miss Winfrey and confirm? I'm sure she's not doing anything."

The guard looked horrified at the thought of disturbing his boss with something like this.

"At least let me call and let them know you're coming."

Rachel leaned back and threw up her arms. "Fine. I just really need to get inside. I'm already late."

He smiled apologetically, then picked up the phone. "Hey, it's Eugene down at the gate. I have a Jasmine Bush here. She says she's supposed to be on the show today." He paused. "Okay . . ."

Rachel's heart raced as he stood silently. This plan had to work, because she didn't have a backup plan — short of bum-rushing the set. She relaxed when Eugene grinned and said, "Thanks a lot. I'll send her up."

He hung up the phone and handed the papers back to her. "All right, Miss Bush, you're all set. They said they were waiting on another person. You can park over there," he said, pointing to his left.

Rachel took the papers, allowing her fingers to linger to show her appreciation. She had no idea who they were waiting on and didn't care. She just wanted to get inside as fast as she could. "Thank you so much. This is my fault for being late and not getting here with the rest of my team."

The man seemed mesmerized, then shook himself out of his trance. "Well, they're aware of you at the back door, so you should be fine."

He stole one last glimpse of her chest and Rachel gave him a finger wave as she drove off. She wanted to squeal with delight as she drove into the parking lot and parked the rental car. She'd considered getting a car service, but she didn't want a witness to everything that could possibly go down. Besides, she might have to make a quick getaway.

Rachel parked, then took a slow stroll up the walkway. She kept her cool, flashing a smile at the female guard who buzzed the door to let her in.

"Do you want me to call the producer down to escort you in?" the guard asked once Rachel was inside.

"No, I'm late," Rachel said. "Can you just

point me to the greenroom? That's where they told me to go."

Rachel was hoping the woman wouldn't question her any further. She breathed a sigh of relief when the guard said, "Okay, go down this hallway, make a left, and you'll see the greenroom."

"Thanks a bunch," Rachel said, ecstatic that her plan was coming together. These folks could keep underestimating her if they wanted, but Rachel Jackson Adams knew how to get what she wanted, and how to stay poised, confident, and in control to get it.

Rachel made her way around the corner and had just reached to open the door when she heard a voice say, "May I help you?"

"Yes," Rachel said, panic setting in. She couldn't get kicked out, she just couldn't. Rachel slowly turned around, bracing herself for the worst. But the woman stopping her looked a little young, with stringy blond hair and too-small glasses; not the least bit threatening. Rachel relaxed and said, "Yes, I'm scheduled to be on today's show and the security guard told me to go into the greenroom."

"Well, you definitely don't want to go in there." The young girl laughed. "That's the archive room and the lock is broken. That door closes and you're stuck. It's sound-proof, too, so you could be forever trying to get out of there."

Rachel raised an eyebrow in shock. "Well, I definitely don't need to go in there."

The young woman smiled warmly. "You want that door, the last one on the right," the woman said, pointing down the hall.

"Thank you so much," Rachel replied. "Are you a producer?"

"I wish," the woman said wistfully. "I'm an intern. Just delivering some scripts to the studio." She held up a stack of papers.

"Well, I'm on today talking about Jacqueline's Hope."

"Okay, if you'll just wait in the greenroom someone from hair and makeup will be in shortly to get you." The young woman scurried off.

Rachel had no idea how she would finagle her way from here. Truthfully, she hadn't even been sure she'd be able to get in, so she hadn't thought much further than that. The one thing she did know? Jasmine wouldn't cause a scene in Harpo Studios and Rachel would take advantage of that fact and calmly sit her behind right down next to Jasmine on Oprah's couch.

She made her way down the hallway, taking in the hundreds of celebrity photos that lined the wall. Oprah and Will. Oprah and Julia. Oprah and Danny. Oprah and Michelle. A small smile crept up as Rachel envisioned her picture up there this time next year. Yeah, the season was ending but she'd heard Oprah was going to keep the studio for OWN, her new network. Rachel's picture would be the perfect addition.

Rachel shook herself out of her daydream and proceeded to the greenroom. She eased the door open, half expecting to see Jasmine poised up, sipping a latte as she waited for her national debut. But the room was empty. Rachel paused to take in the beauty of the room. Just being here gave her goose bumps.

Rachel heard a toilet flush, then glanced up just as the door to the restroom opened.

"What the — ?" Jasmine said, losing her smile when she saw Rachel. "What in the world are you doing here?"

Rachel immediately went on the offensive. She didn't know how Jasmine would react so she had to be prepared for anything. "You didn't possibly think that the American Baptist Coalition would be represented on *Oprah* and *you'd* be the one doing the honors?"

Jasmine took a step toward her. "*I* didn't think anything. I can't help it if I'm the one

Oprah wanted to talk to."

"Well, Oprah will just be talking to us both," Rachel said matter-of-factly. Rachel would never admit it, but her run-ins with Jasmine had proven the old hag was a formidable opponent. Still, Rachel had to remind Jasmine that she wasn't one to be played.

"That's ridiculous. I'm going to get Yvette." She pushed Rachel aside and stormed toward the door.

Maybe Rachel had pegged Jasmine wrong. Maybe she *would* start a scene in Harpo Studios.

Think, think, think.

"Look," Rachel said, moving to block Jasmine from leaving, "I'm not trying to cause any drama. As the first lady, I am above that now."

Jasmine snickered as she folded her arms across her chest. "Oh, so you're above kidnapping kids now?"

"Why you always gotta be bringing up old stuff?" Rachel snapped. Jasmine would never get over Rachel's "borrowing" her daughter for a play date. Just because Rachel didn't tell anyone, Jasmine wanted to say she'd tried to kidnap the little girl. "Besides, I didn't kidnap your daughter," Rachel continued. She caught herself and lowered her voice. "But I will admit I did some dirty things to win the election, and you have to admit you did, too."

Jasmine raised an eyebrow like she didn't have to admit anything.

"Well, I'm a different woman now," Rachel continued with an air. "And my point is, there's room at the top for us both. I think Jacqueline's Hope is a fantastic idea and I am all for it getting the attention and accolades that it deserves. But it is an extension of the American Baptist Coalition, for which *I* am the spokesperson." She tried to keep all trace of arrogance out of her voice. She wanted to get through to Jasmine, and copping an attitude was not the way to do it.

"It's not my fault that they asked for me to come on the show," Jasmine said.

She had a point there and Rachel made herself a mental note to remind Yvette who she really worked for.

"Look, I'm not here to steal your shine," Rachel continued. "I've done enough media on my own."

"Oh yeah, you did do that local access cable show," Jasmine said with a snicker.

It took everything in Rachel's power to ignore Jasmine's condescending tone.

"Well, of course there is nothing bigger

48

than *Oprah,*" Rachel said. "That's why I feel like we need to maximize this opportunity at exposure. Think about it — Jacqueline's Hope will get the attention it deserves and I will get to talk to Oprah about the overall goals of the ABC."

"That's not what the show is about," Jasmine protested. "It's about organizations making a difference. And besides, how do you think you're just going to bogart your way onto Oprah's show?"

"You of all people know what underestimating me can lead to. I know you think I'm some hick-town diva —"

"Umm, I don't know that *diva* is a word I'd use to describe you," Jasmine interrupted.

Rachel had to inhale. She'd tried so hard to leave her over-the-top ghetto ways behind her. And she'd done a pretty good job, until she met Jasmine. Jasmine made her revert back to the conniving, backstabbing woman that she once was. Since she'd taken over as first lady, Rachel had hoped that those ways were gone for good, but Jasmine was determined to make her take a detour with the devil once more.

Rachel released a frustrated sigh. "Jasmine, look, I know you don't particularly care for me."

"Well, that's the understatement of the decade."

"Trust, the feeling is mutual." Rachel glared at her, all niceness gone. Finally, she managed a smile. "But again, the ABC is bigger than the both of us. We just need to learn to work together. Oprah is huge; think about what she can do for the Coalition. Now, Lester is inclined to only do one term as president." Rachel was lying through her teeth but she'd say whatever she needed to. Lester was going to ride that presidency for as long as term limits would allow. "It's natural that Hosea would take his spot, continue the legacy that he's building."

Jasmine let out a laugh. "Hosea doesn't need to continue to build on anyone's legacy!"

"All I'm saying is Lester is laying a foundation upon which Hosea can come later and build. I just want us to find a way to work together for the betterment of the ABC."

Jasmine looked on pensively as if she were weighing Rachel's words.

"Okay, fine," Jasmine said. "But Yvette is the one that set this all up, so we need to talk to her. We don't need to mess up her contact. I'll go get her."

Rachel suddenly felt a flash of panic as

Jasmine walked out of the room. What if Yvette did start trippin'? What if she was adamant that Jasmine do this appearance alone? No, Rachel couldn't risk that.

Think, think, think.

"I saw Yvette go in there," Rachel said, pointing to the large door at the end of the hall.

Jasmine headed down the hall, then swung the door open. "Yvette . . . ?" She stopped in the doorway. "What is this?" she said, looking around the small room.

"Happy reading!" Rachel said, as she pushed Jasmine into the room and pulled the door shut. Rachel smiled at her quick thinking. She hated that she had to resort to such junior high antics, but hey, this was *Oprah* they were talking about. All was fair in love and *Oprah.*

"Hi, I was looking for you!"

Rachel turned toward the high-pitched voice. It was the intern.

"They sent me to find you. We gotta get you into hair and makeup because Miss Winfrey is almost ready for you."

"And I am ready for Miss Winfrey." Rachel smiled, brushed her dress down, held her head high, then followed the intern so she could go get beautiful for her national debut.

CHAPTER FOUR

Jasmine's knuckles were aching, so she switched to the palm of her hand. She banged against the door — one, two, three, four, five more times.

"Help!" she shouted again, though the urgency that had been in her voice just minutes before was replaced by hopelessness now. "Help, please!" This time, her words were barely a whisper.

Breathless, Jasmine twisted around and leaned against the door. It was time to give up the screaming and the banging. Her throat was already sore and now the palm of her hand was red and tender from beating against the solid steel. She couldn't use any more energy that way — after all, she was about to make her appearance onstage with Oprah. She couldn't show up looking beat up.

Jasmine glanced down at her watch. "Oh, God!" she moaned. It was 8:37. In twenty-three minutes, the show was going to start — live. If she wasn't out there, what would they do?

Her eyes widened. If she wasn't there . . . and they had to do a show . . . would Oprah invite . . . Rachel . . . in place of her?

That thought made Jasmine spin around and rattle the doorknob once again. She'd rather have Cecelia King on that stage than Rachel. But she knew Rachel would be the one who would take her place.

She shook the knob again. Nothing. She banged on the door one more time, only now, she imagined that her fist was knocking Rachel right dead in the middle of her chicken-nose face for pulling this *Sesame Street* stunt. Who did this kind of thing? It was ridiculous. It was childish. And it was going to work if she didn't get out of here.

She banged and yelled until she was out of breath once again, then stepped back and imagined that the door was Rachel's head. Going for the goal, she swung her foot like she was on the U.S. soccer team.

"Damn!" she yelped, and hopped across the room on one foot. Now, she was really pissed. She'd probably broken her Louboutins and her big toe at the same time. Her toe throbbed, but she couldn't afford to focus on that. Time was passing; she only had a few minutes to get out of there.

Think, Jasmine, think!

Taking a deep breath, Jasmine's eyes slowly scoped the room. This was nothing like the plush greenroom where she'd been waiting. This room was smaller and filled with nothing but shelves stacked high with rows and rows of videotapes and five-drawer file cabinets pushed against the walls.

Limping over to one of the cabinets, Jasmine glanced at the label on the outside — *Transcripts.* This had to be some kind of archive room. Which explained the steel door. Which explained why no one heard her. And, as she glanced around, which explained why there were no windows.

Think, Jasmine, think!

How was she supposed to get out of here? She stood in the center of the room and did a slow turn, taking in every inch . . . there had to be a telephone somewhere. But there was nothing.

The throbbing in her toe had risen through her body and was now in her head, too. Her thoughts had gone beyond the show. How long would it be before someone found her in here? Suppose no one came for hours, for days? She could die in here.

Thoughts of death took her right back to Rachel. She was going to free the earth of that vermin and kill her for real this time. That wasn't a threat, this was a promise. She'd done it before . . . not by her own hands. But she'd had someone murdered. It wasn't something she was proud of, it wasn't something that she ever thought about. But Rachel brought out the witch in her and if that's what Rachel wanted, that's what Rachel was going to get.

Rachel was going to die.

But first, she had to get out of this windowless, steel-door, soundproof, broken-lock room.

Maybe she could find some kind of letter opener, or a pair of scissors. Then she could pick the lock and once she was free, the scissors would serve double duty: She'd use them to stab that scarecrow right in her heart.

Jasmine paused. She couldn't use up all of her energy thinking about Rachel and her timely death. No, if she did that, she wouldn't be able to hear God. That was something that Hosea and her father-in-law had taught her. There was no way God could bring blessings if you held malice and unforgiveness in your heart.

So she took a breath, leaned against the door, closed her eyes, and prayed for God to take away thoughts of Rachel's death —

at least for now. Next, she prayed for salvation from this situation.

God, please. I don't know what this is all about, but You know my heart. This is about Jacqueline's Hope and all I want to do is give missing children a chance. Being on Oprah, *that's our best chance. Well,* Oprah *and You — I don't want You to think that I'm leaving You out. So please, God. Please show me how to get out of here.*

Exhaling, Jasmine opened her eyes and on the wall right across from her was . . . a smoke detector.

She stood there for a moment, staring at the device and slowly her eyes widened.

Amen!

One last glance at her watch told her that she only had four minutes.

Jasmine kicked off her pumps, then dragged one of the chairs to the file cabinet that was under the smoke detector. She hiked up her skirt and as she climbed from the chair to the cabinet, she prayed that this was just like the device she had at home. Slowly, she stood on top of the cabinet, balanced herself, then reached for the smoke detector.

She had to stand on her toes (even her throbbing one) and stretch, but she reached the cap and twisted. Like the one at home, the cap snapped off and there was the test button.

Jasmine closed her eyes, said another quick prayer, then pressed the red button. The blast startled her at first, but she held the button down. Something would happen now for sure. Something just had to happen.

She held the button, not letting go, for what felt like the longest minutes. But there was still nothing. No people, no sound, no rescue, nothing. Her arm ached from stretching so far above her head and now every one of her toes pulsated with pain. She was dying to just give up, but she'd lived her whole life knowing that one day she was going to be on *Oprah.* She had to keep going.

One minute passed, two, then three.

And then . . .

The door opened.

"In here," she heard a man shout. "The alarm keyboard said that it's coming from in here."

Still, Jasmine held on to the test button until the uniformed man stepped inside, looked up, and said, "What the heck?"

It must've been his shock that held him in place when Jasmine finally released the button and climbed down from the cabinet.

"Thank you," she said. "I was locked in here."

When she jumped from the cabinet to the chair, it wobbled and the security guard rushed to her side. "What were you doing in here?"

"It's a long story." Jasmine slipped on her left shoe, then stuffed her throbbing toe into the right one. It took her a moment to stand up straight, adjust her jacket, and continue. "But I don't have time to explain. I'm the guest on Oprah's show this morning," Jasmine said, hoping that the security guard would rush her onto the stage. "I have to get into the studio."

The guard shook his head. "That's not going to happen. We've cleared the building because of the alarm. Everyone is outside; Oprah, the audience, her guests . . ."

What guests? Rachel?

"What are they doing outside?"

"The fire —"

"But there is no fire."

"Doesn't matter. According to our regulations, we have to clear the building at the first sound of any alarm."

"I set off the alarm."

He shook his head. "We didn't know that before. Gotta follow the rules for insurance purposes." The guard tucked his hand beneath her elbow. "I'm sorry, Miss, but I've got to escort you outside."

Jasmine hobbled beside him, wondering exactly how she was going to fix this. But then, she calmed her brain down. Everything was going to be all right. She'd been rescued and the smoke alarm had even stopped the show. At least now, she wouldn't have to bum-rush the stage and be in the middle of some hot Negro mess in front of a live studio audience.

All she had to do was go outside, find Oprah, let her know that she was here and ready to go. And then that moot Rachel would be stuck on the sidelines, behind the curtain, which is exactly where she belonged.

"Okay, Miss, just go through here," the security guard said as he pushed the door open.

Before she stepped out, Jasmine raised her eyes to the sky and said a quick prayer thanking God for letting everything work out after all.

The sun was almost blinding as Jasmine's eyes adjusted to her freedom. She squinted and did a quick scan of the mass of women who stood packed together in what looked like a huge parking lot. For some reason,

Jasmine felt as if she'd been here before — and then it hit her. This was the parking lot where Oprah had given away all those cars, all those years ago.

Limping, Jasmine roamed through the crowd of what felt like thousands, but really was probably just a couple hundred.

And there, in the front, in the middle of the masses was the Queen.

Trying to straighten up and walk right, Jasmine smoothed down her jacket and staggered over to Oprah.

"Oh, my God, Jasmine! Where have you been?"

Her eyes had been so single-focused that Jasmine didn't even notice Yvette standing to one side of Oprah. Then, right next to Yvette . . . Cecelia King.

Jasmine frowned. Was Cecelia the guest that the security guard had mentioned? But before she had a chance to answer her own question, her eyes zeroed in on the woman who stood closest to Oprah . . . Rachel About-to-Be-Roadkill Adams.

Rachel whipped around and Jasmine could see the blood draining from that vampire's face. Her lips looked like they were cemented together as Yvette continued.

"Rachel said that you had left." Yvette began explaining the lie Rachel had told.

"That you had an emergency at home and had called her to fill in for you."

All this time, Jasmine had really liked Yvette. But right now, she wanted to slap the fool upside her head for even repeating that stupid story. How was she going to call Rachel to cover for her when Rachel was supposed to be in Houston? No wonder no one had come to look for her. Yvette couldn't have two working brain cells if she'd listened to Rachel's lie for even two seconds.

But Jasmine had no time to deal with that mud-duck, or the idiot that she and her husband had hired as a publicist. Jasmine would take care of both of them after the show. Right now, she had one mission.

She held out her hand even before she was in front of Oprah. "Miss Winfrey, I'm Jasmine Cox Larson Bush, your guest for your show this morning."

Oprah frowned as she looked from Rachel to Jasmine. "I also heard that you had left for an emergency."

"No, I've actually been locked inside your archive room."

"What were you doing in there?" Oprah's eyes were as big as Yvette's, but when Jasmine glanced at Rachel, her eyes were cast down as if she was looking for something on the ground.

"I was pushed in there by this heifer," she said, pointing to Rachel.

For the first time, Rachel stood up straight. "Who you calling a heifer?"

"What?" Oprah's eyes blinked rapidly.

"I was pushed in there, locked in there by her." She thumbed her finger in Rachel's direction. "She actually thought she could take my place on your show."

"I don't know what she's talking about," Rachel said, sucking her teeth.

Jasmine's eyes were full of fury. "You know exactly what I'm talking about, you low-life trick, and you need to —"

"Girl, I will cut your old-troll face right here."

"Really? You think you can do that?" Jasmine said, forgetting where she was.

"Watch me, you sleazy ho!"

"Bring it, you country slut!" Jasmine said, one second away from tearing her diamonds out of her ears so that she could drop-kick this slug, right here, right now.

The crowd pressed closer into a cluster around them, their eyes on a performance that no one coming to *Oprah* expected, but one that might be just as good as anything inside the studio.

"Uh . . . uh, ladies." Oprah held her hands

62

up and glanced from one to the other. "I am not Jerry Springer. What is going on?"

Oprah's voice saved Jasmine from a felony murder charge and she had to blink a couple of times to pull herself back from the edge. *Dang!* she thought as she took in the staring eyes around her. She really was in the middle of some Negro mess.

As she looked around, it was Cecelia's eyes that stopped her. Cecelia's eyes told the whole story — that Jasmine and Rachel were back to their old ways, both unfit to represent the ABC.

Behind Cecelia stood Pastor Griffith, wearing his own look of disgust.

She cleared her throat, ignored them all, and turned to Oprah.

"I'm really sorry about that, Miss Winfrey. It was just that I was so upset by what happened. But it doesn't matter..I'm here now and ready to do the show."

Oprah folded her arms. "Well, there's not gonna be a show today."

"What do you mean?"

"There's no time for us to do it."

"Why not?" Jasmine said, feeling her opportunity slipping away. "We can go in there right now."

"Not until the fire department has inspected the entire building."

"But there is no fire!"

As if Jasmine hadn't spoken, Oprah said, "By the time they do all of that, I'll be out of here. I have to be on a plane to Los Angeles for an event I have to do tonight."

"That's why I'm saying let's go in there now, because *I* set off the alarm. You can just call the fire department and tell them that."

Oprah looked at Jasmine, then at Rachel, as if she was trying to decide which one of the two had any sense. After a moment, she turned to Yvette.

"For the first time in twenty-five years, I will miss doing a live show. Do you realize that?"

"Miss Winfrey, I'm so sorry." Yvette had to raise her voice above the sirens that blared, announcing the approach of the fire trucks.

Oprah turned back to Jasmine and Rachel. "I have you two . . . women to thank for messing up my record." Before any of them could say another word, Oprah stomped toward the gate, clearly more interested in talking to the firemen than to the two nutcases behind her.

Jasmine watched Oprah move farther and farther away, before she hissed to Yvette, "You've got to do something. Set it up for

64

tomorrow . . . or later in the week. I'll stay in Chicago."

It was Yvette's turn to look at Jasmine as if she didn't have any working brain cells. "You must not get what just happened here. Do you really think she's going to let any of us anywhere near her stage?" Yvette's eyes darted between the two. "You and Rachel have ruined everything for everybody; do you know what it took for me to make this connection? This. Is. *Oprah!*"

"But she —" Jasmine and Rachel spoke at the same time as they pointed at each other.

Yvette held up her hand, stopping them. "I don't even want to hear it." She stared down Rachel first, but then Jasmine was shocked when Yvette turned her glare of rage to her.

"Look, I was the one who was pushed into a room with no way out. Don't look at me like that. It was this bi—"

"Neither one of you need to say a word right now," Yvette said, stopping Jasmine from cursing and setting it off again. "Both of you need to get your butts out of here so that I can try to smooth it over with Oprah." Jasmine was hopeful until Yvette added, "Not for you, for my other clients!" Shaking her head, she added, "I need to figure this all out with Pastor Griffith."

Then she stomped away, too, just like Oprah had, leaving Jasmine and Rachel standing in the middle of a crowd of women hopeful that some more Negro mess was about to jump off, because if they couldn't get into *Oprah* today, at least they'd have front-row seats to this drama.

CHAPTER FIVE

Everything inside Rachel wanted to sock Jasmine in her left eye. The chance of a lifetime had just slipped through their hands — all because Jasmine had to come raise a scene. And to think, she's the one always acting like she's the epitome of class. Class-*less* was more like it. What kind of woman would start a fight in front of the richest woman in entertainment?

Rachel glared at the woman standing eye-to-eye in front of her. Jasmine was so close she could see the dried Botox in the crevices under her eyes.

"This is all your fault," Jasmine hissed.

"Let me tell you something," Rachel began. Just then, out the corner of her eye, she saw a young woman giggling as she held up her iPhone, pointing it directly at them, no doubt hoping to catch some kind of fight on camera. A fight that would be uploaded to Facebook and YouTube before they made it out of the parking lot.

Seeing that brought Rachel back to reality. As much as she wanted to stomp this troll, she was above that. She'd left her gutter ways behind and she couldn't let Jasmine take her there again.

Suddenly, Rachel heard a voice she'd come to despise in the six months Lester had been at the helm of the ABC. She groaned as Rev. Earl Griffith approached them. His brow was furrowed, his green eyes blazed with rage as he stomped toward them. He was definitely good-looking for his age, but since Rachel literally could not stand that man, she had never been able to see anything other than the ugliness of his ways. He had bogarted his way into every aspect of the ABC, wanting to give his input on every decision that was made. Rachel had told Lester on more than one occasion to put the man in his place. Of course, her husband had yet to do that.

"What in Sam Hill is going on?" Rev. Griffith bellowed.

Rachel couldn't be sure, but she thought she saw a flutter of uneasiness pass over Jasmine as she stepped away from the two. But she didn't have time to read too much into it because the next thing she knew, Rev. Griffith had grabbed her by the arm.

"Have you lost your mind?" he said, pulling Rachel off to the side.

"Me?" Rachel asked, snatching her arm away. "You need to be talking to that old toad over there," she said, pointing at Jasmine. But then the magnitude of his actions set in. He had literally grabbed her and pulled her off to the side. How dare he snatch her up like some child?

"She's not the first lady of the American Baptist Coalition. You are," he hissed. "And I can't believe you're out here acting a plum country fool. You need to leave that ghetto, backwoods mess back in Houston." He pointed a long, scrawny finger in her face. "Don't you dare come up in my city embarrassing me and drawing negative attention to the ABC."

Rachel was dumbfounded. How was she getting all the blame? Come to think of it, what was he even doing here?

By this time, the crowd had eased over their way, no doubt trying to see if the fight would be moving from Rachel and Jasmine to Rachel and Pastor Griffith. Everyone had made their way over, except Jasmine. She still stood off to the side like she didn't want to get involved.

"Are you listening to me, little girl," Rev. Griffith said, snatching her arm again. "I

69

don't need this."

Rachel had had enough. She was tired of being disrespected. It had been that way since she was a preacher's daughter, and didn't change once she became a preacher's wife, despite her efforts to walk the straight and narrow. It hadn't changed until recently, when she took over as first lady of the ABC. Now, people were finally showing her some respect and she wasn't about to let this geriatric caveman treat her like some little pansy.

"Little girl?" It was her turn to point a finger in his face. "Let me explain something to your decrepit behind. I am not some little twit that you can order around. First of all, what happened here today is none of your concern."

"None of my concern?" he asked incredulously, not fazed by her being in his face.

"Yeah, because in case you haven't gotten the memo, my husband runs this organization. Not you. So, number one, you need to stay the hell out of our business. And number two," she stepped even closer, not caring who was watching now, "if you ever put your crusty hands on me again, you will live to regret it."

They stood glaring at each other. Rachel knew Lester would have a conniption fit when he heard what happened, but she didn't care. Rev. Griffith had picked the wrong day to push her.

"Excuse me."

Both Rachel and Rev. Griffith turned to face two burly security guards hovering over them. "Miss Winfrey has asked that we escort you off the premises," one of them said. He motioned toward Jasmine. "All of you."

"You have got to be kidding me," Jasmine mumbled. "We're getting kicked out?"

The guard nodded firmly. "Miss Winfrey just thought that it would be best if we made sure that all of you got back to your respective vehicles."

"I rode with my publicist," Jasmine said, pointing to Yvette, who was standing a few feet away looking frazzled as she talked to a curly-haired woman who looked extremely upset. The woman threw up her hands, then walked away. Yvette took a deep breath, then stomped back over to Jasmine and Rachel.

"I hope the two of you are happy. I have never in my entire career been more embarrassed," she said. "And now, not only did you mess up this interview, but you've put our second interview in jeopardy."

Rachel's left eyebrow raised. "What second interview?"

Yvette cut her eyes at Rachel, but said with exasperation, "On top of the show, we were also doing an interview with *O Magazine.*"

"What?" Rachel yelled, then quickly lowered her voice when one of the guards took a step toward her. "So she was going to be on the show *and* in the magazine? Without me?"

Yvette shot her a "not now" look. Rachel decided then and there that as soon as they got back, Yvette had to go, right along with Pastor Griffith.

"Now look," Yvette said. "The interview is supposed to take place at Rev. Griffith's place." She finally turned to Rev. Griffith and acknowledged him. He grunted his displeasure and she shot him a look to tell him she understood his frustration.

"Why would it be there?" Rachel interrupted.

Yvette ran her fingers through her hair. It was obvious they were working her last nerve but Rachel didn't care. It was Yvette's job to tend to Rachel's needs — at least for the time being.

"It's at my place because Chicago is my home," Rev. Griffith interjected. "And I have historical pictures that would make a good backdrop for the story on the ABC and Jacqueline's Hope." He took a deep breath, trying to calm himself. "I'm the one who called in favors to make the interview happen." He glanced at his watch, then back up at Yvette. "I need to get going," he huffed. "I would hate for the reporter to get to my place and no one is there." He glared at Rachel again. "Besides, I need to get my head together on how we're going to clean up this mess."

Rachel flicked him off as he walked away, then spun back in Yvette's direction.

"So, you had this interview set up and you didn't think I should be included?" Rachel said, not bothering to hide her attitude.

"For your information, this is something that happened last minute and I did give the reporter your number and was planning to call you," Yvette replied.

"Oh, I get *called* and she gets interviewed in person?" Rachel jabbed a finger in Jasmine's direction.

"You know what?" Yvette said, throwing up her hands. "I can't do this with you two. At this point, I don't know if that interview has been canceled as well and that's my priority."

"How can we fix this?" Jasmine asked, rolling her eyes at Rachel.

Yvette dug in her purse and pulled out a

sheet of paper. "Just go on over to Rev. Griffith's place. Oprah's assistant is there trying to find out if we can even still do the interview. But I need you in place in case it's still a go."

"But I rode with you," Jasmine protested. "Can you at least call me a car service?"

"If you wait on a car, you're going to have to wait out on the sidewalk," the security guard interjected as he motioned for them to get moving. "I've been patient, but you two have got to go."

"What's the address?" Rachel asked, snatching the paper out of Yvette's hand. "I drove so I'll head on over there."

"Fine. Jasmine, you can ride with her," Yvette said.

"Are you insane? I'm not going anywhere with that woman."

Rachel shrugged. "Fine by me. Go see if you can catch Pastor Griffith." She smiled as she walked away. "I'll make sure and tell the reporter you said hello in case you don't make it there in time."

Yes, there's a chance to salvage things yet, Rachel thought as she speed-walked toward the car. She would fix this. She would dazzle the reporter and Oprah would be so in love with the story that all would be forgiven. Rachel had just approached her rental car

74

when she heard the click of heels scurrying toward her.

"I don't think so," Jasmine said, snatching the passenger door open.

"What are you doing?" Rachel asked. She really hadn't expected Jasmine to ride with her. She thought for sure she'd flag down Pastor Griffith and ride with him, or call a cab, or catch the train, anything but hop in her car.

"If you think you're going over there without me, you've lost what little mind you have left." Jasmine plopped down in the passenger's seat.

Rachel sighed as she got in, too. "Get out of my car."

"Drive the car, Rachel," Jasmine said, pulling her seat belt over her chest.

Rachel was about to say something when her cell phone rang. She groaned as Lester's name popped up on the screen.

"Hi, honey," she said, answering in her sweetest voice.

"Rachel, what in the world is going on?" Lester bellowed. "Rev. Griffith just called and said that the show didn't happen because you and Jasmine caused chaos."

"Yes." Rachel tsked, trying to decide if she was going to continue her conversation or push Jasmine out of her car. "Jasmine set off a fire alarm and they had to evacuate the place," Rachel finally said.

"Set off an alarm? Why?"

"I have no idea. You know she's old. She's probably in the early stages of dementia and likely thought it was a doorbell."

"I got your dementia, right here," Jasmine said, shooting Rachel her middle finger.

Rachel rolled her eyes. "That's so becoming of you, *Madame First Lady.*"

"Rachel, is Jasmine there with you?" Lester asked. He sounded extremely worried.

"Unfortunately."

"Baby, what's going on? Pastor Griffith was livid."

Rachel really wasn't in the mood for a lecture. "Lester, it's not that serious. Everything is fine now. I'm on my way to Pastor Griffith's place now. A reporter from *O Magazine* wants to interview me."

"She doesn't want to interview *you,*" Jasmine hissed.

"I swear, you act like a middle school girl sometimes!" Rachel snapped.

"Rachel —"

"Lester, hon, I'll call you after this is all over, okay? Love you." Rachel hung up the phone before he could say another word. After the day she'd had, she didn't feel like getting harassed by her husband as well.

Rachel looked over at Jasmine, who was glaring out the window.

"You just remember who's the first lady, and who was the runner-up," Rachel felt the need to remind her.

"Rachel, don't talk to me," Jasmine said.

"Whatever," Rachel mumbled as she reached up to put the address in the rental car's navigation system. She turned on the gospel channel and pulled out of the parking lot. After a minute, Rachel heard Jasmine humming along to a Yolanda Adams tune, so she changed to a hip-hop station just to be spiteful.

As the sounds of Lil Wayne filled the car, Rachel pumped up the volume.

"You can't be serious," Jasmine mumbled.

Rachel ignored her and continued bopping her head. She didn't even like Lil Wayne — anymore — but the irritation on Jasmine's face was giving her immeasurable joy.

"Crap," Rachel muttered when the navigation system led them onto a road closed for construction. "Now what do I do?"

Jasmine turned up her lips and looked out the window. It was obvious she wasn't going to offer any help. And she had the nerve to talk about Rachel. That woman was so childish.

Rachel thought about asking someone for directions, but the few people out in the brisk October weather seemed rather unsavory and not like anyone she'd feel comfortable stopping to talk to.

Rachel sighed as she reached back in her purse and pulled out her cell phone. She didn't need to waste time being lost. She punched in Rev. Griffith's number.

He answered on the first ring and issued a gruff "Where are you?"

"We're lost. The navigation system sent us down a road that has construction." She leaned in and peered at the street sign. "We're on West Twenty-sixth."

"Turn around and get back on the main street and go three lights and make a right. The building is on the left," he snapped.

"Okay, fine. Is the —"

He cut her off. "Just get over here so we can figure out how to clean this mess up before the reporter gets here."

"Okay, but —"

"No buts, I have to go. Someone is at my door. It's probably the reporter."

Rachel stared at the phone as it went dead. These people better recognize who she was. How dare he hang up the phone in her face?

"Are we going to sit here all day or what?" Jasmine said.

"You can walk, you know."

Suddenly, a homeless man banged on the hood. "Got some spare change?" he shouted.

Rachel jumped, then quickly pulled away. She followed the directions Rev. Griffith had given her, and in minutes was pulling up to his building.

"Why don't you just drop me off and you go park," Jasmine said as Rachel pulled into the circular driveway in front.

"I wish I would," Rachel replied, stopping for the valet. "I'm Rachel Jackson Adams, here to see Rev. Griffith," she told him.

"Yes, he is expecting you. The concierge stepped away a minute so you can go on up," the young man said as he took Rachel's keys and helped her out. He raced over to open Jasmine's door, but she was already out and stomping inside.

"What's the unit number?" Jasmine asked once they neared the elevator.

Rachel glanced down at the 404 written on the sheet of paper in her hand. "It's 804," she said.

That heifer didn't even say thanks as she pushed the Up button.

Suddenly, Rachel started shifting from

79

foot to foot. "Dangit. I need to use the rest-room and I don't want to go into this man's home, using his restroom. Can you wait a minute so that we can go up together? That's only fair."

Jasmine looked at her like she was crazy, then smirked. "Sure."

Rachel smiled appreciatively, then darted into the restroom at the end of the hall. As soon as she stepped in, she peeked out and as expected, Jasmine stepped onto the eleva-tor. That had been too easy. As soon as the elevator doors closed, Rachel raced back to the elevator and jabbed the Up button.

If she played her cards right she'd get a chance to make the first impression on the reporter before Jasmine tracked down Rev. Griffith's actual apartment number.

When the elevator doors opened on the fourth floor, Rachel spotted an elderly woman looking frazzled as she picked up what looked like a bunch of stuff that had spilled out of her purse.

"Are you all right?" Rachel asked, kneel-ing to help the woman retrieve her belong-ings. Rachel didn't have much time — she needed to get inside before Jasmine got here — but the woman was visibly upset.

The woman shook her head. "I just don't understand people today. No respect for their elders. Some fool was in such a hurry and just plum knocked me over, didn't stop to say excuse me, to help, or anything." She smiled as Rachel handed her her wallet. "Thank you, baby." She squeezed Rachel's hand. "Thank God for nice angels like you."

"You're welcome," Rachel replied. How anyone could be so rude to the elderly was beyond her. Well, with the exception of Jasmine. She could understand how someone could be rude to that old hag.

"Well, my name is Ms. Martha. I'm a seamstress. I'm working on a dress for the lady that lives there." She pointed to unit 412. "She'll vouch that I'm pretty good." The woman handed Rachel a card. "So if you're ever in need of someone to sew you some nice dresses, please don't hesitate to call." She pointed to an awful plaid dress with lace around the collar she was wearing. "I made this myself."

Rachel took the card, even though she had no intention of ever using it. She'd come too far to resort to homemade dresses.

"Thank you, have a good day," Rachel said, dropping the card in her jacket pocket.

"You, too, baby." Ms. Martha made her way toward the elevator. Rachel scanned the hall, looking for apartment 404.

She spotted the unit at the end of the

hallway, took a moment to compose herself, then marched over and knocked on the door.

"Knock, knock," she said, tapping on the front door, which was cracked open. She assumed the Reverend had left the door open for them.

After a few seconds, Rachel pushed the door open and eased inside. "Rev. Griffith. It's Rachel Jackson Adams," she called out.

No one answered. Rachel surveyed the plush living area. This man sure lived well for a retired minister. Paintings by John Biggers lined the walls. African statues sat in the corners and a thick African rug stretched across the hardwood living room floor. Rachel didn't know much about art, but this stuff definitely looked expensive.

"Reverend, it's Rachel. I'm here," she called out as she walked into the kitchen area.

Historic pictures from the Coalition were strewn across the dining room table, so he obviously was preparing for their visit.

"Doggone it," she said, when she noticed the reporter wasn't here. She had really wanted to get to the reporter before Jasmine. "Hello!" she called out again. Rachel hated wandering around the man's house but it was obvious the old man was hard of hearing.

She noticed a long hallway that must've led to his bedroom. Maybe he was in there. She headed to that room. "Reverend," she said, knocking. When she still didn't get an answer, she eased the door all the way open.

Rachel's heart dropped as she noticed Rev. Griffith on the floor beside his bed. "Rev. Griffith!" she said, panicked. Had the old man fallen? Had a stroke? "Oh, my God, are you okay?" she asked, kneeling down beside him. She immediately put two fingers to his neck to check for a pulse. She felt nothing and reached under him to turn him over when she felt something wet and sticky. It was then that she noticed the blood pooling around his head. Rachel felt a scream building in the pit of her gut as she backed against the wall. Pastor Griffith was dead! He was really dead!

CHAPTER SIX

Jasmine pressed the number eight on the elevator panel, then jammed her thumb on the Close Door button so that the door would close before two of Rachel's brain cells had time to rub together and she figured out what Jasmine had just done.

When the elevator began its ascension, Jasmine leaned back against the wall and laughed out loud. Sometimes, Rachel made things just a bit too easy. She was such a simple girl, not much going on between her ears at all. How dumb was it for Rachel to give her the apartment number and then leave her by the elevator? Really? Please! That girl was so dumb it probably took her two hours to watch *60 Minutes*.

Well, Jasmine was going to use this little bit of time she had. Hopefully, the interviewer would already be here because Jasmine wasn't all that anxious to be anywhere near Earl Griffith. That man not only gave her the creeps, but he was off the Richter scale when it came to being dangerous.

According to her sources (through Mae Frances) Griffith and his drug cronies were moving major weight and funneling most of that money through the ABC. The drug cartel had tripled its financial foothold in the ABC and really, Jasmine couldn't understand why none of this had come out. She had thought that by now, Lester Adams would've been dragged away in shackles. But it seemed that the Reverend was just as dumb as his wife — he didn't have a clue to what was happening, and how they were being set up.

But that was okay; surely, it was just a matter of time and when the ABC began to crumble, Hosea would be ready to step into that cornball preacher's position. Up to this point, Jasmine had been willing to just sit and wait for what was naturally going to happen, but after what Rachel pulled today, Jasmine was ready to take over now. As soon as she returned to New York, she was gonna talk to Mae Frances to see what they could do to expedite the Adams family's return to the backwoods where they belonged.

When the elevator doors parted on the eighth floor, Jasmine stepped quickly; she wasn't going to have that much time advantage on Rachel, and every minute counted.

She knocked hard on 804, then inhaled as she wondered what it was going to be like to be alone with Pastor Griffith for the first time since the ABC election in which he'd been so invested. That man had worked hard to make sure that Hosea won and Jasmine had a feeling that the pastor had already figured out that she'd rigged the election so that Lester Adams had the victory. And if Pastor Griffith knew that, he was probably also aware that Jasmine knew about his extracurricular activity. But, he had to know that she wouldn't say a word; that must be why he'd left her and Hosea alone.

Well, at least this would just be one meeting, a short meeting.

As the door to 804 opened, Jasmine exhaled, pasted on her best smile, then frowned.

"Come on in!"

Jasmine stared for a moment at the white man — well, actually, he was more of a boy. The sandy-haired, blue-eyed young man couldn't have been more than twenty, twenty-five years old. Dressed only in a pair of beige cargo shorts, he made a grand gesture with his arms, motioning for her to come in.

What in the world? Who was Pastor Griffith hanging out with now?

"Is the pastor here?" Jasmine stepped slowly past the young man and entered the apartment.

He laughed. "Pastor? Is that what you call him?" His chuckles continued as he shook his head, then yelled out, "Hey, the other stripper is here!"

"Stripper?"

She couldn't believe Pastor Griffith was going to play her like that. At the convention, he'd found out (because of Rachel) that she'd stripped in her younger, naïve days. But that was a long-ago life. Why would he bring that up now?

"I am not a stripper," Jasmine said just as another guy stumbled out of a back room. This one was older than the one who still stood at the door; he was at least twenty-seven. But Jasmine wasn't sure how she exactly figured that out because she could hardly see his face — not with the way the two *strippers,* who were clad only in G-strings, were hanging off him.

"Hey, we weren't expecting you for another hour," the twenty-seven-year-old said. Then he paused. "I'm gonna like you. I haven't had a black girl in a long time. But I guess you gotta have variety in an all-day

87

bachelor party!"

Jasmine's fingers curled into a fist. *Rachel!*

Without saying another word, she pivoted and rushed through the door.

"Hey!" one of the boys called behind her. "Where you going?"

Jasmine ran down the hall and punched the button to the elevator until her finger turned red. "Ugh!" She couldn't believe she'd been tricked by that troll . . . and twice in one day. Who did this kind of thing? Who played these games over and over? Now Jasmine knew for sure that Rachel had never gotten out of the sixth grade because clearly, she was still living her life like she was in middle school.

But her games were working, and as Jasmine jumped into the elevator, she blocked out thoughts of murder and focused on how she was going to find the right apartment.

In the lobby, she rushed to the concierge. "Excuse me. I'm here to see Pastor Earl Griffith," she spoke quickly, imagining that the interview had already begun. "Can you tell me his apartment, please?"

The concierge said, "I can't give you that information, but I can call up for you."

She tapped her fingers on the edge of the marble counter. "Go ahead," she said, wanting to tell the man to just give her the apartment number. But there was no time for fighting — too much time was passing.

The top hat that the man wore tipped a little as he glanced down at a directory, then dialed four numbers. From where she stood, Jasmine could hear the phone ringing . . . and ringing . . . and ringing.

Before he returned the phone to its cradle, Jasmine was pointing at it and telling him, "You need to call again, 'cause he's waiting for me."

"I don't know what to tell you, Miss," the concierge said. "But I can't send anyone up without letting the pastor know."

"Hey, Stan. The pastor is waiting for her."

Jasmine exhaled as she turned around and faced her angel. She wanted to kiss the valet who'd taken Rachel's keys earlier.

"Yeah," he continued, "the Reverend called down while you were helping Ms. Johnson up with her packages. He said to let the ladies right up." Then he turned to Jasmine. "There are supposed to be a couple more, right?"

"Yes," Jasmine said breathlessly. That meant that the reporter and Yvette hadn't arrived. *Ha!* Rachel was up there with Pastor Griffith and after the argument the two of them had had at Harpo Studios, Jasmine was sure that by now, her nemesis was probably wishing that she'd never sent Jasmine on a wild-pastor chase.

"You can go right up to apartment four-oh-four," the valet attendant said.

Jasmine strolled to the elevator, then stopped and turned around. Why was she going up there? By now, Pastor Griffith was surely torturing Rachel in some kind of way and Rachel deserved it all. Plus, if she waited down here, Jasmine could intercept the woman from *O Magazine* and Yvette right in the lobby. She could tell them that Rachel had her own emergency, and now she was gone.

Then, the interview would just belong to her — the way it was supposed to. That would be the ultimate payback for the games that chickenhead had been playing all day long!

But just as Jasmine aimed her butt for the sofa in the lobby, she had that tug on her heart.

Dang! She'd been having that a lot lately — whenever she was getting ready to do something that she shouldn't do, she'd get this little pull in the center of her chest. The first time it happened, about six months ago, she thought for a second that she was having a heart attack.

When she'd told Hosea about it, he'd

chuckled. "It may be just the Holy Spirit, darlin'."

That made her laugh, but since that first time, it had happened at least another ten times — and she was beginning to believe that maybe Hosea had been right.

She tried to settle into the couch, but then, Jasmine sucked her teeth and marched to the elevator.

"This is ridiculous," she muttered to herself as she rose to the fourth floor. "Why am I going to save this middle school drop-out?"

Jasmine was still pissed about her decision when she knocked on Number 404 with an attitude. She hit the door so hard that it pushed open. She paused for a second, but then stepped inside.

The space was silent, almost eerily so.

"Hello," she called out.

And then . . .

A blood-curdling scream. At first, the sound made Jasmine freeze, but only for a moment. She dashed toward the cries that followed and just a couple of seconds later, she was in what had to be the master bedroom suite.

She gasped at the sight — Pastor Griffith lying on the floor and Rachel pressed up against the wall, trembling in fright.

"What the hell?" Jasmine's eyes were wide as she moved closer, though she carefully stepped around the pool of blood that was seeping from a deep gash in Pastor Griffith's head. "What did you do to him?"

Rachel shook her head. "I . . . I didn't do anything," she whimpered as she pushed herself up from the floor.

Jasmine's glance moved from the dead pastor to Rachel. "There's blood all over your dress!"

Rachel's chin dropped to her chest as she tried to glance down beyond her Wonderbra-enhanced DDs. Jasmine could see the scream rising within Rachel and she knew that if Rachel let it out, the girl would never stop.

"What happened?" Jasmine asked as she motioned for Rachel to step away from the body.

Rachel's head whipped from side to side. "I don't know. I just came in here and he was like that. I checked his pulse. I felt blood — wiped it on my dress. He-he's dead," she cried. "We have to call the police."

Jasmine felt that tug again, as if her subconscious was ahead of her — ahead of the thoughts that were just now coming to her. In an instant, memories scanned through her mind, of all the things Rachel had done to her. From kidnapping Jacqueline, to exposing her as a stripper, to the stunts she'd pulled this morning.

This lady deserved payback . . . and Hosea deserved to be the president of the ABC.

The idea must have been somewhere in her heart already because it came so quickly.

"No!" Jasmine shouted, and grabbed Rachel's hand. "We have to get out of here!"

"What? No! We have to call the police," Rachel cried.

"You can't do that." With a final glance at the pastor, Jasmine dragged Rachel down the hall, toward the front of the apartment.

"But I have to," Rachel wailed. "We have to let the police know that there's a dead man back there."

Jasmine stopped moving. At least she had Rachel out of that room. "And what do you think is going to happen when you call the police?"

Rachel's eyes were so filled with tears that Jasmine wondered how she could even see. "What do you mean?"

"Rachel," Jasmine said, keeping her voice stern. "You are the first lady of the American Baptist Coalition."

"So?"

"So, how is this going to look? One of the

board members is found dead by the wife of the president."

"But that's what happened!"

"And people have been convicted of murder on much less."

"Murder!" she shrieked.

Jasmine felt her opportunity slipping away. On one hand, Rachel's hysteria would work for her — she couldn't think straight right now. But that would be the downfall of her plan, too. Rachel was so distraught that it didn't seem like she'd be able to function beyond putting one foot in front of the other.

But this was just too good an opportunity to let slip by. She had to give it her best try. And, she'd have to do it within the next few minutes because surely, Yvette and the reporter were on their way.

"All I'm saying is that you don't need that drama, Rachel, especially —" Jasmine stopped. She glanced at Rachel for a moment, then turned away as if she couldn't face her. Then, she shook her head.

"What?" Rachel cried. "What were you going to say?"

"Well, you don't want this drama with all that's going down with the ABC and the investigation with your husband and Pastor Griffith —"

"What? What are you talking about?" She was still crying, but it sounded a little different now. Hysteria with some sense.

When Jasmine faced Rachel this time, her eyes were wide. "You don't know?" Jasmine asked. "I don't have time to explain it all now because we have to get out of here. But let's just say that your husband is going to be the first one the police will look at. And since you found him —"

"No," Rachel screamed. "No. Lester had nothing to do with this."

"I know that." Jasmine lowered her voice as a clue for Rachel to do the same. "I know that and you know that. But there will still be lots of questions asked and you don't need to get involved in this. Let someone else find Pastor Griffith," she said, taking Rachel's hand once again. "Don't get involved, Rachel. Trust me."

It was her last two words that made Rachel stop and snatch her hand away. Rachel wasn't hysterical enough to trust Jasmine.

"All right," Jasmine said. "You do what you have to do, but I'm leaving." She was going to leave no matter what. This was Rachel's drama, not hers. "I didn't find the pastor, you did; so don't even give them my name. I'm out."

"No, no," Rachel said, sounding desperate

once again. "I'm going with you."

Her smile was instant, but Jasmine pivoted slowly to give herself time to compose a serious, concerned expression.

"Okay, we've got to move quickly because Yvette will be here with —"

"Oh, God," Rachel moaned.

Jasmine wanted to slap Rachel and tell her to "snap out of it!" like Cher did in that movie *Moonstruck*. But the girl was young and pitiful and Jasmine had to be patient . . . since she was setting up Rachel for the biggest fall of her life.

"Did you touch anything?"

"I . . . I . . . don't know. Maybe the door . . . and maybe . . ." Rachel shuddered. "I touched him," she said, with tears spilling out once again.

"Okay, you have your purse, right?"

Rachel nodded.

Glancing around quickly, Jasmine grabbed an afghan that was tossed over the sofa. Using the blanket, she wiped the door handle — especially since she had touched the knob as well. She tossed it back onto the couch, looked around, and then took Rachel's hand again as if she was leading a two-year-old.

Inside the hallway, Jasmine pointed to the staircase. "Let's go down that way."

As she went down the stairs, Jasmine organized her thoughts. She really needed to make this as much of a cloak and dagger operation as she could. She needed Rachel to trust her.

On the first-floor landing, Jasmine said, "Okay, I want you to go out the back door, and I'll talk the valet into giving me your car."

"Why?" Rachel asked, her eyes still filled with tears.

"Because I'm trying to protect you and I don't want you to walk out the front door of this building with all of that blood on your dress."

It was as if she'd forgotten and when Rachel looked down, her hysteria returned.

"Don't worry," Jasmine said, trying to calm her. "I'll get your car and meet you out back."

When all Rachel said was "Okay," Jasmine knew that she had this girl right where she needed her.

This petrified Rachel wasn't going to last; Jasmine knew that. At some point, Rachel would look back and regret this. But shock was a beautiful thing. And as long as Rachel stayed in this state for a few more minutes, Jasmine would be able to move forward with her plan.

"Don't say anything to anyone," Jasmine reminded Rachel. "Keep your purse in front of you in case you see anyone. And here, take my sunglasses." Jasmine handed Rachel her Chanels. "I don't want anyone to remember you. I'll take the risk for both of us."

Rachel adjusted the glasses on her face, then nodded at Jasmine.

As Rachel slipped out the back door, Jasmine turned toward the lobby.

Wow! Pastor Griffith was dead. She only wondered for a moment what had happened because that man was into so much mess, it was a wonder that he'd lived this long.

She'd call Hosea and have him say a prayer or something for Pastor Griffith, though she was sure there wasn't much anyone could do for that man's soul.

This was such a tragedy. But like folks said, one person's tragedy was another's triumph.

This was going to be her triumphant day.

CHAPTER SEVEN

You've got to calm down.

The sane, rational part of Rachel was trying to garner control.

Ohmigod! Ohmigod! Ohmigod!

But the erratic, panic-stricken part refused to listen.

Rachel had alternated between extreme fear, complete hysteria, and utter disbelief for the past hour. She'd never seen a dead man up close before, especially someone she knew. She felt like Rev. Griffith's lifeless image would forever be embedded in her mind.

Rachel had finally stopped crying, but her despair hadn't subsided. In fact, she knew she probably looked a hot mess right now, with puffy eyes and a mascara-stained face.

"Here, clean yourself up." Jasmine's words brought Rachel back to reality. They were sitting in the small room at the LaQuinta Inn. She didn't remember much, except Jasmine saying they had no choice but to come to this dump because she "wasn't about to take a bloody, hysterical Rachel back up to my hotel room at the Omni."

Rachel took the towel, slowly coming out of her daze. She looked around the bare room. Although she'd upgraded to more exclusive hotels, she wasn't above a LaQuinta. But being here had to be killing Jasmine.

Yet, Jasmine was here anyway.

Rachel sniffed as she thought about how Jasmine had literally taken control of everything. Here Rachel had been scheming and conniving just a little while ago, and now Jasmine was being nothing but a friend.

"And put this on." Jasmine handed Rachel an oversized sweat top and pants.

"What is this?"

"Look, its not like Walgreens sells designer duds and I didn't have time to run to your favorite store, T.J.Maxx."

There was the old Jasmine, Rachel thought. Normally, she would've had a comeback for Jasmine's condescending dig, but right now, that was the last thing on her mind.

"Or you could just stay in your blood-soaked clothes," Jasmine said when Rachel didn't move.

Rachel glanced down at her dress, the blood now dried and flaking. Just the sight made her heart race all over again. She took the hideous outfit and made her way into the bathroom. She caught a glimpse of herself in the mirror again and the tears welled back up. Her dress was covered in blood. Her hair was all over her head. Just like she thought — a hot mess.

Rachel turned the shower on, getting the water as hot as she could stand it, then stepped inside. She wished she could wash away the madness of the last few hours. Shoot, at this point, she wished she could turn back the hands of time and not even have boarded that plane to Chicago in the first place.

Rachel didn't know how long she'd been in the shower when Jasmine banged on the door. "Hurry up, Rachel," she said.

Rachel dried off and put on the clothes Jasmine had bought, grateful that her nemesis had even thought to get underwear.

"I still think we should've called the police," Rachel said as she walked out of the bathroom twenty minutes later.

"We've been over this a thousand times, Rachel. And say what?" Jasmine said. "I told you, if you want to call, fine, just drop me off at the airport, then you deal with the paparazzi."

"Paparazzi?"

"Yes, Rev. Griffith is well known in Chicago. I'm sure the media will be all over this story. And I'm sure they'll believe your story that you didn't kill him, even though all of Oprah's audience heard you threaten the man just a couple of hours ago," she said sarcastically.

"I *didn't* kill him." Rachel felt herself hyperventilating again as her mind raced back to their argument. She was just talking noise with her threat. No one could've believed she really would do any harm to Rev. Griffith, would they?

The ringing cell phone kept Rachel from going off the deep end. She picked it up and looked as Yvette's name popped up on the screen. Rachel pressed Talk just as Jasmine hissed, "Don't answer it."

Rachel gave her a "too late" shrug, then said meekly, "Hello."

"Rachel! Where are you guys?" Yvette said, panicked.

"Ummm, ummm," Rachel stammered.

"I mean, thank God the reporter is running late," Yvette continued. "You're not here. Jasmine's not here. Pastor Griffith's not here. I swear, I feel like I'm fighting an uphill battle with you people."

Rachel paused as her words sank in. *Here?*

"Where are you?" Rachel asked.

"I'm at Pastor Griffith's apartment. Where you're supposed to be."

"Wh-what are you doing there?" Her eyes widened in horror.

"We have an interview, remember?" Yvette said, exasperated. "I pulled all these strings to keep this interview and you guys aren't here."

Rachel no longer cared about any interview. She didn't want any part of this anymore.

"Where are you guys?" Yvette snapped. "I need you to get over here ASAP."

"Umm, ummm." Rachel looked to Jasmine for help, but Jasmine was just staring at her, confused.

"What's going on?" Jasmine mouthed.

Rachel covered the mouthpiece. "Yvette is at Pastor Griffith's," she whispered.

Jasmine's eyes grew wide as well.

"Rachel, where are you?" Yvette repeated.

"Ummm, we were hungry, and umm, Jasmine . . . she wanted some Harold's Chicken."

Jasmine rolled her eyes in disgust, but Rachel ignored her and continued talking. "So, we came here to get something to eat."

"Come again," Yvette slowly said. "You

already blew one opportunity. You're about to blow another one because . . . You. Wanted. Some. Freakin'. Chicken? Are you serious?"

"Exactly where are you in Pastor Griffith's apartment?" Rachel asked.

"I'm in the living room," she huffed. "What kind of question is that? I thought you guys were around somewhere since the door was cracked."

"Ummm, have you looked around?" Rachel said slowly.

"Why would I go wandering around this man's house?"

"I don't know. Maybe he's in the bedroom taking a nap."

Yvette huffed, then it sounded like she was moving through the apartment. "He's not back here."

"What do you mean?"

"I mean, I'm in the man's bedroom and he's not here."

"Did you look on the floor? Maybe he fell or had a stroke or something."

"I'm walking all over the man's bedroom and he's not here," she snapped. "This is ridiculous. This is an opportunity to clean up the mess from earlier, so I need you guys here ASAP!"

"Oh, my God," Rachel pushed the End

button and slowly turned to Jasmine.

"What?" Jasmine asked, frantic.

Rachel plopped down on the bed, stunned. She looked up at Jasmine as she weighed the magnitude of Yvette's words. "You're not going to believe this. Pastor Griffith is gone."

"Gone where?"

"I don't know. Just gone."

"I thought you said he wasn't breathing."

"He wasn't!"

"How do you know?"

"Because there was blood and I checked for a pulse!"

"Maybe you didn't know what you were doing. Maybe he wasn't really dead."

"Or maybe whoever killed him was still there, hiding or something, then moved the body when we left!"

Now, Jasmine looked just as frazzled as Rachel. "Well, what else did Yvette say?"

"She said we need to get back over there because the reporter from *O* is on the way."

Jasmine looked like she was thinking. "Okay, let's go."

Rachel stared at her incredulously. "Are you crazy? I'm not going back over there!"

"Rachel, the man must not be dead. Maybe he just got up and left."

"Or maybe the killer moved his body."

105

"Either way, are you prepared to be looking over your shoulder constantly? We need to go back and see what's going on."

Rachel cut her eyes at Jasmine. "You just want to do the interview."

Jasmine looked like she wanted to curse Rachel out. "Girl, I'm not thinking about that interview. But you know what? Fine! Go on home and let Yvette tell the police that instead of coming back over there, you disappeared, left town. If that isn't the act of a guilty woman, I don't know what is!"

"I'm not guilty of anything," she said, panic setting in again.

"Look, Rachel, if you say you didn't kill Pastor Griffith, then I believe you."

"I didn't!"

"Well, obviously, someone did. And now, it looks like they moved his body. The problem is you have phone records showing you called him."

Rachel didn't say it, but they also had Ms. Martha as a witness, the argument at Oprah's studio, and the fact that she was very vocal in her disdain for Pastor Griffith. The thought made her sick to her stomach. "Yeah, but the valet saw us both coming in," Rachel managed to say.

"But if they pinpoint the time of death, they'll see that I was downstairs trying to find the right apartment." She paused. "And if they ask me under oath, I'll have to tell them the truth — you sent me to the wrong apartment."

Rachel's mouth dropped open. "Oh, my God. You know I just did that to mess with you. Not to buy time to kill anyone!"

"I know that, but a good prosecutor can make it seem like that was exactly what you were trying to do."

Rachel fell down onto the bed. "Ugggh," she said, running her hands through her hair. How had a trip that was supposed to be a turning point in her career taken such a disastrous detour?

"So, I guess we have no choice. We've gotta go back."

Jasmine handed Rachel her purse. "Come on. Let's get this over with and see what we can find out." She eyed Rachel's hideous outfit. "But first, we need to get you a change of clothes."

CHAPTER EIGHT

"Don't you dare say a word!" Jasmine warned as she rolled Rachel's rental car to a stop in front of the building they'd just left about two hours ago. "Let me do all the talking."

Rachel said nothing, just stared straight through the windshield, and Jasmine prayed that the girl would be able to pull this off. Since she'd spoken to Yvette, Rachel had hardly said a word, and the few she had spoken came with a boatload of tears.

Jasmine jumped out of the driver's seat and handed the keys to the same valet who'd taken care of them earlier.

"You're back," he said.

On the drive over, Jasmine had tried to think of all kinds of things to say to the valet in case he was ever questioned by the police. But she'd decided that the best thing was to stay as low-key as possible.

So, she merely nodded. "We won't be

here long."

"No problem, just go right on up." The attendant nodded to the concierge. "They're Pastor Griffith's guests."

Just before Jasmine stepped through the double glass doors, she glanced over her shoulder. With a sigh, she pivoted and marched back to the car where Rachel still sat in the front seat, her eyes still straight ahead as if she couldn't bring herself to even look at, let alone enter, the building where she'd found the dead body.

Jasmine's voice was low when she coaxed, "Come on, Rachel."

She shook her head and said, "I . . . don't think I can go back up in there," sounding as if another bout of tears was on the way.

"Do you think I want to go?" Jasmine hissed. "I saw his body, too. This is not just about you."

Now Rachel faced her. "I know it's not just about me. That's why both of us need to get out of here. Let's just call Yvette and tell her we changed our minds. Tell her we don't care about the interview," Rachel pleaded. "We can tell her that too much crazy stuff was going on and we decided to just get on our planes and go home."

Any other time, Jasmine would have left Rachel's butt sitting right there, gladly taking this interview by herself. But she wasn't about to do that. This child was so traumatized Jasmine didn't know what Rachel would do if left alone.

All she wanted to do was grab a handful of Rachel's weave and drag her from the car. But she kept her tone as soft and kind as she could. "We're gonna do that, Rachel. We're gonna go home as soon as this interview is over." Still, Rachel did not move and Jasmine had to hold herself back. "Come on, Rachel," she said, her tone a bit stronger this time. "We've got to play this through. If we don't, everyone will wonder, and then everyone will question, and then the police will come, and then . . ."

"Okay, okay," Rachel said as she swung her legs out of the car. "I'll go just so I don't have to hear your motor mouth anymore."

In the past, Jasmine would have had a comeback and a smackdown for Rachel, but this time, she stayed silent. She hardly had any more energy after all she'd been through in the past couple of hours.

When she'd first found Rachel and Pastor Griffith, her plan had been to use this situation to her advantage. That was still the plan, but she hadn't realized that before she could take Rachel down, she'd have to hold her up. That's what she'd been doing over

110

the past hours; she'd taken on a caretaker's role. From taking Rachel to that filthy motel, to stopping by The Limited on Michigan Avenue and buying Rachel a new dress for this interview, Jasmine had jumped in, taken over, and cared for Rachel as if she didn't hate her.

But even though Jasmine had to do all of it with gritted teeth, she knew that if she just kept playing it straight like this, in the end, the presidency of the American Baptist Coalition would belong to Hosea, the man who should have rightfully had it in the first place.

Now, with Pastor Griffith dead, the path was clear. There would be no one in the way to stop Hosea from doing great things. And she would be right by his side — the first lady of the world.

Inside the elevator, Jasmine asked Rachel if she was all right. Rachel nodded, and Jasmine repeated her question when they stood outside Pastor Griffith's door.

"I'm fine," Rachel snapped, though she looked like she was about to throw up.

"I'm only asking because we both have to pull this off."

"I know." Her voice was softer this time, sounding like she was ten years old.

For a moment, Jasmine felt sorry for her,

111

but then she shook those feelings away. Emotions had no place in business, and this was all about business. She had a job to do and this mess was going to help her get what she wanted.

Rachel stood behind her as Jasmine knocked on the door and before she had a chance to pull down her hand, Yvette swung the door open.

"Okay, they're here," Yvette said into the earphone that was pressed inside her ear. There was a pause and then, "I got it." The intensity in her voice made Jasmine frown.

Yvette pressed the End button on her earpiece, and then faced Jasmine and Rachel with an expression that revealed her thoughts before the words came out of her mouth. "Where have you been?" she asked as if she was speaking to children.

If it had been any other situation, Jasmine would've shut Yvette down right there, but her focus was to just get in here, do this interview, and get out.

"I'm really sorry we're late."

"I've been calling and calling you."

"We had to make a stop. Rachel spilled something on her dress and we had to get her something else to wear because she couldn't come to the interview that way."

For the first time, Yvette glanced past Jasmine and stared at Rachel as she stood with her back pressed to the door. "Well, you wasted your time," Yvette said, directing her words to Jasmine, "because this interview isn't going to happen."

"Why not?"

"I can't find Pastor Griffith, and then the reporter never showed up and when I called her, she said she'd gotten a call from her editor telling her that this interview was canceled."

"What?" Rachel and Jasmine said together.

"Yeah, that's why I was trying to reach you guys. This whole thing is off. It's a mess. I don't know what's going on."

"Okay, bye," Rachel said as she turned around and grabbed the doorknob.

"Wait!" Jasmine stopped her. When Rachel turned around, Jasmine tried to calm her down with her expression. "Just wait a minute." Turning back to Yvette, Jasmine asked, "So, Pastor Griffith isn't here?"

Yvette spread her arms wide as if she was one of the show girls on *The Price Is Right.* "Do you see him anywhere?"

"So, how did you get in?" Jasmine asked.

She shrugged a little. "The door was cracked open. I thought Earl . . . Pastor Griffith had left it that way 'cause so many of us were coming up here."

Jasmine frowned. She remembered closing the door, but then, someone obviously had been in there after her and Rachel.

Yvette continued, "So I came in, looked around, and I've called his cell a million times."

"Did you check his bedroom?" Rachel asked. "Did you check in there?"

Yvette's eyes became thin slits as she shook her head. "What is your fascination with the man's bedroom? Go back there yourself if you don't believe me."

"Nuh-uh!" Rachel's eyes got wide. "I'm not going back there!"

While Yvette looked at Rachel as if she was nuts, Jasmine again tried to calm her without words. She nodded and spoke slowly, "Why don't I just check back there."

"Go ahead," Yvette said as she turned her attention back to her phone.

"It's just that this all seems kind of strange to me," Jasmine said as she took slow steps down the hall that led to the bedroom. "I mean," she kept talking so that Yvette and Rachel would know where she was at all times, "Pastor Griffith said he was going to meet us here himself." She tiptoed into the bedroom.

Just like Yvette said, there was no one,

nothing there. She took an extra moment to stare at the space where she knew for sure she'd seen the body. There was a bit of a stain on the carpet. Blood. But against the brown carpet, it just looked like someone had spilled a small amount of wine or Kool-Aid.

Her eyes scanned the space slowly. Just like when she'd walked into the room before, nothing else was disturbed.

All afternoon, Rachel had been so worried. First with who had killed Pastor Griffith, and then after Yvette's call, her distress had turned to what had happened to the man's body. But neither of those questions had concerned Jasmine. Pastor Griffith was in knee-deep with some of the baddest dudes in Chicago. It was a wonder that he'd lived this long.

Now though, this whole thing did seem too bizarre. A body, then no body. And for the first time, she wondered if she and Rachel would be involved. Did the person who killed the pastor know that they'd been there? Had the person who'd come back for the pastor seen them?

Why was she thinking about any of this? This had nothing to do with her. She just needed to get her butt back home to New York and do what she had to do.

She rushed back into the living room, not wanting to leave Rachel alone with Yvette for too long. She was already shaking her head at Rachel when she stepped back into the living room. Rachel was gulping down a bottled water.

"Sorry," Rachel said when Jasmine looked at her as if to ask what she was doing. "Yvette offered me some water because I'm feeling dizzy."

Jasmine ignored Rachel and turned to Yvette. "You were right." She shrugged. "He's not back there. So, what should we do now?"

"Well, there's no reason for either of you to stay here." She glanced at her watch. "Jasmine, you can still make your flight . . . you're scheduled for six, right?"

Jasmine nodded.

"What time are you heading back to Houston, Rachel?"

"Now. My plane leaves right now."

"What?" Yvette asked.

"She means we have to leave now if we're going to make our flights." Jasmine hugged Yvette, then almost pushed Rachel out the door.

"So, he wasn't in there?" Rachel whispered the moment they were in the hall.

"No," Jasmine hissed back.

116

"Well, did you check everywhere?"

She tilted her head when she asked, "Everywhere like where?"

"Did you check the closet or under the bed or behind the door?"

Jasmine shook her head. This child was losing it, though she couldn't say that she blamed her. How weird was this — a disappearing, dead, drug-lord pastor. It made for quite a novel.

But it was a plot that didn't have anything to do with her.

"So what are we gonna do now?" Rachel asked as they slipped back in the car.

"We're gonna do exactly what we told Yvette," Jasmine said as she turned the key in the ignition. "We're gonna head to the airport and go home."

"That's it?"

"What else is there to do, Rachel?"

"I don't know. I still think we should've called the police."

"If we did that or if you do that now, then kiss that first lady's position that you love so much goodbye."

Rachel sighed and Jasmine did, too.

Jasmine said, "So, I'll drive us to the airport, you can drop me at United, and then take back this car. What time is your flight?"

After a moment, Rachel said, "I wasn't supposed to be leaving tonight."

Jasmine frowned.

"I was gonna leave in the morning 'cause I figured that after Oprah and I met, we were gonna hang out for the rest of the day. I heard she likes having pajama parties with her girlfriends."

So much had happened in the last few hours that Jasmine had almost forgotten what this heifer had done. So, Rachel was just gonna leave her in a locked-up room while she hung out with Oprah?

Oh, yeah. There was no doubt now. Jasmine couldn't wait to get back to New York. Rachel was going to pay, big-time.

But all she did right now was smile and say, "Well, maybe the next time you come to Chicago, you and Oprah can have that pajama party."

Rachel looked at her sideways. "Are you making fun of me?"

"I would never do that."

"Yeah, right!"

And neither one of them said another word all the way to the airport.

CHAPTER NINE

Rachel had never been so happy to be home. Thankfully, she'd been able to get a seat on the last flight. She'd had to do something she hadn't done in a long time — take a drink of Jack Daniel's on the plane ride home. She might have a glass of wine from time to time, but she'd long ago given up the hard stuff.

It's amazing what seeing a dead man could make you do.

Rachel had left Jasmine with the understanding that they'd pretend the whole incident at Pastor Griffith's place never happened. When Jasmine had first suggested that just before they went their separate ways at the airport, Rachel thought she was stone-cold crazy. There was no denying it — they had both seen Pastor Griffith dead as a doorknob.

So what in the world happened to him?

Rachel pushed the thought from her head

as she navigated her Benz into the four-car garage of their Southwest Houston home.

"Mommy!" Rachel's two youngest children — Brooklyn and Lewis — met her at the door. At two, they were only days apart. She'd given birth to Brooklyn, and Lewis — well, Lewis was a long story. He was actually the son of her husband's one-time mistress. That woman, Mary, had claimed that Lewis was Lester's child, but right before she was carted off to jail they'd proven Mary had lied. It had taken a lot of prayer, but Rachel had taken in Lewis anyway rather than send him to foster care. And now, she loved the child as if she'd given birth to him herself.

Too bad both of his mommies might end up in prison.

That thought had been haunting her all day. She could get a little ghetto from time to time, but Rachel knew she was in no way cut out for prison.

No! Rachel shook off that thought. *No body. No crime.* She repeated the mantra she'd been mumbling all the way home, then focused her attention on her kids.

"Hey, sweet peas," she said, dropping her Louis Vuitton duffel bag and hugging both children tightly. They should've been in bed, but when she'd called Lester and told him she was on her way home, she knew he'd let them stay up until she got there. "Where is everyone?" she called out.

"Daddy's upstairs playing Xbox with Jordan," her eight-year-old daughter, Nia, said from the sofa. As usual, her head was buried in a book.

"Well hello to you, too."

"Hi, Mom," Nia said, standing, then kissing Rachel on the cheek before disappearing up the stairs.

The twins, as she called Brooklyn and Lewis, immediately raced back over to the sofa to continue watching their TV program. Rachel took a deep breath as she made her way upstairs to the family room to face her husband. She hesitated at the doorway, debating whether to turn around, go back to her room, and climb under the covers, because she wasn't in the mood to answer a bunch of questions. But she knew she needed to go ahead and get it out of the way.

"Rachel!" Lester exclaimed when he noticed his wife in the doorway. He jumped up to greet her. "Is that a new dress?" he asked, surveying her outfit.

Leave it to her husband to pick that up. "Long story," she said.

" 'Sup, Mom?" her fourteen-year-old son

Jordan said, not missing a beat in his game.

Rachel waved to her son. Normally, she would've chastised Jordan about his slang but she had more important things to concern herself with right now.

Lester leaned in and hugged her tightly. His embrace actually felt good. Momentarily, she felt safe.

Lester must've known Rachel was stressed because he ran his hand over her back and said, "Come on, let me fix you some tea, then we can sit and talk."

She let out a sigh, then followed her husband down the stairs. Lester sent her to their room to change clothes while he made her a cup of raspberry tea.

"Okay, what in the world happened?" he asked once they were finally settled at the kitchen table.

Rachel took a moment, weighing what to say. Everything inside her wanted to tell him about Pastor Griffith. Maybe if she shared this burden with Lester, he could help her figure out what to do. But Jasmine had convinced her that no one needed to know — especially their husbands.

"Umm, it was just a nightmare," she finally said, sipping the tea. "A great opportunity with Oprah, ruined." She wanted to say more — tell him how Jasmine had ruined everything, but for some reason, she just didn't feel comfortable throwing Jasmine under the bus like that anymore.

"Well, I've been trying to get in touch with Pastor Griffith," Lester continued, worry lines creasing his face, "but he's not answering my calls."

At the mention of Pastor Griffith's name, Rachel tensed.

"Babe, are you okay?" Lester asked, stroking her hand. His touch was soothing. She'd come a long way in her love for Lester. He'd pursued her since they were thirteen years old. She'd never given him the time of day — other than to use him for his money. But his love had endured. It still did. It had taken her years to realize it, but Lester was a good man. That's why she couldn't drag him into this mess.

"Yeah, I'm fine." She took another quick sip of her tea, flinching as the hot liquid seemed to pierce her tongue.

Lester glanced at his watch. "Oh, no, it's almost nine. I need to give your brother a ride to work."

Rachel knew he was talking about David. His car had been broken for the past three weeks and he was constantly bumming rides.

David!

Her brother hadn't exactly led a stellar lifestyle. His ex-girlfriend Tawny was a bona fide crackhead and was always getting them in trouble and hooking up with unsavory characters. David didn't hang with those folks anymore, but he knew that criminal element. Maybe if Rachel talked to him, he could help her figure out what to do.

"I need to get out of the house. Why don't I go give David a ride?" Rachel said.

"Get out? You just got here."

"I know, but I need to" — she paused, debating whether to lie — "I need to go pick up some sanitary pads." She forced a smile. She knew Lester wouldn't touch that. Anything else, he would've insisted on doing for her.

"Are you sure?" Lester asked.

Rachel was already standing before he could finish. She didn't know why she didn't think of this in the first place. Her other brother, Jonathan, would give the most sound advice, but David was the one with the criminal background, so he was the person she needed advising her in this case.

"You just get the kids in bed. I'll be back in a bit," Rachel said, grabbing her keys and heading out the door before her husband could say another word.

Thirty minutes later, Rachel was pulling in to her brother's apartment complex. She bore down on the horn.

"Hey, you," David said, climbing in the car. She'd sent him a text to let him know she was coming to pick him up instead of Lester.

"Hey, big brother," she replied. "Where's my nephew?" she asked, referring to David's two-year-old son, whom he was raising.

"He's with Dad and Brenda because I'm working the night shift all week." He eyed her suspiciously. "But I know you didn't offer to give me a ride to work to check on D.J." He leaned back in the passenger seat. "So, what's really going on? Because I know you're not here out of the goodness of your heart."

Rachel bit her bottom lip, then said, "Nothing. I was just heading your way."

He shook his head like he knew she was lying as she pulled out of the complex. David made small talk while she worked to get up the nerve to ask for his advice.

Finally, when they'd reached his job, Rachel stopped the car, then turned to her brother. "Look, I just need to ask you something."

He smiled. "I knew it was something. You

all holy now, but I know the real Rachel and she isn't just offering up rides, especially when she just got back in town."

"Hypothetically speaking," she continued, ignoring his sarcasm, "if a person were to, like, see a dead body and they didn't do anything about it, what would happen?"

He lost his smile, stared at her for a minute, then said, "Rachel, what in the world have you gotten yourself into now?"

"Me?" She feigned shock. "Why does this have to be about me? This is someone that, ummm, told me some things in confession."

"Umm, you're not a priest," he chuckled.

"You know what I mean," she said, exasperated. "They confided in me, so I can't share who it is but I want to figure out how to help them."

"Okay, whatever," he said, obviously not believing her. "But to answer your question, I'm no lawyer, but I think you have a legal obligation to report it when you know a crime has been committed. Not only that, wouldn't it be the Christian thing to do?" he said with a smirk.

"David, I'm being serious."

He sighed heavily, and shook his head like he knew his sister was headed for trouble.

"I just want to know. The D.A. can't prosecute without a body, can they?" Rachel questioned.

"Happens all the time. Do you really want to go to trial over murder?"

"Oh, my God! Murder? I would go — I mean, the person I'm talking about could face murder charges?"

David narrowed his gaze at her. "All right, sis. I don't know what type of mess you've gotten caught up in, but I'm telling you, you don't need to be doing anything that could put you behind bars."

She tried to laugh it off, but inside, she was terrified. "Boy, I know that. I'm a prominent first lady. I'm not committing any crimes."

He raised his eyebrows. "All right, then. Let me put it like this. My boy Mase is doing twenty-five to life for murder after DNA put him at a crime scene. They never found the dude he was accused of murdering, but they convicted him anyway."

DNA? She hadn't considered DNA evidence. Yes, Jasmine had wiped the doorknob off but what if they'd missed something? What if the police found out she'd been there?

Rachel tried to keep the panic from setting in. Maybe if she and Jasmine could find who stole Pastor Griffith's body, they could find the real killer. "Look, don't you know someone that can, umm, find dead people?"

David looked at her like she was crazy. "Yeah, let me call Bruce Willis," he said sarcastically.

She swatted his shoulder. "This is serious, David! My life is on the line!"

His eyes widened in shock. Rachel wanted to kick herself. The last thing she needed was someone getting suspicious.

"Look, sis," David said, "all I can tell you is if you're caught up in some mess, you would need to make sure you cover all your bases because there aren't too many people who get away with murder these days."

"I didn't murder anyone," she said, her voice cracking.

He looked at her skeptically. "Well, if you know about a murder and didn't do anything about it, you can still get in major trouble. So, clean it up and don't tell anyone anything," he said sternly. "The people you trust the most with your dirt are the same ones that will turn on you when their back's against the wall. So whatever you — or the person who confided in you — did, keep it between you and God." He put his hand on the door handle. "And you know what? That includes me. I wouldn't snitch on you, but I'm just now getting my life together. I'm not trying to be an accessory to any crime.

Love you, though." He kissed her on the cheek and got out of the car.

Rachel sat for a moment, taking in everything he'd said. Jasmine wouldn't turn on her, would she? She couldn't because at this point, Jasmine was in just as deep as she was.

The buzzing of her cell phone snapped Rachel out of her thoughts.

Hope u made it home safely. Keep it together. JB

Speak of the devil. Rachel couldn't believe Jasmine was texting her. She guessed Jasmine was just as worried as she was.

Keep it together.

Keep it between you and God.

Rachel composed herself. Both her brother and Jasmine were right. She needed to keep it together. No one else needed to know anything. In fact, maybe Jasmine was on to something when she said to pretend it never happened. *That's it,* Rachel thought, nodding. In fact, maybe the stress of the day at Harpo Studios had caused her to imagine the whole thing.

"Yep, that's it," she mumbled, finally smiling as she pulled her car out of the parking lot of the building where David worked as a security guard. "It never happened," she repeated.

She'd never been at Pastor Griffith's apartment. She'd never seen a dead body. For all she knew, Pastor Griffith had run off to Costa Rica with his young lover. She didn't know nothin' about nothin'.

That was her story, and she was sticking to it.

CHAPTER TEN

The moment Jasmine opened the door to her apartment, she grabbed Mae Frances's wrist and dragged her inside, which was quite a feat since Mae Frances had at least four inches and fifty pounds over Jasmine's five-foot-five, one-hundred-and-fifty-pound frame.

"What the . . . ?" Mae Frances said as she stumbled across the foyer. "Jasmine Larson! What in the heck is wrong with you?" She brushed her fingers through the hairs of her coat as if Jasmine had somehow messed up her thirty-five-year-old mink.

"What took you so long to get here?" Jasmine whispered.

Her best friend frowned. "You just called me thirty minutes ago. What was I supposed to do, fly across town and land my helicopter in the middle of your penthouse?"

Jasmine ignored her friend's sarcasm. "I called you all day yesterday, but you didn't answer."

"Oh!" A slow smile crossed Mae Frances's face. "Sorry 'bout that, but I had company. Herman was in town."

Jasmine twisted the lock in the door, then started down the hallway before she asked, "Herman who?"

"Herman Cain."

"Who's he?"

"A black Republican who thinks he can give President Obama a run for his money. He's thinking about entering the race, so he wanted my advice on how he could get past Newt."

"Newt who?"

"Newt Gingrich, 'cause you know, I used to hang out with him back in the day."

Jasmine stopped and slowly pivoted to face her friend. Mae Frances grinned and nodded like she had a secret.

Jasmine frowned. "You're not saying . . ."

"That's exactly what I'm saying, Jasmine Larson. Herman came into the city because he wanted my advice on getting past Newt and the rest of them clowns."

Jasmine's eyes widened, but then she wondered why she was surprised. Of course Mae Frances would know Newt Gingrich and this Herman Cain guy. Mae Frances knew everyone — living and dead.

Jasmine led her friend back to the study, her mind once again focused on why she'd sent out the 9-1-1 to Mae Frances.

"Why are we going all the way back here?" Mae Frances grumbled. "I prefer sitting in the living room."

Jasmine didn't say a word until she stepped inside the last bedroom, which had been converted into a home office for her and Hosea. She made sure the door was completely shut before she spoke. "Mrs. Sloss is in the kitchen with Zaya and I don't want her to overhear this," she said as she directed Mae Frances toward the small sofa.

"What did you do now, Jasmine Larson?" Mae Frances grumbled.

"What do you mean?"

"Any time you call me for a secret meeting, that means I have to get you out of some mess." Mae Frances shrugged her mink from her shoulders, then leaned back and crossed her arms. "So, who did you sleep with? What I gotta do?"

"I didn't sleep with anyone," Jasmine said, rolling her neck with each word.

Mae Frances twisted her lips as if to say, "Yeah, right."

"Mae Frances," Jasmine continued, "I haven't slept with another man since I married Hosea."

Mae Frances tilted her head and raised her eyes toward the ceiling as if she was trying to calculate. "So if it's not another man, why did you drag me over here like someone died or something?"

Jasmine raised her eyebrows. "Do you know already?"

"Know what?"

Jasmine took a deep breath before she said, "Pastor Griffith *is* dead!"

"What?" her friend screamed so loud Jasmine leaned over and covered her mouth with her hand.

"Mae Frances! I told you; Mrs. Sloss is right down the hall."

"Well, what did you expect me to do?" Mae Frances started fanning herself and rocking back and forth on the edge of the sofa as if she was having a heat flash. It took her a minute or two to settle down enough to say, "Now, repeat that . . . slowly, this time, Jasmine Larson."

Jasmine nodded. "It's true. Pastor Griffith is dead."

"Well, how did he get dead? Did you kill him?"

"Mae Frances!" It was Jasmine's turn to yell.

"Well, you know you've done some scandalous stuff in your lifetime."

"I've never killed anyone. At least not directly. But this time, it has nothing to do with me. It's all Rachel."

"Rachel who? Not that country chick?"

"Yup," Jasmine said. "This is why I was trying to get in touch with you all day yesterday. Really, from the moment my plane touched down at JFK the other night."

"Okay, you need to back up and explain this to me," Mae Frances said. "Like I said, slowly."

So, Jasmine began at the beginning: from the moment she arrived at Harpo Studios to the point where she came out of the restroom and saw Rachel standing there.

"You mean to tell me that she showed up at *Oprah*?"

Jasmine nodded and continued with the story.

When Jasmine got to the part about the archive room, Mae Frances shouted, "No! She didn't lock you in there like that!"

Then Jasmine told her friend about finding Oprah, Yvette, Cecelia, and Pastor Griffith all in the lot . . . with Rachel.

"What were Cecelia and Earl doing there?"

"Yvette invited them, but can you focus?"

But when Jasmine got to the part about confronting Rachel in the parking lot, Mae

Frances sat back and hollered, "That must've been something." Her shoulders quivered as she laughed. "The two first ladies duking it out in front of the big O."

"Mae Frances, this isn't funny. I told you, Pastor Griffith is dead."

"Oh. Yeah. I forgot." She lowered her eyes as she wiped away her tears of laughter and then slumped her shoulders as if that was the appropriate thing to do. Her voice was softer when she said, "So, is he really dead?"

Jasmine nodded and filled Mae Frances in on the rest of the story until Mae Frances screamed again. "What do you mean he disappeared?"

This time, she jumped up from the sofa, so there was no time for Jasmine to cover her mouth.

"Please!" Jasmine hissed. "Keep your voice down 'cause you're the only person I'm telling about this."

"What do you mean? You didn't tell Preacher Man?" she asked, calling Jasmine's husband by the name she'd made up for him years before.

"Of course not! Hosea would tell me to call the police."

Her eyes were wide when she asked, "So, you *didn't* call the police?"

Jasmine leaned back on the sofa, crossed

her legs, and smiled. "If you sit down, I'll fill you in on the greatest scheme I've ever had."

The deep lines in Mae Frances's forehead looked like they'd been branded into her skin. She took slow steps back to Jasmine. "A man is dead, his body is gone, and all you're thinking about is some scheme?"

Jasmine's eyebrows seemed to rise to the top of her forehead. Was Mae Frances really coming at her like that? She . . . who was the master schemer? "Look, you know who Pastor Griffith was and what he was involved with. And you know how he was just setting Hosea up to become president of the Coalition because he thought he'd be able to control my husband." She waved her hand in the air. "I'm not about to shed one tear for the man who sold all those drugs to all those people, and who had no problem trying to mix my husband up in the middle of his mess."

Mae Frances sighed. "He wasn't like that when I knew him all those years ago." She paused. "Plus, word on the street is that he was trying to get out of it all because of, you know, his daughter."

Jasmine rolled her eyes. Ever since she and Mae Frances had uncovered the pastor's illicit activities months ago, Mae Frances had filled Jasmine in on whatever she learned about Pastor Griffith. Mae Frances insisted that she found Pastor Griffith's involvement with drugs just so hard to believe since Pastor Griffith's only child, Eleanor, had struggled with crack her entire adult life.

That was exactly why Jasmine thought that Earl Griffith was a low-down, dirty dog to the nth degree. Jasmine was convinced that Pastor Griffith was responsible for his own daughter's addiction, though Mae Frances always said that could never be true. But Jasmine believed that not only had Pastor Griffith poisoned his community, he'd poisoned his own blood, too.

Right now, Jasmine had no idea what had happened to Pastor Griffith, but she wasn't about to shed one tear over that man. And in fact, with the way he'd been using people, Jasmine was going to use his death for her own profit.

Mae Frances said, "Well, he really was a good man."

"Once upon a time, but now he's nothing but a dead drug dealer."

Mae Frances glared at Jasmine for a moment as if she wanted to know where her compassion was . . . and Jasmine stared right back at her.

It was Mae Frances who blinked first.

"Okay," she began, "so what's your plan?"

"Okay," Jasmine said, shifting to the edge of the sofa. "Like I said, Rachel was the one who found Pastor Griffith; I just walked in on her. So technically, she was the one who should have called the police."

"Why didn't she?"

"Because I told her not to."

Mae Frances frowned. "I'm not sure, but I think there's something illegal in there. Sounds like a bunch of trouble to me."

"Exactly. Trouble for Rachel, nothing for me."

"You're gonna have to explain this to me, Jasmine Larson. Because nobody in the world knows how to put a scheme together better than me and I don't see anything here."

That was exactly what Jasmine had been waiting for. She jumped up and, as if she were in the middle of a dramatic movie scene, she swooped a piece of paper off the desk and presented it to her friend.

Mae Frances frowned. Her eyes scanned over the letters, cut from magazines, that were glued onto the page, then widened as she read aloud, " 'We know what you did to Earl Griffith and soon the police will know, too. Stay tuned for further instructions!' "
Her mouth opened into a wide, perfectly

139

shaped *O.* "Jasmine Larson, what is this?"

"It's exactly what it looks like. I'm black-mailing Rachel."

"To get what?"

"The presidency of the American Baptist Coalition for Hosea."

Mae Frances shook her head as if this was all so sad. "I thought I taught you better than this. Even that girl with her borderline-special IQ will be able to figure out that this is from you."

Jasmine let her friend rant a bit more about postmarks and everything else that could go wrong. When she settled down, Jasmine asked, "Are you finished?"

Mae Frances rolled her neck as if she was twenty years younger. "I'm just sayin'."

"Then let me *just say* how this is gonna go down. First, we're gonna use one of your connections in Chicago and have them FedEx the letter from some fake address, then I'm going to get one of these letters, too." She handed Mae Frances another paper with cut-out letters and as Mae Frances read, Jasmine recited the words she'd glued onto the paper, " 'We know what your friend did. We're calling the police. Stay tuned for further instructions!' "

"I'm going to call Rachel first, before her letter arrives. And of course, I'll be so upset and scared for her . . ."

Mae Frances was still staring at the notes, but then she slowly began to nod her head. "This . . . just . . . might . . . work."

Jasmine clapped her hands. "See? I am your student. Now, of course, I can't make it obvious. I'll send her a couple of other notes and finally demand that she make Lester step down."

"And what kind of demands will be made for you?"

She shrugged. "I don't know; I may say that Hosea has to give up his television show or something like that . . . it won't matter. Rachel will be running so scared, she won't even be thinking about what the blackmailers are asking of me. She'll be too worried about keeping her butt out of jail."

Mae Frances nodded as if she agreed with all that Jasmine was saying. But there was something in her eyes that made Jasmine ask, "What's wrong? What's bothering you?"

Her friend shook her head. "I don't know. It seems like it could work, but still, it doesn't feel right. I mean, Jasmine Larson, you're still ignoring the fact that a man is dead."

"So? What am I supposed to do about that?"

"Or maybe he isn't," Mae Frances added.

"Why aren't you upset about the fact that at first his body was there, and then it was gone?"

"Because I just don't care about a man who never cared about anyone else. But anyway, trust me, Mae Frances. The man was dead. There was a gash and there was blood. Maybe the people who killed him decided they didn't want any evidence. Maybe they took his body to dump him in the Chicago River. I couldn't care less."

"Well, you should care, Jasmine Larson, because —"

Jasmine held up her hand. "It doesn't even make sense to talk about this anymore. The fact is that man was mixed up with some really bad people. You were the one who told me how deep he'd been in."

"And I also told you how I'd heard he was trying to get out."

"It doesn't matter if he was in or out. Whatever happened with Pastor Griffith doesn't have anything to do with me. It doesn't even have anything to do with Rachel. I'm actually really glad that someone took his body because now we won't have to deal with the police coming around asking any questions. I can just concentrate on using this situation for what it is — the chance to get Hosea into the position that I took away from him because of Pastor Griffith. It feels like justice to me."

"All right, Jasmine Larson. I'll take these," Mae Frances said after a moment, picking up the letters. "I'll have them sent by one of my connections from Chicago, just like you wanted. Rachel will get hers the day after tomorrow."

Jasmine grinned. "Let's do the daggone thing." She clapped. "A month from now, Hosea will be in his rightful place."

Mae Frances nodded as she stuffed the letters deep into her purse. "I hope you're right. I hope he'll be the president of the Coalition." She moved toward the door. "And I hope you won't find yourself inside somebody's jail . . . or someplace even worse."

Jasmine laughed, but then her laughter faded when she saw the expression on her friend's face.

"Mae Frances . . ."

But she didn't have a chance to say another word. Her friend just marched out of the room, with her mink coat dragging behind her.

Was she kidding? Jasmine wondered. "Yeah," she whispered. "She was kidding." And then she laughed again. Only along with her laughter, her heart pounded deep inside her chest.

CHAPTER ELEVEN

When she was younger, Rachel's mother used to tell her she sometimes lived in a place of denial. Denial about her schoolwork. Denial about her chores. Denial about anything she didn't want to deal with.

Right about now, denial was a great place to be.

"Let the church say amen!"

At the pulpit podium, Lester closed his bible. He had just delivered a rousing sermon and the congregation was on their feet. Sister Ida, who had to be pushing ninety, had caught the Holy Ghost again (as she did every Sunday) but this time, it seemed for real.

Rachel smiled at her husband. Being president of the ABC had energized him. He didn't preach as much on Sundays anymore because he traveled a lot, but when he did, it was with a fire Rachel had never seen before.

As the associate pastor began the altar call, Rachel felt her phone vibrating in her purse. She frowned. Who in the world would call her on a Sunday morning? She carefully eased her purse open as if she were looking for a tissue because Lord knew if she pulled that phone out, it would be the talk of the church for the next month. She'd texted her friend Twyla during service one Sunday and you would've sworn she'd broken out a romance novel and started reading the way these folks acted.

Rachel's heart dropped when she noticed the name on her screen. *Bug-a-Boo* — the name she had in her phone for Jasmine.

Rachel quickly closed her purse and tried to focus her attention back on the front of the church. She hadn't heard from Jasmine in over a week and that had been just fine with her. Not talking to Jasmine made it even easier to pretend that Chicago had never happened.

But now Rachel couldn't focus. What if Jasmine was calling her with some news about Pastor Griffith? Lester had said yesterday that still no one had heard from Pastor Griffith. Part of Rachel was hoping that he did surface, at least that way she would know he wasn't dead and she didn't have to worry about anyone thinking she killed him.

The phone vibrated again. *Don't look,* the little voice in her head said. But Rachel's gut told her it was important. So, once again, she eased her purse open and glanced down at the phone.

It was a text from Jasmine. *Call me ASAP!* Fear gripped Rachel, and she had to raise her index finger and excuse herself. She felt the eyes on her back as she eased out of the sanctuary, but right now only one thing was on her mind — what in the world did Jasmine want?

Rachel didn't exhale until she was sitting in the back of Lester's SUV. She'd actually thought about ducking into the ladies' room but she couldn't chance anyone overhearing her conversation, and Lester's secretary was sitting outside his office so she couldn't go there. So she went to the only place where she could safely talk: Lester's Chevy Tahoe. The windows were tinted so she hoped no one saw her, but she ducked down in the seat just in case. She felt kind of silly hiding, but that's how paranoid this whole situation had her.

"Jasmine?" she whispered once Jasmine picked up the phone.

"Rachel!"

"What's up?"

"Why are you whispering?"

Why was she whispering? She was in a locked car in a parking lot in the back of the church. She shook her head. *Get it together, girl,* she told herself.

"Umm, no reason," Rachel replied, a little louder.

"Where are you?"

"Duh, in church. I am a first lady."

"You're still in church? It's almost three o'clock!" Jasmine exclaimed.

"It's only two here," Rachel snapped. "We ran a little long today, but regardless, we don't have microwave services." She took a deep breath. Now was not the time to be getting into it with Jasmine. "Look, what's going on? You wanted me to call right away. Have you heard anything about Pastor Griffith?"

Jasmine was momentarily quiet, then said, "No, at least I don't think so." Her voice was shaky and that scared the bejesus out of Rachel.

"What do you mean, you don't think so?" Rachel was back to whispering.

"I . . . I got a letter."

"What kind of letter? And who sends letters these days?"

"Someone that wants to blackmail you."

Rachel didn't think her heart could drop

any further, but it did. "Excuse me?"

"Y-you haven't gotten anything?"

Rachel sat up straight in the truck. "No! What did you get? What did it say? Who sent it? Oh, my God!"

"Rachel, calm down." Jasmine took a deep breath. "I just assumed you got one."

"Got one what?" Rachel shouted.

"Got a letter. A blackmail letter. Mine said: 'We know what your friend did and soon the police will, too.' "

A wave of panic roared through Rachel's body. "I didn't do anything," she said meekly.

"I know that and so do you, but whoever sent this letter thinks otherwise. I just assumed you had gotten a letter, too."

"I didn't," Rachel said, the tears now falling down her face. "I knew we should've called the cops. Now, I look like I had something to hide."

"Rachel, you've got to hold it together. Now, obviously, whoever sent this wants something so we just need to wait and see what they want."

"How do you know they'll contact us?"

"Because the letter ended with 'stay tuned for further instructions.' "

Rachel fell back against the seat. "Ohmigod. Ohmigod."

"Let's just wait and see what they want."

"I don't have any money." She caught herself. She was distraught, but she wasn't about to let Jasmine know her financial situation. The ABC presidency was about power, not money, and Lester didn't even draw six figures as pastor of Zion Hill. "I mean, I don't have blackmail kind of money."

"Well, let's just wait and see," Jasmine said soothingly.

"No, I need to tell Lester and the police about this."

"Rachel, you said yourself, Lester has made huge strides with the ABC. As much as it pains me to say this, you've even brought a positive light to the ABC. Can you imagine what the negative publicity of you being involved with a murder could do to Lester, to you, to the ABC? No. We just need to wait and see how all of this plays out."

Rachel heard her, but she wasn't convinced. This was already spiraling out of control. Now someone was blackmailing Jasmine? "Jasmine, I think —"

The sound of someone knocking on the window caused Rachel to jump, then yank her phone away from her ear.

"Sister Adams?" the old man said, leaning

150

in and peering through the window. Rachel groaned at the sight of Deacon Willis. Why wasn't his old behind in church? "You okay? Pastor sent me to check on you."

Rachel composed herself and quickly wiped at her eyes. At least they sent the half-blind deacon in search of her. She eased the door open. "I'm okay. I felt a little dizzy and a chill creeping up on me so I needed to come sit in the car under the heater."

He looked at the truck, then back at her. "But it's not on."

"I, um, I just turned it off. But I was just taking a moment."

He eyed her skeptically. "Oh, okay. You sure you don't need anything?"

I need you to leave me alone, she wanted to shout. Instead, she said, "No, I'm okay." She brushed her dress down, then reached back inside the truck for her purse and phone. "As a matter of fact, I'm going to go on back inside now. I feel a little better and want to stand by my husband's side as we bid the members goodbye."

He smiled, revealing his crooked and decaying teeth. "Yes, sireee. That's what I'm talking about," he said as he motioned for her to walk in front of him. "Even in sickness, you goin' to be by your husband's side." He nodded his head in satisfaction.

"You truly are a woman of God."

The words made Rachel sick to her stomach.

CHAPTER TWELVE

"Bye, sweetheart!" Jasmine blew a kiss to her son before she closed the door behind him and his nanny. She had never been so grateful for a seventy-degree day in October.

When she suggested that Mrs. Sloss take her son, Zaya, out for a walk, the nanny didn't hesitate. It would be a couple of hours before they came back from their journey through Central Park. And that would give Jasmine all the time she'd need.

Once alone, she ducked into her bedroom closet and gathered the magazines that she'd stuffed in the back. She laid the publications across her bed — six in all. This would certainly be enough to create the second letter to send to Rachel.

"Hey, darlin'!"

Jasmine jumped at the sound of her husband's voice. "Hosea!" She pressed her hand against her chest as if she were trying to keep her heart inside. "What are you doing here?"

He frowned as he walked into the room. "I don't know if you've noticed, sweetheart, but I live here. I've been here with you and our children for how many years now?"

"Very funny," she said, though she didn't smile. "I'm just sayin', I thought you were going to be at the church all day."

"We have Jacquie's parent-teacher conference," he said as he rounded the bed and came toward her. "Did you forget?" He picked up one of the magazines.

"No." She took the publication out of his hand, then piled together the ones that were still on her bed. Tucking them under her arm, she replied, "You're the one who must've forgotten. We were supposed to meet at the school, remember?"

He shrugged. "I just decided that I wanted to walk into the school with my beautiful wife." He eyed the magazines that she tried to hide as best as she could.

"What's all this?"

"Nothing. Just some reading I'm trying to catch up on."

The way he frowned, Jasmine knew that he was contemplating, calculating. They'd been married so long, Hosea could smell her lies. "What's really up with you, darlin'?" He squinted as if he was trying to see

154

her better.

"I told you . . . I got behind and there're some articles I want to check out. Why are you so suspicious?"

He held up his hands in surrender before the battle even began. "I'm not suspicious; I've just been married to you for a long, long time."

"And?"

He chuckled. "And, I'm totally in love."

"Good answer," she said as he kissed her cheek.

"Anyway," he said as he stepped back. "I had an interesting call this morning."

"From who?"

As he shrugged off his jacket, he said, "From Jeremiah Wright. Seems like you and Rachel aren't the only ones causing havoc in Chicago."

"Uh, excuse you! But I was not the one. It was that Adams chick."

"I'm not trying to get into anything with you about Rachel."

"I'm just sayin' that if you stood me next to that over-age delinquent, I wouldn't be the one who would be picked out of a lineup."

"Jasmine, can we just focus on what I was saying?" he said before he stepped into his closet. "I was trying to tell you that Rever-

155

end Wright told me that Earl Griffith is missing."

She was glad that Hosea couldn't see her because she was sure that he'd be able to tell that her heart was beating just a little harder.

"Pastor Griffith?" she asked, giving herself some time to think about how she was going to play this. She hadn't said anything to Hosea about seeing Pastor Griffith when she was in Chicago. If she'd mentioned that she'd seen him at Harpo Studios, she'd have to add that she'd seen him in his apartment and since she was never going to admit that she was there, she'd said nothing about Pastor Griffith — not dead or alive.

"Yeah," Hosea continued, "you know, Reverend Wright and Pastor Griffith have been on the outs ever since Reverend Wright dismissed Griffith from his church."

"Did you tell me that?" Jasmine asked, remembering that she'd found all of that out from Mae Frances and not Hosea.

"I thought I did. But anyway, Griffith was running around with some bad dudes; a major drug ring in Chicago. And now, the word on the street is that he's missing. That he was taken."

"Taken? Taken where?"

"Kidnapped. Or maybe even something

worse." Hosea shook his head. "Reverend Wright said that it's all over the streets, though his disappearance hasn't hit the news yet."

"Wow!" Jasmine leaned back on the chaise. "This sounds pretty bad."

"It may be. I'm gonna give Lester Adams a call to see if he's heard anything. I know he was working closely with Griffith. I think Griffith was trying to change his ways, trying to become more legit by working with the Coalition."

Yeah, right. "Okay . . . well . . . let me know what he says." Jasmine leaned back, crossed her legs, and opened a magazine across her lap.

Hosea glanced at Jasmine sideways. "That's it? You're not going to follow me, stand over my shoulder, and pretend that you're *not* listening to my conversation with Reverend Adams?"

"Nope!" she said as if she couldn't possibly care less.

"Okay, darlin'. I know something is up with you now, because my wife would never pass up any kind of gossip."

"You're the one who's always telling me that gossip is a sin. Didn't you just preach on that?" Before he could respond, she added, "I think your exact words were 'For

157

by your words you will be acquitted and by your words you will be condemned.' "

"Well, looka here." Hosea grinned. "My wife is actually listening in church."

"Yes, I am," she said. "I'm listening and putting it all into action. I'm watching my tongue. Because death and life are in the power of the tongue, right?"

He stepped back a little and let his eyes roam over her as if he was seeing her for the first time. "Look at you, my scripture-quoting wife. I remember when you didn't even know where to find the Book of Genesis in the Bible."

As he laughed, she grabbed a pillow from behind her and tossed it at him. "Stop making fun of me," she said, though she laughed, too. "Go on and get out of here. Go make your call."

He was still chuckling when he strolled out of their bedroom. Jasmine kept her grin until he was out of her sight.

Dang!

There was no way she was going to be able to sit up in this bedroom and cut out letters from a magazine with Hosea on the other side of the apartment. But she really needed to get this letter to Mae Frances so that she could mail it out. Rachel was so filled with fear and Jasmine had to strike again, now!

She dumped the magazines into a tote bag, then grabbed her purse and jacket before she scooted down the hall to their office.

"Hey, babe." She peeked in the door. Hosea had the phone pressed to his ear, so she whispered, "I'm going to Starbucks. Want something?"

He shook his head.

She said, "I'll be back in an hour," and waved. She took an extra moment to stare at her husband and wonder if he would appreciate all that she was doing for him.

Probably not. Hosea was such a leave-it-up-to-God kind of guy. Well, he would appreciate it when he was sitting in the president of the Coalition's chair. And if Jasmine had anything to do with it, Hosea would be taking that seat within the next thirty days.

Jasmine was talking before Mae Frances had the door completely open. "Okay, I have another letter for you to mail to Rachel," she said, stepping over the threshold. "I have to cut out the letters, but it won't take me long."

She rushed over to the dining room table, but then stopped when she glanced over her shoulder. Mae Frances hadn't moved from the door.

"What's wrong?" Jasmine asked.

"Uh . . . excuse me, Jasmine Larson," her friend said in a huff. "Good afternoon."

Jasmine waved her hand in the air. "I'm sorry. It's just that there is so much to do and I'm getting kind of excited. Even though I always planned to get Hosea the presidency, I never thought it would happen this quickly." Jasmine shrugged off her coat. "So, as I was saying, about this letter to Rachel . . . I'm gonna need you to help me cut out some of these letters —"

"No."

Jasmine's head snapped up. "What did you say?"

"I said, no. Very clearly, I might add."

"No, what?"

"No, we're not going to do this. We're not going to send any more letters."

"Mae Frances," Jasmine whined. She didn't know what her friend's problem was, but she didn't have time for this. While this was the highest priority on her list right now, she had so many other things to do — like going to Jacqueline's school this evening. So, she didn't feel like making too much of an effort to cajole Mae Frances. "I told you, this isn't for fun. This is business. Even you said Hosea should've been the president."

"Yes, I did. And that's exactly why we shouldn't be doing this."

Jasmine tossed the magazines down on the table. "You're not making any sense."

"You and I put that plan together to make sure Preacher Man didn't win because we knew Earl was involved with some really bad people. And those bad people are back. They killed the man."

"Well, he's not officially dead."

"What?"

"Jeremiah Wright called Hosea today and told him that right now, Pastor Griffith is missing. That's all."

"Well, I've been speaking to people, too. My own connections. And that man is dead."

"Well, I'm glad to hear that. That means I can move forward as planned. All I need is for you to mail another letter to Rachel."

"I'm not doing it." Mae Frances crossed her arms and shook her head. "I've known a lot of dangerous people in my life, and the way I've been able to stay alive is by staying out of their way. I know when to stay away from trouble, and Jasmine Larson, this is trouble."

"What kind of trouble are you talking about?"

Mae Frances grabbed Jasmine's hand and

161

led her to the sofa. "I don't know, but you can't convince me that there's anything right about this," she said as she pushed Jasmine down. Sitting next to her, Mae Frances continued, "Look at what we're dealing with. Some people say he's missing. Some say he's dead. You saw a dead body. And then it was gone. Oh, no." She whipped her head from side to side. "Add all of that up and it's trouble to me! Nope, I'm not mailing another letter and neither are you."

"I cannot believe you're backing out on me now." Jasmine wanted to stand up and slap some sense into her friend. "This is for Hosea and I need your help."

"I am helping you. I'm helping you to stay out of a whole bunch of mess. My connects in Chicago are telling me all kinds of things. Nobody knows anything for sure except that Griffith is missing and money is missing. And you know you better not mess with no drug dealer's cash."

Jasmine jumped up from the couch as if she was ready to fight somebody. "What I'm doing has nothing to do with drug dealers or even Pastor Griffith. I don't care about him. I don't care if he's dead or alive. After the trouble that he was planning to cause my husband —"

"That's what I'm talking about. That same

trouble has followed him to the grave."

"And it has nothing to do with me!" She marched over to the table and snatched up the magazines. "Fine. If you don't want to help me, I'll just do it myself."

"Listen to me, chile." Mae Frances held Jasmine by her shoulders and looked into her eyes. "You know I love you like a daughter, so I can't let you do this. Whatever is going down out there is really, really bad. I need you to back away."

Was that fear that she saw in her friend's eyes? If it was, this would be the first time. Jasmine couldn't remember Mae Frances ever backing away from anything. No one scared her, no one could threaten her. So what was this about?

Mae Frances kept on, "If you want Preacher Man to get that president's chair, then I'll help you do it. We'll sit down and think of another way. But we're not going to do it this way."

Mae Frances had never sounded more like a mother to Jasmine, and when she pulled Jasmine into her arms, Jasmine melted into the embrace.

Mae Frances held her until Jasmine said, "All right."

"You promise me, Jasmine Larson," Mae Frances began as she stepped back. "You

163

promise me that you'll just let this go."

"I will."

"And I promise you that after this settles down, we'll figure out something to take that presidency away from that sow and her husband."

Jasmine cracked up. "A sow, Mae Frances? Really?"

Mae Frances bowed her head. "I'm sorry. That wasn't nice, huh? Calling Rachel a sow and insulting all the female hogs out there."

This time they laughed together, though Jasmine knew this was Mae Frances's game — to get her to step back and away from the situation.

But it wasn't going to work.

"See, Jasmine Larson," Mae Frances said. "It's gonna be fine. Just you wait. You'll see. We'll figure out something."

"Okay." Jasmine slipped on her coat and tucked the magazines under her arm, but Mae Frances held out her hand.

"Give those to me."

Jasmine frowned.

Mae Frances repeated her demand. "Give me those magazines so that you won't be tempted and then find yourself all caught up in that mess."

Jasmine chuckled, but Mae Frances kept her hand stretched out in front of her as if she had no plans of letting Jasmine leave with those magazines.

With a sigh, she slipped the magazines from under her arm and gave the bunch to Mae Frances.

Mae Frances smiled and hugged Jasmine again. But when Jasmine stepped outside of her friend's apartment, she had her own grin.

Please! As if that was supposed to stop her. Yes, Mae Frances had always been in the mix and Jasmine always had her friend's help when she needed her most. But she had been in trouble before and gotten out of it way before she ever knew Mae Frances.

If her friend didn't want to help her, no problem. She'd find a way to make it happen. She was definitely going to send another letter to Rachel. And she was definitely going to use this to bring Lester Adams down.

"Trust that!" Jasmine whispered, as she stepped from Mae Frances's building and headed toward home.

CHAPTER THIRTEEN

The eight-by-ten piece of paper trembled in Rachel's hand. She hadn't been able to stop shaking since she first saw the words, which now seemed to be leaping off the page.

You killed him! And we have proof!

Fear filled her body as a river of tears found their way down her cheeks. How in the world had she gotten caught up in something like this? She was actually being blackmailed!

After Jasmine had told Rachel about her letter, Rachel had said a silent prayer all the way home. She'd prayed that God would make this whole mess go away. She'd prayed that there was no letter waiting for her since she hadn't checked Saturday's mail. There wasn't and for a minute, Rachel thought God had answered her prayers — until the mailman appeared this morning, right after Lester left for a meeting.

The mailman, who usually just dropped

their mail in the brick box out front, had personally walked the stack of mail to the front door, where Rachel had been peeping out. Rachel knew her mind was playing tricks on her, but it seemed like he needed to hand deliver this devastating news, when in actuality he was just coming up to have her sign for another Express package for Lester.

The postman hadn't gotten back to the sidewalk when she noticed the long, manila envelope with no return address. Everything inside her said, "Don't open it," but it was as if some greater force took over. She'd nervously torn the envelope open and pulled out the ivory paper with the cutout magazine letters.

You killed him! We have proof!

"Mama!" Rachel jumped at the sound of her son's voice.

She clutched her heart and said, "Boy, you scared me to death. What?" Why today of all days did Jordan have to be home sick? She wanted to be alone. She *needed* to be alone right now.

"Dang, I've been calling you a hundred times," he said through a stuffy nose. "Telephone."

Rachel snatched the cordless phone he extended toward her, just as he turned and

167

stomped back inside. Rachel wished he hadn't answered the phone. She wasn't in the mood to talk with anyone.

"Hello," she snapped.

"Rachel?"

Rachel took a deep breath. "Oh, hey, Yvette," she said, massaging her temples.

"Are you okay? You sound stressed," Yvette replied.

"I'm fine. What's going on?" Then suddenly, Rachel added, "Any word from Pastor Griffith?"

Yvette was silent a minute, then said, "Actually, that's why I'm calling. He's still missing and his daughter, Eleanor, is ready to call the police."

Rachel groaned as she made her way back inside. Why couldn't Pastor Griffith's cokehead daughter be off somewhere on a binge? Last Rachel had heard, the young woman had been clean for six months. Rachel knew it was mean, but she wished the girl was off somewhere getting high so she didn't go looking for her father.

"Well, why does Eleanor think he's missing and not just away on vacation or something?" Rachel asked, trying to compose herself.

"Well, apparently, Earl — I mean, Pastor Griffith — was supposed to be at her rehab graduation ceremony yesterday and he didn't show up."

"And?"

"And, she said he wouldn't have missed it for the world."

Rachel paced back and forth across the living room, the letter still clutched tightly in her hand. "So what? There's a first time for everything."

"There's more."

More? Rachel fell down on the sofa to brace herself for the rest.

"So, Eleanor asked around at his building and the doorman recalled seeing Pastor Griffith go up, but says he never came down."

Rachel's heart raced like it was a contender in the Daytona 500.

"And here's what's confusing to me," Yvette continued. "The valet says he remembers someone named Rachel saying she was there to see Pastor Griffith."

Rachel's heart sank into the pit of her stomach. This nightmare was getting worse by the minute. And why would the valet only remember her? Jasmine was there, too!

Play dumb, the voice inside Rachel's head screamed.

"Huh?" was all she could manage to say.

"I said, the valet remembered a Rachel

169

going upstairs," Yvette repeated. "You said you weren't at Pastor Griffith's apartment until you met me there."

Think, think, think!

Rachel couldn't believe how convoluted her thoughts were. She was usually on top of her game when it came to scheming and conniving. But then again, she'd never been involved in a murder before.

"It wasn't me."

Again, silence on Yvette's end.

"What other Rachel would be going to visit Pastor Griffith?"

"Don't know," she replied as calmly as she could. "Maybe he's confusing the name from when Jasmine and I came to see you. Yeah, that's it. I think I gave him my name then," she said, even though she knew she hadn't said two words the second time they arrived at Pastor Griffith's building.

Yvette let out a long sigh. "Pastor Griffith was not only supposed to go to his daughter's event, but he was supposed to pick up a donation for the ABC from a Chicago church yesterday and he didn't show, so something is definitely wrong."

Why was he picking up checks for the ABC? Rachel wanted to scream. He wasn't the treasurer. Shoot, he wasn't even an officer. This man was more trouble than he was worth.

"Are you sure you don't know where Pastor Griffith is?" Yvette asked again.

"Of course I don't." That wasn't a lie. Rachel had no clue where his *body* was.

"Well, this is getting crazy. Eleanor will file a police report on Wednesday. They're making her wait seventy-two hours. Maybe then the cops can pull the surveillance video at his building and we can get some answers."

Rachel let out a small gasp. *Surveillance video?* Why in the world hadn't they thought about surveillance video? That stupid Jasmine. Trying to take control of the situation like she was a professional criminal, and she forgot some basic facts. Like the fact that in such an upscale building, of course there would be surveillance video.

"Rachel, are you there?"

"Huh? Y-yeah, I'm here," Rachel stammered. "J-just wondering what happened to Pastor Griffith."

"Everybody is wondering that. It's already the talk of the town. I heard it's gonna be on the news tonight. But maybe the video will give us some answers." She paused. "Rachel, there's nothing you need to tell me, right? I mean, there aren't going to be any surprises?"

If Rachel wasn't so doggone guilty, she would have taken offense at Yvette's tone. "What kind of surprises? I told you, I don't know where Pastor Griffith is. I didn't see him."

"Maybe Jasmine knows something."

"No!" Rachel caught herself and lowered her voice. "I mean, Jasmine was with me. She knows what I know."

"Okay," Yvette said skeptically. "I'll keep you posted."

"Do that." Rachel hung up the phone without giving her a chance to say goodbye.

Rachel glanced at the TV. A commercial with a smiling Oprah Winfrey filled the screen. Rachel tossed a throw pillow at the TV. "This is all your fault!" she yelled at Oprah. "If you had just let me on the show, I wouldn't have ended up at Pastor Griffith's and in the middle of this mess."

"Mama, why are you screaming at the TV?" Jordan asked, appearing in the doorway.

"I'm not. Go lie down."

"Can I go play football with Terrence and Dave?"

"You're sick, boy. And you're not hanging with those juvenile delinquents. Go lie down."

"I'm bored," he groaned.

Rachel glared at her son. "Jordan, I am not in the mood," she hissed. "Get your little behind in your room and take a nap."

He frowned. "Dang, I feel like I'm in jail," he said, stomping off.

Jail. The word sent chills up Rachel's spine. Could she really be facing jail time? It's not like she killed anyone.

But you lied about seeing him. Jasmine saw you standing over his body. She could testify against you.

She shook her head. No, if Pastor Griffith was chopped up in a Dumpster somewhere, it had nothing to do with her.

But then a glance at the blackmail letter brought Rachel back to the cold, sobering reality. Earl Griffith was dead and people would think she was to blame.

Rachel knew what she had to do. She had to erase all evidence that she'd ever been at Pastor Griffith's building. She had to get the surveillance video. She didn't know how, but she had faced tougher tasks before and had always come out on top.

Rachel took a deep breath and gathered her strength. Enough of the crying. She had to save her behind, and the first step would be to return to Chicago. Only this was something she couldn't do alone.

"Okay, God, this plan has to work," she said, picking up the phone and scrolling through until she found the number she was looking for.

"Jasmine, it's Rachel," she said, not giving Jasmine time to say anything other than "hello." "Pack a bag. We need to get back to Chicago ASAP."

CHAPTER FOURTEEN

Jasmine could not believe this!

Here she was, thirty thousand feet in the air, heading west across the country from New York to Chicago. What was she doing on this plane? No one could have paid her money to believe that she would be on her way to Chicago to help Rachel Jackson Adams. The only help Jasmine wanted to give that girl was help her get arrested.

And that was the reason she was on the plane.

When Rachel had first called yesterday and told her to pack a bag, Jasmine was sure that the dimwit had lost that single brain cell that she was working with.

"Pack a bag for what?" Jasmine had asked Rachel.

"I got one of those letters!"

Jasmine had tried to keep the laughter out of her voice as she listened to Rachel wail on the other end of the line. "You should have been expecting it. I tried to warn you."

"Well, it's worse than just the letter. Yvette just called me. Pastor Griffith's daughter is waiting to report her father missing." As Jasmine listened to Rachel go on about the pastor's daughter and the police probably going after the videotape in Pastor Griffith's building, another plan began to form in Jasmine's mind.

With this trip, Jasmine could have a multifaceted plan.

First, she'd have Rachel all over Chicago asking all kinds of questions about the missing/dead pastor. Then, she'd leak information to the police about Rachel. Not to have her arrested (though that would be a bonus) but to have the police sniffing around so much that there would be outside pressure for Lester Adams to step down from his position.

"So that's why you need to go with me." Rachel had broken through Jasmine's thoughts. "Because you're on that surveillance tape, too."

"True," Jasmine said, calculating it all in her mind. "But the tape will clearly show that I came back down to the lobby after you sent me to the wrong apartment. And, I can easily say that I met you in the hallway when I finally got to the right apartment and you told me that Pastor Griffith wasn't there."

"So you're just gonna lie!" Rachel's tone sounded like she couldn't believe it. As if she had never lied before.

"Please. As if you would help me if I needed it."

"I would," Rachel said. "I would help you any way I could." Then Rachel had coughed as if she was choking on her words.

"Look, Rachel, I'm sorry for what you're going through, but I don't want to get any more involved in this." Just to push Rachel closer to the edge, she added, "I've been doing some research and the people Pastor Griffith was involved with, the people who are blackmailing you, are some really bad folks. I don't want to put myself in danger like that. So, good luck and . . . God bless."

She'd hung up on Rachel, but that was only for effect. Jasmine had already made up her mind — she was going with Rachel, but she needed the girl to stew a bit more. By the time she called Rachel back, Jasmine wanted the skinny simpleton to be on her knees with gratitude.

And so, half an hour later, Jasmine had called, told Rachel that she couldn't let her go through this by herself . . . and just like she expected, Rachel had been tripping over her words, thanking Jasmine.

But while Jasmine had the reaction she'd wanted from Rachel, all was not good on the home front. It was easy enough to tell Hosea that Yvette wanted her in Chicago for another publicity event, but Mae Frances wasn't happy to hear of Jasmine's plans.

"I thought I told you to leave this alone, Jasmine Larson," the woman had said as the two shared chai teas at Starbucks yesterday afternoon.

"I was. I was going to do exactly what you said, but then, Rachel called me."

"And you should have told her that you weren't going to Chicago and neither should she."

"I couldn't do that," Jasmine said. "I can't leave Rachel out there like that."

Mae Frances's frown was so deep, so tight, her eyebrows became a unibrow. "I know you don't care a daggone thing about that girl. What are you really up to?"

"Nothing. Just what I said. I want to help Rachel."

Mae Frances had leaned so far over the table that she was right in Jasmine's face. "Stay away from this, Jasmine Larson. Those people are bad news and if you end up in the middle of this, it will be a disaster for you, too."

Jasmine had been sorry that she'd confided in Mae Frances. It was just that she'd been so used to working with her friend on everything. But this time, Mae Frances didn't want to have anything to do with this. And every time Mae Frances talked about Pastor Griffith, she spoke with such fear in her eyes.

It was a little disconcerting to Jasmine. She'd never known her friend to fear anything. But there was no need for Mae Frances to be afraid over this. Jasmine had no intention of getting involved with Pastor Griffith's people. Everything she was going to do in Chicago was just for show. Rachel was going to be the one out there, out front, for the whole world to see.

Jasmine knew she'd be just fine.

Still, Jasmine lied and told her friend that she wouldn't go to Chicago, even though she knew that Mae Frances would find out. Her hope, though, was that by that time, she would be back and Lester Adams would be writing his resignation letter.

As United Flight 87's wheels skidded across the tarmac in Chicago, Jasmine formulated the last of her plan in her mind. This was all happening so quickly, she hadn't had a chance to cross every *T* and dot every *I,* and she didn't have the benefit of Mae Frances and her calculating ways. But she still had enough of a plan to make Rachel look hella guilty to anyone looking back over all of this.

Jasmine was almost giddy with anticipation when she stepped through the jet-bridge, but then she stopped the moment she passed through the gate.

"What are you doing here?" Jasmine frowned as she almost bumped into Rachel, who was standing right at the edge of the doorway. "I thought we were meeting in baggage claim."

"I wanted to make sure that you didn't slip off to do your own thing."

"My own thing? I'm only here to help your sorry behind."

"Well, I just wanted to make sure that your *old* sorry behind was right next to me so that I could keep my eye on you."

"You know what? I can get right back on this plane, go back to New York, and mind my business like I was doing before you called me. Because I am not the one who found a dead pastor and didn't report it."

"Ssshhh!" Rachel hissed. "Do you have to be so loud?"

Jasmine raised her eyebrows. "Look, do you want my help or not?" She folded her arms and waited. She wasn't going to take another step until Rachel gave her the right answer.

Rachel pressed her lips together, turned around, and then marched away, as if her apology was somewhere in her silence. With a shake of her head, Jasmine followed. From behind, she took in her enemy and Jasmine almost busted out laughing.

It was Rachel's ghetto ninja outfit that had her wanting to roll on the floor. She had on a thick black turtleneck, black leggings, black boots. Even a black skullcap. While she was trying to be incognegro, she stood out like a flashing light.

But Jasmine didn't say a word as she swung her cashmere cape over her shoulders. The two made their way from the terminal to the car rental in total silence. Even as they stood in line for the car, they ignored each other as they studied their phones, read messages, sent texts, and checked their emails.

Right before Rachel stepped up to the counter to rent the car, Jasmine excused herself to go to the restroom. She didn't step inside the ladies' room, though. She just wanted to make sure that only Rachel would be remembered. Only Rachel would be on any surveillance tapes here.

They didn't speak to each other until they

slid into the car. Jasmine asked, "So, do you have a plan, Miss Ninja?"

"Why you calling me that?" Rachel asked with an attitude.

"Oh, I don't know," Jasmine said as she looked Rachel up and down.

"Look, you can waste time calling me names or we can get to work and figure this out."

"That's what I asked you. Do you have a plan?"

Rachel rolled her eyes. Just hearing Jasmine's voice annoyed her. "I haven't figured it all out yet, but I know for sure that we have to talk to the valet at Pastor Griffith's building because he's already identified me."

"Identified you? To who?"

"Yvette told me that he said someone named Rachel had visited Pastor Griffith on that day."

This is getting better and better. "So, you're going to walk into the building and ask him what?"

"I said I haven't figured it all out yet," Rachel snapped.

"Well," Jasmine began, her tone calmer than Rachel's. She was going to show this trick that she was the grown-up in this car. "You can't just walk in there and say, 'Show me your surveillance tapes.' But, I've given some thought to what you could say. You can tell them that you're a graduate student, working on your thesis about security systems. Then, you can ask some questions about how their system works, where they keep their videos, you know, stuff you want to know."

"Hmmm," Rachel said.

"But I found out that most of these buildings don't keep the tapes past two weeks. So, after you talk to the concierge, we should try to see if we can meet up with Pastor Griffith's daughter. Maybe if you talk to her you could stop her from going to the police so soon, and by the time she goes, the tape would be gone and there won't be any signs of you being in that building."

"Or you."

"Like I told you, I'm not worried about me. And if you want, we can test it. We can go straight to the police and you can watch me convince them that you are far more guilty than I am."

Jasmine could almost see the steam rising from Rachel's head, but though she was sure Rachel wanted to throw her out of the car, it was clear that she was the one doing all the thinking.

"Okay," Rachel said finally. "So, if we can talk Pastor Griffith's daughter into waiting

183

a little while, we won't have to worry about the tape at all. Maybe that's all we need to do. Maybe we don't need to go to Pastor Griffith's building at all."

"You need to do both," Jasmine said, wanting to encourage Rachel. She needed Rachel to be in front of as many people in Chicago as she could. "It won't hurt to talk to the concierge so that you can have a backup plan. And who knows? Maybe the tapes are someplace where you'll be able to get them anyway. Maybe they keep the tapes right there at the front desk. Plus, you do need to know how long they keep their tapes before you talk to his daughter."

"Okay, you're right. So, we'll do both."

"Uh . . . you're going to have to be the one to speak to the concierge and valet."

Rachel frowned. "Why just me?" she asked, her voice filled with distrust.

"Remember I said you're going to pretend to be a student? Well, honey, I'm a little bit older than you. I can't pass for a graduate student."

Even from her profile Jasmine could see Rachel's wide smile. *Oh, yeah.* This chick loved calling Jasmine old but the one thing she was too dumb to know was that with age came wisdom. And as good as Jasmine looked, Rachel could only hope that she looked half as good when she got into her . . . forties.

For the rest of the ride, the two went back to their silence. The scenario was playing out in Jasmine's head: Rachel all over Chicago asking questions about videotapes and the missing pastor. This was going to play out so well.

"Okay," Rachel said finally. "Pastor Griffith's building is in the next block. Should I park in there or on the street?"

"Go up to the concierge. He wasn't at the desk when you came to visit Pastor Griffith, so the chances of him remembering you are slim. Use that to your advantage to get information from him."

"Okay, that's a good idea."

"And just drop me off around the corner."

"What?" Rachel slammed her foot on the brake and both of them jerked forward. "Why? Why don't you want to go in there with me?"

"Because," Jasmine began, though she looked at Rachel like she wondered if the girl was trying to kill her, "if you're supposed to be here just doing some research, why would I be riding around with you?" Before Rachel could protest any more, Jasmine added, "Plus, I have my own investigative work to do. I want to check out the whole building. While you're in there talking to the valet and concierge, I want to check out the number of different ways Pastor Griffith's body could have been taken from the building. I'm trying to find everything I can to prove that you're innocent."

"I am innocent!"

"I know that. I'm just saying if there is ever a question, we will already have all the answers." When Rachel twisted her lips, Jasmine added, "Look, I'm trying to help you, Rachel. Just go in there, do your part. Ask them all kinds of questions about the tapes, where they keep them, how long, even ask them what company they use. And I'll be checking out everything around the building."

"Okay," Rachel mumbled as she edged the SUV to the curb.

Jasmine jumped out. "I'll meet you right back here." She watched Rachel drive off, then turn into the curved driveway that led to the front of the pastor's luxury high-rise. With a smile, Jasmine stepped around the corner and into the Starbucks that she'd noticed when she and Rachel were here last week.

"May I have a grande, soy, no-water, chai?" Jasmine gave her order to the barista.

186

Then she pulled her Kindle from her tote and sat down at one of the tables.

She would be able to get a good fifteen minutes of relaxation in before Rachel came back. She leaned back in the chair, sipped her tea, and wondered in what other ways she could set Rachel up while she brought her husband down.

CHAPTER FIFTEEN

Rachel caught a glimpse of herself as she passed a mirror in the foyer of Pastor Griffith's building. Okay, maybe the skullcap *was* a bit much. She pulled it off, stuffed it in her purse, then fluffed out her curls. She frowned as she thought of Jasmine belittling her outfit. Rachel was just trying to be prepared for anything. And although she knew how to get down and dirty, she wasn't proficient at *real* criminal activity like Jasmine, so she thought the outfit was fine.

The concierge was sitting behind the front desk. He was tall, with a protruding stomach that made him look like he was seven months pregnant. But he was clean shaven and immaculately dressed in a gray uniform, so Rachel forced a smile as she approached him. Jasmine's idea of being a college student working on a thesis might work. But then again, judging from the way the man's eyes lit up as she strutted toward him, Rachel thought her idea would work so much better.

"Good evening. May I help you?" the man said with a cheesy grin.

"Hello," she said, tossing her hair over her shoulder. "I sure hope you can help me," she added sweetly. "My name is Lois Lanegly," she quickly corrected. She needed to seem legit. "I am a reporter with *Ebony* magazine and I am doing a story on people behind successful people."

He looked confused as she continued. "See, I was thinking about doing a story on successful Chicago residents, but then I thought, why don't I look at the people who make the successful people's lives flow smoothly. Like assistants, maids, and" — she pointed at him — "doormen."

He smiled. "Technically, I'm not a doorman. I'm more of a front-desk security." He stuck his chest out. "But I definitely keep things in order around here."

"Oh, I can only imagine," she cooed. "You probably make life so much easier for the rich people that live in this building and they don't appreciate or recognize you for all that you do."

He looked at her in awe. "Wow, somebody gets me."

"So, what's your name?"

"Victor. Victor Swanson."

"Victor, do you mind talking to me?"

He looked around nervously. Rachel had purposely come late so there wouldn't be much traffic in and out of the building. "Ooooh, I don't want to get in any trouble."

"Oh, no, this is a positive feature story. But if you can't do it, I'll go talk to the guy at the building across the street."

"You mean Felipe?"

"Yeah," she said, shrugging. She just assumed that the ritzy building across the street had front-desk security as well. The disdain on his face told her there was more to their story.

"Well, I could tell you so much more than Felipe. I mean, he's only been around the last two years."

"I'm sure you could." She stuck out her lip in a playful pout. "But if you're uncomfortable, I don't want to make you do anything you don't want to. But I would much rather spend my time interviewing a hunk like yourself."

He blushed as Rachel looked him up and down and licked her lips. "Because Felipe doesn't have anything on you," she added.

He looked at her pensively. "The story is positive, right?"

"Of course." She looked into her purse

190

and silently cursed herself for not bringing a notepad. It would look pretty tacky for her to pull out her light bill and start writing on the back.

"Do you mind if I record this?" she asked, pulling out her BlackBerry after it dawned on her that the phone had a voice recorder. "It won't take long. I just want to ask what a typical day is like for you."

Rachel hoped Victor wouldn't be long-winded as he began explaining his very boring day with the enthusiasm of a rocket scientist.

Back in the day, she'd wanted to be a reporter, but since she never quite made it through college, that was a dream she'd never realized. She asked Victor a few other questions about being appreciated and his dream job — which was to be a Calvin Klein model. As if.

Finally, she said, "I'm sure part of what you have to do involves protecting the place?"

"I'm kind of a jack-of-all-trades."

"I'm sure it's difficult keeping track of everything. Do you have any help? I mean with a place like this, I'm sure there is some top-notch security."

"You would think, wouldn't you? But no, we just have a regular old video camera system," Victor said, pointing to a desk that showed several cameras. "Nothing ever happens around here. But just in case, we record everything to the back office." He pointed over his shoulder.

Rachel asked him a couple more questions, then said, "Okay, if you don't mind, I'd like to get a few more pictures for my story." She pointed the BlackBerry at him. He frowned at the sight of her camera phone.

"Oh, you know technology these days. This is a high-tech camera phone so we don't have to carry around bulky equipment anymore." The answer seemed to appease him. She looked around, turning up her nose. "You know, this area is so dull and bland. It isn't doing you justice. Maybe we can go in the back office."

"Well . . ." he hesitantly began.

Rachel couldn't believe what she was about to do, but desperate times called for desperate measures.

She slithered closer. "I mean, I would really love to go in the back, to, umm, take the photo, then see what else we could get into."

He looked at her, stunned, as it dawned on him what she was saying.

Rachel ran a finger across his protruding

stomach. "It's something about a man with some meat on his bones that turns me on," she said seductively.

A big grin spread across Victor's face. Rachel glanced back to see if she could spot Jasmine, but of course, that skank was staying out of sight.

"Well, it is kind of quiet right now. Guess I could spare a few minutes to, umm, take some pictures," he said with a sly grin.

"So, do you keep a stack of tapes?" Rachel asked once they were in the back office. "That might make a good visual, standing you next to that."

He laughed. "Tapes? Nah, everything is digital. Stored on the server." He pointed to a massive electrical unit. "So, let's get your photo so we can, ummm, get to know each other better. I'm gonna have to get back up front in a minute."

Rachel's mind raced as she tried to think. She hadn't accounted for technology. She thought she was just going to have to figure out a way to steal a tape. She hadn't thought about the fact that everything would be digital.

"Okay," she said, taking out her phone again. "Oooh, hold on. My boss is texting me." She pulled the phone to her and began typing.

Jasmine, I'm in the back office trying to get the video. Need u to come create a major distraction ASAP. No questions. Just hurry!

She hoped Jasmine didn't try and be a butthole and not come. Right now, a distraction was the only way she could get to that server.

Victor cleared his throat. "Ahem."

"Sorry," she replied. "Okay, stand over there." She pointed to the corner. While he posed, Rachel took picture after picture, praying Jasmine wouldn't let her down.

"Okay, that's enough," he finally announced. "Told you, I don't have much time." He licked his lips. "And I have something else I'd much rather be doing." He flashed a wicked grin and stepped toward her. Rachel felt bile building in the pit of her stomach.

"Bring your fine behind to daddy," he said with a throaty moan.

Rachel held out her hand to stop him just as he leaned in to kiss her. "Umm, do you have some wine or something? I'm a little nervous."

"No, no drinks allowed in here. Can't have liquid around the server. Plus, they overwork me and I haven't had a chance to back up anything in the last two weeks."

That was music to her ears. "Oh," she

said, pouting when she really wanted to rejoice. That meant the only copy of the surveillance video was on that machine. "That's a shame. Because, I tell you. If you want to see me get wild and loose, just give me even a half a cup of wine." She giggled.

His eyes danced in anticipation. "Well, I do keep some Boone's Farm and some weed in my car. We could go out there."

Boone's Farm? Rachel guessed the immaculate appearance was just for the job. Underneath it all, he was just a Chicago hoodrat. "Or you could go get it," she said, running her hands up the center of his thigh. "The wine at least. I'm not a smoker."

"I'll be right back," he panted. "Hot diggity dog! My boys ain't gonna believe this," he sang as he raced out the door.

Rachel raced over to the server. She had no idea where to even begin. All the switches, buttons, and levers were completely foreign to her. "Where the heck is the Delete button?" she muttered.

She punched a host of buttons but nothing happened. She heard Victor shuffling back in, so she had to quickly turn around.

"Time to get wild and loose," he said, holding up the bottle of strawberry Boone's Farm. Rachel forced back her groan. What

195

type of man actually kept cheap wine in his car?

He handed her a Styrofoam cup, quickly screwed the top off, then poured some of the beverage into her cup.

"Drink up. Time's a'tickin'."

Think, Rachel, think. Where the heck was Jasmine? If that heifer didn't come through . . .

She slowly sipped her drink while Victor eyed her like a hawk about to move in on its prey.

"Okay, I don't have time to wait for the wine to go to work," he said, taking her cup from her and sitting the bottle on the counter next to the server. She needed to figure out how to get him to show her how the server worked. Maybe she should just come clean. Maybe he would help her delete the video if she told him the truth. Or maybe he would be so mad about her leading him on that he'd turn her in to the police. No, she couldn't chance it.

But as she watched Victor remove his belt and start unbuttoning his pants, she knew she couldn't go so far as to sleep with this man either.

"Ummph, I can't believe I'm about to get with a woman this fine," he said, thrusting his crotch toward her. "I'm about to rock your world, girl."

Rachel was about to abort the whole mission when she heard a loud crash coming from the lobby area.

"What the — ?" Victor said, jumping back.

He raced out to the front and Rachel jumped up to once again try to figure out how to delete the files on the server. After a few seconds of pounding keys to no avail, Rachel spotted the bottle of wine on the counter. Without thinking, she reached over, grabbed the bottle, then proceeded to dump the entire contents onto the server. She immediately heard sizzling, then hissing, then finally a plume of smoke rose from the machine.

She'd just set the bottle back down when Victor raced back into the room. "You're not going to believe this. Someone just broke the big glass table in the lobby. Then —" His words stopped midsentence when he saw the smoke. "Holy crap!"

He raced over to the server. "What's going on?" he said, panicked.

"I have no idea! When you jumped up, you knocked over the wine and it spilled onto that thing," she said, pointing at the server.

"Oh, my God!" he yelled, grabbing his shirt and trying to dab the keyboard. "It's destroyed! This is a thirty-thousand-dollar machine!" The sizzling continued, followed by a few snaps, crackles, and pops.

Rachel suppressed a smile. *Destroyed?* Oh, this worked out better than she expected.

Victor began pounding his head, muttering a string of obscenities. "I am in so much trouble," he cried.

"Well, look, I see things have gotten kind of hectic." She grabbed her purse. "So I'm going to get going." She squeezed his arm. "Thanks for everything. Hope it all works out!"

Thankfully, he was so frazzled that he didn't pay her any attention as she darted out the door. She stepped over the broken glass covering the lobby floor. A few people had started to gather, eyeing the damage. Rachel smiled to herself. So Jasmine had come through.

But she wouldn't give Jasmine all the glory. She'd destroyed the video — something that Jasmine had zero confidence that she would be able to pull off. But that's what Jasmine got for underestimating her. Sooner or later, Jasmine and everyone else would realize that she always came out on top.

CHAPTER SIXTEEN

Jasmine kept her eyes on her cell phone screen.

What in the world did that child get into? Jasmine wondered as she read Rachel's text again.

At first, when she'd received Rachel's SOS, Jasmine had chosen to ignore it. After all, isn't this what she'd come to Chicago to do? To make sure that Rachel created havoc and drew major attention to herself at the same time?

But as she sat sipping her Starbucks, Jasmine read the text over a few times. There was something about the last words — *Create a major distraction ASAP. No questions. Just hurry* — that made Jasmine decide that she couldn't just sit there. Maybe it was the "just hurry" that had Jasmine going. She could hear the panic and fear in those words. There was no telling what kind of idiotic move that girl had made, but no matter what, Jasmine couldn't just leave Rachel out there like that. Her goal wasn't for Rachel to end up dead or even physically hurt — she just wanted her arrested.

So, Jasmine had left Starbucks and done something. She just prayed that it had worked.

"Jasmine!"

She'd been so focused on her cell, reading Rachel's text once again, that she didn't even notice Rachel drive up. She hopped into the car, slammed the door, then turned to Rachel as she swerved away from the curb.

"What happened?"

Rachel shook her head. "You don't even want to know."

"Uh, yeah, I do. I had to sneak in the side door and destroy that beautiful glass table, then run like some criminal before anyone saw me! So don't tell me that I don't want to know. Girl, please!" Jasmine sucked her teeth. "You better tell me."

"Okay!" Rachel exclaimed as she maneuvered the car with one hand and pressed the other against her chest as if she was trying to tell her heart to calm down. She was silent for a while, putting her thoughts together. Then, "It was just horrible," she said, before she began to tell Jasmine the story of Victor. "He was all over me," Rachel said when she got to the part of how she got him into the security room. "And I didn't know what else to do."

"So you had me put myself in jeopardy of being arrested because you were trying to get your freak on?"

"Have you not heard a word of what I said? It was just a ploy to get him back there."

"A stupid ploy!"

"A ploy that worked!" She paused and then grinned as she waited a moment to appreciate the look of surprise on Jasmine's face. "That's right," Rachel said. "I destroyed the server. The whole thing went . . . up in smoke." Rachel giggled as if she was replaying that part in her head.

"You've got to be kidding me."

Rachel finished the story, telling how she'd destroyed the server with half a bottle of Boone's Farm.

Jasmine shook her head as she listened. She had to give it to Rachel — she'd helped her cause . . . and kind of blew up Jasmine's cause at the same time.

Rachel said, "So, now that I did what I came to Chicago to do, we can go home."

"Really? Just like that?"

Rachel gave Jasmine a quick glance, then

turned her eyes back to the road. "All I wanted to do was get that videotape. Whether it's in my hands or destroyed doesn't matter to me. As long as no one will be able to see me," she paused and glanced once more at Jasmine, "or you on that tape, we're good."

"So you're going to just head back to the airport right now? Without really taking care of business?"

Rachel slammed on the brakes, deciding not to run a red light, and jerking Jasmine forward at the same time. Now, she faced Jasmine full-on. "Didn't you hear a word I said?" she asked, raising her voice. She slowed her cadence. "There's . . . no . . . need . . . for . . . us . . . to . . . stay." She spoke as if Jasmine was deaf and dumb. "We're . . . good."

Jasmine wanted to slap the Chihuahua-faced ninny, but she had to play nice until her deed was done. "I'm just saying there is one more thing that we need to do."

Rachel looked at her quizzically.

"You need to go see Pastor Griffith's daughter."

"What? Why should we do that now? It's totally unnecessary."

"Because coming to Chicago wasn't about just the videotape. We have to protect you.

Get all the information we can, and that includes you talking to Pastor Griffith's daughter."

Rachel was already shaking her head. "I told you, I'm good. Did what I came to do and now I'm out of here."

"But what about the letter? Rachel, you really need to take this seriously. Someone saw you."

"So what? They can't prove it. Not without the tape."

"You don't know what kind of proof they have. There could be several eyewitnesses who saw you walk into Pastor Griffith's apartment. And they won't need the video-tape. One eyewitness can corroborate another's story." Jasmine paused as Rachel squinted her eyes, thinking. She added, "Are you sure you didn't see anyone when you went up to Pastor Griffith's apartment?"

Rachel slowed the rental car as they came to another red light. And Jasmine watched Rachel remember that day. "There was someone, but I know she's not sending me any letters."

"Who?"

"An older lady. She was kneeling on the floor when I got off the elevator; she said she'd been knocked down by some fool." Rachel stopped and Jasmine could almost see Rachel's brain ticking as she connected the dots.

Rachel said, "Do you think whoever knocked that lady down has something to do with all of this?"

Jasmine nodded slowly. "That's what I'm thinking. That's why we need to talk to Eleanor."

"But what is that crackhead gonna tell us?"

"First of all, she's not a crackhead anymore. And aren't you related to a crackhead?"

If Rachel's head wasn't covered by her weave, Jasmine was sure she would've seen the smoke rising from her brain. "Don't be talking about my family 'cause I don't want to have to —"

"Look." Jasmine stopped her. "I'm not trying to start a fight. I'm just making a point. Your brother —"

"You don't know nothin' 'bout my brother! And how do you even know I have a brother?"

Jasmine raised an eyebrow. After all she'd put this girl through, was Rachel really asking this question? "Okay, so your brother's not a crackhead, but he was and now he's fine. That's all I'm saying about Eleanor. She's fine, in her right mind, and you don't know what she may be able to tell us. She might have information about her father that she doesn't realize she has."

"And how is this supposed to help me?"

"You never know where a clue can pop up. Look, Rachel, all I'm saying is that since we're here anyway, let's play this out. Your flight doesn't leave 'til tomorrow, right? So what do you have to lose?"

Rachel blinked over and over as if that motion was the motor that got her brain moving.

Jasmine pushed on. "The worst that could happen is we get nothing. The best . . ." She stopped, knowing Rachel was at least smart enough to finish that.

"All right," she said finally, reluctantly. "But I don't know where she lives."

"I have it right here." Jasmine held up her iPhone. She glanced up at the traffic light. It was green. "Let's go."

Rachel turned off the ignition, then clicked the door handle to open the car door. But when Jasmine didn't move, Rachel frowned.

"I'm not going with you," Jasmine explained before Rachel could even ask the question. "You need to talk to Eleanor by yourself."

"What!" Rachel exclaimed. "You just said

that we needed to get over here."

"We needed to get over here, but you need to be the one who talks to her. You're the one being blackmailed."

"What does that have to do with anything?"

"You're the one who needs the information. No one is coming after me."

"So you think Eleanor has something to do with what's going on?"

"No, but she may have information and she's more likely to talk to one person she doesn't know rather than two."

Rachel paused, blinked, thought. "You made up some excuse not to go with me into Pastor Griffith's building." She frowned. "What's really going on, Jasmine?"

Jasmine sighed. "Look, Rachel, I was in New York, minding my own business. If I was trying to do something to you, I wouldn't have flown halfway across the country to help you. If I was trying to hurt you, I wouldn't have come up with all of these ideas. So you need to know, if you keep coming at me like this, I'll just get on the plane, go home, and maybe send you a letter when you get your prison number assigned. Because if you don't take care of this, trust . . . you will end up in jail."

Rachel's lips were pressed together as if

she was holding back the verbal whip-ass she wanted to give to Jasmine. She slammed the door, then trotted across the wide street. Rachel had to pass one, two, then three buildings before she got to the walk-up that was Eleanor's.

Jasmine laughed as Rachel disappeared behind the glass door of the building. Rachel may have destroyed the server, but this was still working out. Depending on how that server worked, Rachel could very well be on the video today. (Jasmine had taken great pains to stay out of sight when she broke the table.) So it would still show that Rachel was in the building, just not on the day the pastor disappeared. But the question would be raised . . . What was she doing back?

And even without the server, the concierge still saw her and Jasmine was sure that the valet did, too, since Rachel had parked the car and was wearing the stand-out ghetto ninja gear. Yup, two people would be able to say that Rachel had been back in Chicago asking crazy questions. And now Eleanor would make three. When Jasmine contacted the police anonymously and put them on Rachel's trail, there would be enough questions as to why this woman was so interested in videos and the missing pastor.

As she waited, Jasmine glanced around. Eleanor may have only lived five miles from her father, but this was a world away. Just blocks from where the Robert Taylor homes had stood, the neighborhood still hadn't gone through gentrification and as Jasmine took in the brick building with cardboard covering some of the windows that she sat in front of, she wondered if she should have gone with Rachel, rather than just sit here like a target.

Glancing at the ignition, she frowned. Dang . . . Rachel had taken the key. She tightened her coat around her as if that would give her some kind of protection. She should have told Rachel to just ask a question or two and not sit down for a cup of tea.

Jasmine's gaze moved to the other side of the street and her eyes fixed on two men approaching. There was nothing that made either of them stand out or seem out of place. Two black men, in their twenties, one with a short haircut, the other with locks. One tall and lean, the other muscular. Both in jeans and dark leather jackets.

Nothing special, except for the way they walked. Their swagger was tough, determined, as if they were on their way to take care of serious business.

Jasmine checked the car locks, just to make sure that she was safe inside. The moment she turned her eyes back to Eleanor's building, the door opened and Rachel walked out.

That was fast, Jasmine thought and wondered if Eleanor had even been home. Whatever. Sitting in that rental car had Jasmine ready to agree with Rachel. It was time to get out of Chicago.

But then . . .

Rachel took two steps down just as the men Jasmine had seen jumped in front of her. She watched Rachel try to sidestep out of their way, but they blocked her.

There were words. Rachel backed up. Then there was the scream.

Jasmine grabbed the handle of the rental car, jumped out, and yelled, "Hey!" She dashed across the street as fast as her boots allowed, yelling all the way. "Hey! Get away from her!"

She was still feet away when the men stepped back, jumped down the steps, and ran in the opposite direction. Jasmine's gaze followed them, but that was as close to the thugs as she planned to get.

She ran the rest of the way to Rachel. "Are you okay?" Jasmine asked.

Rachel stood frozen, with her back pressed

against the brick wall. Her eyes were filled with tears and her lips trembled.

"It's okay," Jasmine said softly. If she had liked the girl just a little bit more, she would have given her a hug. Instead, she came close as she rounded her arm across Rachel's shoulders. "You're okay," she assured her as she led her down the steps.

At the car, Jasmine put Rachel into the passenger seat. Then she took the key and slid into the driver's side. It wasn't until she tried to stick the key into the lock that Jasmine realized her hands were shaking, too.

"What was that?" Jasmine asked as she twisted the car away from the curb. She wanted to ask Rachel more, but she also wanted to get away from this place as fast as she could. "What did they want? Your wallet?"

The light was red at the end of the street and Jasmine was tempted to run through it anyway. But as she waited, she turned to Rachel who sat still stiff, still stunned.

"It's okay, Rachel," Jasmine said, wishing there was more that she could have done to assure her. "You got away. You're safe. All they did was take your wallet, right?"

For the first time, Rachel moved. She shook her head, and now the tears fell from her eyes. "They didn't want my wallet."

Oh, God! This was going to be even more traumatic. *Were they going to try to rape her?*

Rachel said, "They told me that they know what's going on with Pastor Griffith and if I didn't tell them what they wanted to know, that I would be the one who would end up dead next."

"What?" Now Jasmine was really trembling.

"They said they knew I'd come back to take care of the business and they wanted to know what I knew."

"What kind of business? What are you supposed to know?"

"I don't know," Rachel cried. "But they think I'm involved. Jasmine, what is going on?"

She wanted to cry with Rachel. This was not the way this was supposed to go down. All Jasmine wanted was to get Rachel in a little bit of trouble. Just enough to make Lester have to step down.

But this was much more than trouble. This was knee-deep danger. Jasmine shook her head. This was exactly what Mae Frances had warned her about.

"I'm afraid, Jasmine," Rachel whispered. "How did they know I was in Chicago? How did they know that I was going to be at Eleanor's apartment at that moment?"

"Did you talk to Eleanor?"

Rachel shook her head. "She wasn't home, but I left her a note." She paused and hit herself on her forehead with the heel of her hand. "Oh, no. I left my name and cell number for her to call me. So those thugs have my information. Who are these people and what am I gonna do?"

It was her tone, it was the way she sat, it was her tears that flowed faster than any river that made Jasmine's heart break. But she had to give it to the girl; at least Rachel was still standing. Jasmine was sure that she would've fainted if those men had stepped to her that way, with all of that information.

"Don't worry, Rachel," Jasmine said sincerely. "We're going to figure this out. I promise you. I'm going to help you."

And when the light turned green, Jasmine sped through the intersection, knowing that she'd just told Rachel the truth. This was one of those situations where she could pick on Rachel, she could bring Rachel down, but no one else could.

Jasmine had no idea how she was going to make her promise come true, but she would.

From this point forward, she and Rachel would be on the same team. No longer enemies, though Jasmine wasn't trying to be the girl's friend. At least not completely.

No, they wouldn't be friends, but they wouldn't be enemies, either. They'd be frenemies, just doing whatever they had to do to make this right.

CHAPTER SEVENTEEN

Rachel toyed with the spinach salad that sat in front of her. She felt like they needed to be doing something — searching for clues, calling for help . . . running for the hills — anything but sitting in this restaurant, sipping tea and wolfing down salads.

"Rachel, you have to eat something," Jasmine said. Her tone was gentle, yet persuasive. It almost reminded Rachel of her mother. Rachel felt her eyes mist at the thought of her mother. Loretta Jackson was probably turning over in her grave at the predicament her daughter had found herself in.

"I told you, I'm not hungry," Rachel muttered, moving the leaves around with her fork.

Jasmine reached over and gently touched Rachel's hand. "You've got to keep your strength up."

Rachel glanced up at Jasmine and for the

first time since she'd met the woman, she felt a real connection. She didn't know if it was just because they were bonded by this disaster, or if Jasmine was being genuine. Either way, she was simply grateful for Jasmine's presence.

"I just don't have an appetite," Rachel finally replied.

"I understand that," Jasmine responded. "But you're not going to be able to think straight if you're famished. We've been running around all day and you haven't eaten anything."

Rachel exhaled briefly, then forced a forkful of spinach into her mouth. She chewed, swallowed, then said, "So what's the plan?" At this point Rachel had no clue what they were doing. If she had it her way, she'd go straight to the airport, get on a plane, and head back to Houston like she'd never known anyone named Pastor Earl Griffith. But Jasmine was right. Her ignoring it didn't mean it would go away. She couldn't take this drama back to Houston and embarrass Lester, her father, and her whole church family. No, she and Jasmine needed to figure out what in the world was going on. Those men today had looked like they weren't playing around; and the fact that they knew Rachel was in Chicago, let alone

215

at Eleanor's apartment, meant that these weren't some two-bit hustlers.

"I don't have a plan because I thought we were getting the video, talking to Eleanor, and leaving," Jasmine said.

"Then what are we going to do?" Rachel said.

"That's what we're here to talk about," Jasmine snapped.

Any other time, Rachel might have told Jasmine off for snapping at her, but the situation was tense, so Jasmine's angst was understandable. "The first question is, Who would want Pastor Griffith dead?" Rachel finally said.

Jasmine's eyes flashed knowingly and Rachel leaned in and narrowed her eyes. "Jasmine, do you know something?"

Jasmine didn't respond as she tensed up.

"This is serious. If you know something, you need to tell me," Rachel said in a panic. If Jasmine knew something and was leading her further into danger . . .

Suddenly, Jasmine relaxed. "Of course I don't know anything. I know what you know."

Rachel was just about to say something else when her cell phone vibrated. She glanced down, noticed the 312 number, and froze.

"It's a Chicago number," Rachel said softly.

Jasmine motioned for her to answer it. "It's probably Eleanor."

Rachel inhaled slowly. Of course it was Eleanor. She had just left the woman a note to call.

She picked up the phone and spoke into it. "Hello."

"Yeah, this is Eleanor Griffith," the woman said. She sounded young and her tone was ripe with worry. "I got your message. Why are you asking about my father? Do you know where he is?"

Rachel paused as she tried to gather her thoughts. "Umm, I'm with the American Baptist Coalition," she stammered, shrugging at Jasmine. Shoot, she hadn't thought a lot of this whole plan all the way through. She just wanted to clear her name. "Well, we were just concerned. We heard that your father was missing."

The woman let out a small sob, like she'd been holding it in. "He is. And my gut tells me something is wrong. He wouldn't have just up and disappeared."

Jasmine eyed Rachel, probably anxious to know what the woman was saying.

"So, do you have any idea what could've happened to him?"

"I don't know. I filed a police report this morning."

"Can you think of anyone who would want to harm him?"

"No. My father worked hard in the church. He committed his life to God, to the church. And he was very proud of me. I had an event that he was supposed to be at and he didn't show up." She was actually in full-fledged crying mode now.

"Maybe something just came up," Rachel said.

"That's what I thought at first. But my dad checked on me every day," she said, her voice cracking. "I haven't heard from him. Something is not right."

"Maybe he's with some friends." Rachel knew she didn't sound convincing, but she had to try to gather as much information as she could.

"I've talked to everyone. No one has heard from him. His girlfriend doesn't even know where he is."

Rachel raised an eyebrow. *Girlfriend?* She didn't know Pastor Griffith had a girlfriend.

"Look, I gotta go," Eleanor continued. "I thought you might've had some information or something."

"No, we just wanted to offer our assistance. Let us know if there's anything we can do to help."

Rachel hung up and relayed the details of the conversation to Jasmine.

"Okay, so that means neither Eleanor nor the police are on to you," Jasmine said.

"On to me?" Rachel hated that Jasmine made it sound like she was some kind of criminal hiding from police.

"Ladies, is there anything else I can get for you?" the waitress asked, approaching their table. Both Rachel and Jasmine turned to reply when Rachel's eyes caught the television just above the bar.

"Oh, my God!" Rachel jumped up and raced to the bar.

Jasmine, who'd quickly followed her, said, "What?"

"Look," Rachel said, pointing to the TV. It was the local nightly news and the anchor was talking as a picture of Pastor Griffith flashed on the screen. "Can you turn that up, please?" Rachel asked the bartender, who picked up the remote and pumped up the volume.

"A Southeast minister is missing tonight and authorities need your help in locating the woman last seen with him. Prominent pastor Earl Griffith was last seen at his home in the exclusive South Shore Drive community. Police aren't saying foul play is involved, but they tell WGN that they are looking to question an unidentified woman who is believed to have been with the minister just before he came up missing. The woman is described as a black female, about five-six, one hundred and forty pounds, with curly brown hair."

Rachel watched in stunned horror as the anchor continued talking. "Police say they may be close to identifying the woman, but have yet to release those details. Of course, we'll stay on top of the story and keep you posted."

"Jasmine, what are we going to d—" Rachel turned around to face Jasmine and was shocked to find her gone. Jasmine was back at their table, gathering up her things.

"Did you see that?" Rachel asked, pointing toward the TV.

Jasmine took out two twenties and tossed them on the table. "I saw it."

"So what are we going to do?"

"I don't know about you, but I'm going home." She started walking toward the exit.

Rachel grabbed her arm. "You can't leave."

Jasmine spun toward her. Rachel couldn't be sure, but was that fear she saw in Jasmine's eyes?

"Look, Rachel, this is turning into more

220

than I bargained for. I want to help you."
She took a deep breath. "I mean, I never
thought I'd be saying this, but I genuinely
do want to help. But this" — she pointed to
the TV — "I can't get caught up in this
madness."

Rachel couldn't help it. The dam burst
and all the tears came flooding out.

Jasmine released a small groan, then
stepped toward Rachel and took her into
her arms. "Okay, please stop crying," she
said, awkwardly rubbing Rachel's back. Rachel wanted to stop, but everything just
came to a peak. The whole day had been
too much and now the one person she had
in her corner was about to bail on her. She
simply didn't have the strength to go
through this alone.

"I-I'm sorry," Rachel sniffed, trying to pull
herself together.

Jasmine exhaled, shifted her purse to her
other arm, and said, "Don't be. Like I said,
we'll figure this out."

"Y-you're not going to leave?"

It took everything in her power, but Jasmine finally said, "No, I told you we're,
we're" — she cleared her throat, swallowed
— "we're a team," she continued. "We'll
figure this out, together."

CHAPTER EIGHTEEN

"I'm not sure," Jasmine said into the phone as she paced the width of the hotel room. "I don't know how much longer Yvette wants me to be here."

"Well, what is it exactly that Yvette wants you to do?" her husband asked.

"A couple of interviews," Jasmine said, purposefully being vague with Hosea. "And she might even get us another shot with Oprah. But if she does, it'll have to happen quickly. That's why she wants me to stay close by, you know?"

Jasmine had tried to leave her lying-to-my-husband-all-the-time days behind, but there was always something that pulled her back to the woman she used to be. This wasn't her fault; she hated that the lies slipped so easily from her mouth, but these untruths were being told for a good cause.

"Okay, darlin'," Hosea said, sounding as if he believed every word Jasmine said. "But tell Yvette to hurry up. The kids miss you and I miss you the most."

"There you go. Making me want to hop on the next plane back to New York."

"It's true," he said. "This house is not the same without you."

"Well, I'll call tonight so that I can speak to Jacquie and Zaya. And maybe by then, I'll have a better idea on when I'll be home."

"Perfect," he said. "Oh, and call Mae Frances. When I told her this morning that you'd gone back to Chicago, she was upset."

"Really?" Jasmine closed her eyes as she remembered the last conversation she'd had with her best friend two days ago. The conversation that had warned her to stay away from Chicago. The conversation that had warned her that there was so much danger here.

"Yeah," Hosea continued, "I couldn't figure it out. I told her it was for business, but she seemed really shook up. What's up with that?"

"I don't know. You know how Mae Frances is. It's probably just because I didn't tell her I was leaving," Jasmine said, before she fell onto the bed. She never had to worry about Mae Frances saying a word to Hosea. Her friend wouldn't give her up for anything, so Jasmine didn't have to worry about Hosea

223

finding out about what she'd done to Rachel.

But Jasmine did miss her friend. Mae Frances knew everybody and everything. And right now, Jasmine could use some of her friend's knowledge.

"I'll call Mae Frances and settle her down," Jasmine said, not sure if she was lying or not. She wanted to call her friend, but she didn't want to hear what Mae Frances had to say.

"Do that. I love you, darlin'."

"I love you, too, babe," she said, then clicked off her cell. She tossed the phone onto the bed beside her, then glanced around the bedroom section of the suite. She couldn't believe she was back here at the Omni, one of her favorite places to stay in Chicago. But not even the luxury of this four-star, all-suites, Oprah-favorite hotel could take the edge off the fear that was simmering inside of her.

This had begun as just a little ploy to get back the American Baptist Coalition position that rightfully belonged to her . . . and Hosea, of course. But now, she felt like she was in the middle of some James Bond saga. What bothered Rachel the most was not knowing how those thugs had found out that she was in Chicago. But what had Jasmine on edge was thugs were involved in this at all! Her instincts told Jasmine to get on a plane and head back to New York. Let Rachel handle this, and if the thugs came for Jasmine, at least she'd have the protection of Hosea and Mae Frances.

But there was something inside Jasmine that just would not let her quit. A feeling inside that told her there was so much more to this story and she might be onto something big.

She glanced at her phone, once again wanting to call Mae Frances, but knowing that she couldn't. Mae Frances would probably get on a plane and try to drag her back to New York. But how could she leave Rachel out there like that, when she could very well be part of the reason Rachel was in this mess?

Jasmine was grateful for the knock on the door; at least now she and Rachel would be able to take some action instead of sitting around thinking about this.

She opened the door, and Rachel stepped inside quickly, glancing back over her shoulder as if she was being chased.

"So, are you settled in?" Jasmine asked as if this was just another ordinary day.

"Yeah." Rachel walked around the front room of the suite, checking the wide open space for anything that was hidden. "I called Lester and told him the story that we'd come up with." Stopping and looking at Jasmine, she added, "He wanted to know when I was coming home. I do have small children, you know."

Jasmine's eyebrows arched. "As if I don't."

"Oh, yeah," Rachel said. "I keep forgetting that 'cause you're so much older than me."

Jasmine folded her arms.

"I don't mean anything by that. I'm just sayin' I forget sometimes." Rachel lowered herself onto the couch. "So, what exactly are we going to do? And really, why are we going to do it?"

"Why?"

"Yeah, why." Rachel ran her hands up and down her arms as if she were cold. " 'Cause I've been thinking. Why are we doing this? Why don't we just go home and pretend like none of this ever happened?"

"So you really think going home will make this all go away?"

"I don't know," Rachel said as she stood up once again. As she paced, she added, "Going home can't be any worse than staying here."

"I'm not sure about that," Jasmine said, her eyes following Rachel as she moved.

"Suppose you leave and suppose the thugs follow you. And suppose they follow you home, to your husband . . . and your children."

Rachel stopped walking and it looked as if she'd stopped breathing. "My children?"

Rachel's tears were instant and Jasmine regretted her words. "I'm not saying that will happen," she said quickly. "I'm just trying to get you to see all sides. And there is a side that could affect your children."

Rachel covered her mouth.

Jasmine added, "That's why we've got to stay here, for just a few more days. We'll find out what we can and maybe we'll have enough answers so that we can go to the police and get them to stop looking for you."

"Where are we gonna look for answers?" Rachel cried. "It's not like we know anyone in Chicago."

"Actually, we do. We know Yvette."

Rachel frowned. "Yvette? What can she possibly tell us? She's just a publicist."

"She's from Chicago, she knew Pastor Griffith, and she might have heard something by now. Like you said, she's a publicist and those people always have their ears to the ground. They know everything that's going on around them."

"Are we gonna tell her what's going on?"

Jasmine shrugged as she grabbed her jacket. "I'm not sure. Let's see what she says and then we can decide if we should bring her in to help us."

Even as Jasmine moved toward the door, Rachel stood stiffly in her place. "Jasmine, are you trying to set me up?"

She released a long sigh. "No, Rachel. If I wanted you to go to jail or get in any kind of trouble for this, I would already be on a plane to New York." When Rachel's lips twisted in doubt, Jasmine added, "Look. We're gonna have to trust each other and work together from this point on or nothing will get accomplished."

Still Rachel did not move. "Let me ask you something."

"What?"

"Why do you want to help me? You don't even like me."

"Well, that's true." In an instant, so much went through Jasmine's mind: the fights that she'd had with Rachel as they fought for the presidency of the ABC and the battles they'd had ever since the Oprah fiasco. But what was stuck at the front of Jasmine's thoughts was the letter that she'd sent Rachel and the guilt that was attached to that. She knew that somehow that letter had something to do with this. She'd sent the letter and now Rachel was in trouble that was beyond what Jasmine had intended.

But of course, Jasmine said none of these things. She said, "I want to help because I know you didn't kill Pastor Griffith. And I'd like to think that if this was turned around, you'd do the same thing for me."

It took a moment, but Rachel finally swung her purse over her shoulder and marched out of the room. With a shake of her head, Jasmine followed her.

The GPS unit led the two straight to Yvette's condo and Jasmine was surprised and pleased to find out that their publicist lived just a few blocks away from Pastor Griffith. It was already after ten, so the last thing she wanted was to be roaming around Chicago late at night.

This close proximity might give Yvette an edge that she didn't even know that she had. Jasmine had never asked Yvette, but maybe she and Pastor Griffith crossed paths beyond the ABC, maybe she even attended Pastor Griffith's church, maybe they'd been to social functions together.

"So tell me," Rachel began as they stepped into the high-rise building. "What exactly are we going to say to Yvette? What exactly is the plan?"

Inside, Jasmine screamed. This was Rachel's drama, yet she was the one doing all the mental work. What Jasmine wanted to say to Rachel was, "Why don't you come up with a plan for once?" But since she knew that Rachel was hanging on by an unraveling emotional string, and Jasmine was trying to be a kinder, gentler friend, she only said to Rachel, "I don't know exactly. It'll depend on how receptive Yvette is; just follow my lead."

Rachel nodded as she followed Jasmine into the building and stepped through the glass doors.

A huge cherrywood desk sat in the middle of the lobby and the woman behind it greeted them with a smile. The woman put down the book she'd been reading as Jasmine and Rachel moved past her as if they knew where they were going.

"Uh . . . good evening, ladies, how may I help you?" the woman called out to them.

"Oh, we're fine," Jasmine said, not stopping. "We know where we're going."

But before Jasmine and Rachel could even make it to the elevator, the woman was at their side.

"I'm sorry, but you can't just go up. All guests have to sign in and then I have to call the resident."

"Oh," Jasmine said lightly as she waved her hand. "That's okay. Yvette is expecting us."

The woman never lost her smile as she said, "I'm sorry. But those are the rules. And," she leaned closer to Jasmine as she lowered her voice, "you wouldn't want me to lose my job, would you?"

Inside, Jasmine sighed. Her goal had been to get to Yvette's apartment undetected by anyone. What had just happened to Rachel had her paranoid and Jasmine wanted as few people in Chicago as possible to see her face and know her name.

Still, she followed the woman back to the desk. As she glanced down to sign the guest book, Jasmine noticed the book the woman had been reading.

Jasmine only had an instant to decide how to handle this, then she asked, "Are you enjoying the book?"

The woman smiled. "Oh, yes. Pastor Bush is one of my favorite TV evangelists."

"He's one of mine, too." Then, coyly, she added, "He's my husband."

Jasmine didn't think it was possible for the woman's smile to spread any wider. "You're kidding?" She turned to Rachel. "She's kidding, right?"

Both Jasmine and Rachel shook their heads.

"Oh, my God . . . I love him!"

Jasmine laughed. "So do I."

The middle-aged woman blushed like she was a teenager. "I didn't mean it like that." She lowered her eyes and turned the book over to Hosea's picture on the back. "But honey, if I was twenty years younger." She giggled, then stood up straight. "It is so nice to meet you, Mrs. Bush," she said, shaking her hand. "Please tell Pastor Bush that Sherry from Chicago said hello."

"I'll tell him," Jasmine said, "but . . . ummm . . ."

"Yeah, yeah. Let me call up to Miss . . ." She paused and glanced down at the sheet that Jasmine and Rachel had just signed. "Miss Holloway's apartment."

As the woman dialed the number, Jasmine studied the lobby. From the gold brocade couches to the crystal chandeliers, it was obvious to Jasmine that this was an upscale building, though not as luxurious as Pastor Griffith's. But still, it was clear that Yvette was living well.

"Yes," the woman said. "They're here now." She frowned a little before she handed Jasmine the phone. "She wants to speak to you."

"Hey, Yvette," Jasmine said in a tone that sounded like she was just stopping by to say hello.

"Jasmine?"

"Yeah, Rachel and I are in the lobby."

"What are you guys doing here?"

Jasmine twisted her body around so that Sherry couldn't hear her words. "We have to talk to you about something. It won't take too long."

There was a long pause before Yvette said, "I wasn't expecting you."

"It won't take long," Jasmine repeated. More silence that made Jasmine add, "I promise."

Yvette's long sigh filled the telephone. "All right."

Jasmine handed the phone back to Sherry, then waited as the woman spoke to Yvette.

Rachel whispered, "She wasn't happy to hear from us, huh?"

Jasmine shook her head.

"Do you think she's still mad at you for messing up the Oprah interview?"

Jasmine heard the dig, but didn't respond. Instead, her mind was on Yvette — her words and her tone. Jasmine had been in the middle of enough deception to recognize duplicity when she heard it.

"All right, you can go up now," Sherry

said, pointing to the elevators behind her. "It was so nice meeting you."

Inside the elevators, Jasmine was silent as she thought, as she wondered. In front of Yvette's door, she paused for just a moment before she knocked. When Yvette swung open the door and Jasmine took one step inside her apartment, the reason for Yvette's tone was right in front of their faces.

"Come on in," Yvette said as she motioned with her hands. "I'm sorry if I seemed a little shocked. It's just that I was." She paused. "What are you doing here? And so late?"

But though Jasmine heard her words, her attention was beyond Yvette. Her eyes were on the woman who sat at a small dinette table on the other side of the living room.

"Ladies," Cecelia King said as she stood up from the table where two empty plates had been set as if Yvette and Cecelia had just shared a meal.

"Cecelia," Jasmine responded.

Rachel stepped ahead of Jasmine, her eyes focused on Cecelia. "What are you . . . ?" But before Rachel finished her question, Jasmine touched her arm, stopping her, then they both turned toward Yvette.

Yvette said, "So, like I said, I'm really surprised to see the two of you here." Her glance moved between Jasmine and Rachel. "What are you doing in Chicago?"

There was so much that Jasmine had planned to tell and so many questions she'd wanted to ask. But Cecelia King, the woman who'd tried to take her and Rachel down, stood right in front of them. So Jasmine began to weave a new tale. "A friend of mine has a start-up magazine," Jasmine said, "and she wanted to interview me and Rachel for the Coalition."

Yvette's eyes thinned as she crossed her arms. "You set up an interview without me?"

"It was for a friend."

"What's her name? What's the name of the magazine?"

"I told you. It's small. She's just launching. I'm doing her a favor."

Now, Jasmine turned back to Cecelia and changed the focus of the inquisition. "So, you two are friends, huh?"

"I've known Yvette for a long time," Cecelia said. "We almost hired her to work for the Coalition when my husband was the president."

Jasmine nodded. "So how long are you going to be in Chicago, Cecelia?"

Cecelia raised an eyebrow and without parting her lips, told Jasmine it was none of her business.

So Jasmine turned and directed her questions to Yvette. "This little meeting doesn't have anything to do with the Coalition, does it?"

Yvette frowned. "Why would you think that?"

"Because she tried to steal the election from my husband," Rachel piped in.

"If you must know," Cecelia spoke up, "I'm here because my husband and I are pitching a show to Oprah for her new network."

Yvette added, "And that is confidential, so I'd appreciate it if neither one of you said anything to anyone about this. But," she paused, before she turned the tables back, "I'm still trying to figure out why you came by here since you didn't tell me you were coming back to Chicago."

"We just came by to say hello," Jasmine said and beside her, Rachel nodded. "And see if you had heard anything about Pastor Griffith."

Cecelia was the first one to speak. "No. Still nothing. Such a tragedy. But I have heard that police are looking to question someone regarding his disappearance."

A brief silence filled the room before Yvette stepped up. "You said you wanted to talk to me about something?"

Jasmine kept her glare on Cecelia, so Rachel responded. "We wanted to ask if there was any chance that we could get back on *Oprah*."

Yvette shook her head as she folded her arms. "I wouldn't go back to Oprah's people with the two of you, not when I have big projects on the line." She glanced at Cecelia. "I'm sorry, but there's no chance of that."

Jasmine and Rachel shrugged at the same time. "Okay," they said in unison as if they were both fine with her answer.

Jasmine added, "So that's all we wanted."

Again moving in sync, Jasmine and Rachel turned toward the door.

"So that's all?" Yvette asked.

They nodded.

"Plus," Jasmine added, "it looks like you were busy."

"Yeah, you know, with pitching your show," Rachel said.

"Well." Yvette glanced at Cecelia and when Cecelia nodded, Yvette went on, "You can join us."

Jasmine and Rachel exchanged their own glances. "No, thank you," they said together.

"It might be nice for us all to sit down and talk," Cecelia said.

The frown was on Rachel's face and in

her voice when she said, "We don't have anything to talk to you about."

"We'll talk to *you* soon," Jasmine said to Yvette as she and Rachel walked out the door.

The two didn't speak a word as they marched down the hallway, into the elevator, and out the building. It was not until they were sitting in the rental car that they turned to each other.

"What the hell was that?" Rachel asked.

"I know, right?"

"I'm glad we stayed in Chicago just for that," Rachel said as she started the car. "I'm gonna call Lester and have Yvette fired. How can she be consorting with the enemy like that?"

Jasmine leaned back in her seat and stared at Rachel. "Consorting?"

"Yeah." Rachel grinned. "Consorting! I keep trying to tell you that I ain't no country hick. I know a little somethin' somethin'."

"I see."

But then, Rachel's grin went away. "Well, that was a bust. We didn't find out a thing."

"At least, nothing that has to do with Pastor Griffith," Jasmine said. "But we did find out that we might not want to trust Yvette too much."

"Yvette? I'm not worried about her sorry behind. She wasn't a good publicist anyway. I'm worried about Cecelia and that whole story about why she's in Chicago. I don't believe Oprah would give her a show. Talking about what? How to be a snake?"

Jasmine shook her head. Those were good questions, but she couldn't spend too much time on Yvette and Cecelia. She had to figure out what she and Rachel should do next.

And right now, Jasmine had no idea.

CHAPTER NINETEEN

Jasmine might be ready to move on, but something about Cecelia King being chummy with Yvette was gnawing at Rachel's gut. Cecelia had proven she wasn't to be trusted and she would stop at nothing to get what she wanted. Prior to the election, she had made it clear that she wanted to be president of the ABC and Rachel doubted that Lester's winning the election had squelched that desire.

Rachel shifted to get comfortable in her queen-size bed. It was only eight a.m., but she was ready to get up and moving around, searching for answers. But Jasmine had been adamant that they'd be no good to anyone if they didn't "get a proper night's sleep."

But Rachel was tired of waiting and ready to make a move.

She was just about to get up and go tell Jasmine that when her cell phone rang.

"Hello," she said, answering it.

"Rachel!" Lester sounded relieved to hear her voice, which was strange since she'd just talked to him last night.

"Is something wrong with the kids?" she asked, panic sweeping through her body.

"No, the kids are fine. Why are you sounding like that? Rachel, the Coalition has learned that Pastor Griffith is missing and they think foul play may be involved."

Rachel sat in silence for a minute.

"Did you hear me?" he asked.

"Y-Yes, I heard you," she said. "Why do they think that?"

"I have no idea. But I don't like the way all of this is going down. I think you need to come home."

She thought so, too. But not yet.

"Lester, Pastor Griffith's disappearance has nothing to do with me." She hoped that she sounded more confident than she felt.

"Something just doesn't feel right."

Rachel loved that about her husband. Even when she wouldn't admit it, he knew her so well.

"Sweetheart, I'm fine. I should be home tomorrow."

He didn't sound convinced. "I don't understand why you can't come home today. If your interview is today, why can't you just catch a flight back after that?"

Rachel immediately began trying to formulate the lie in her head. She hated lying to her husband, but "Hey, honey, I'm trying to clear my name of murder" just didn't seem like the right thing to say.

Luckily, her other line buzzed, giving her a reprieve. "Hold on." She glanced at the phone and her heart jumped when she recognized the 312 number. Eleanor Griffith.

Rachel jumped out of the bed and headed into the connecting living area. "Hey, hon, I need to grab this other line. I'll call you back," she said, hurriedly.

"Rachel, wait!"

"Love you. Kiss the kids." She disconnected the call, then tapped on Jasmine's door as she answered the other line. "Hello."

"Come in," Jasmine called out. She sounded like she was awake, which meant they could've been up and out already.

Rachel quickly muted the phone then turned to Jasmine. "It's Eleanor."

Jasmine jumped out of the bed and stood in front of Rachel. "What does she want?" Jasmine replied.

Rachel shrugged. "I have no idea."

"Hello," Rachel said, again.

After a brief hesitation, Eleanor said, "Yes,

Mrs. Adams, ummm, it's ummm, it's Eleanor Griffith. Pastor Griffith's daughter."

She sounded strained. Maybe she had some news about her father.

"Hi, Eleanor, what can I help you with?"

Another beat. Then finally, "Ummm, I got some information. I know you were wondering about my dad, and well, I found out something you might want to know."

"What?" Rachel asked, her heart racing.

"Well, I can't really get into it over the phone. I was wondering if maybe you could come back over."

Rachel muted the phone again and faced Jasmine. "She wants me to come over."

"For what?" Jasmine asked.

"I don't know."

"Well, ask her."

Rachel unmuted the phone and returned to the call. "Can't you just tell me over the phone?"

"Actually, I can't." She paused. "I really need to talk to you in person."

Rachel debated the woman's request. The last thing she wanted was to return to the spot where she'd had her run-in with those goons. But if Eleanor had any information that could help them find out what really happened to Pastor Griffith, she needed to go see her.

"Please." Eleanor must have sensed her hesitation. "It involves you and my father."

"I'm on my way," Rachel finally said.

"Okay, come alone," she added.

Rachel hung the phone up and stared at Jasmine, who stood with her head cocked, her arms crossed.

"You're on your way where?"

"I'm going back to talk to her," Rachel said, heading out of Jasmine's room. The whole "come alone" demand sent chills up her spine, but she had to find out what Eleanor knew.

"Rachel, don't be ridiculous," Jasmine said, following her. "Has yesterday slipped your mind?"

Rachel stopped in the living area and spun around to face Jasmine. "Of course not. But what other choice do we have? You're the one who said we need to do something. Well, this is something."

"I don't know," Jasmine finally admitted.

Rachel exhaled in frustration. "Then I say we go see what she's talking about. Maybe she can give us some answers." Rachel didn't want to tell Jasmine what Eleanor said about its involving Rachel and Pastor Griffith. That piece of news would surely send Jasmine barreling toward O'Hare Airport.

Jasmine continued shaking her head. "I don't have a good feeling about this."

"I don't have a good feeling about the whole thing," Rachel said, turning to head back across the suite. "Now, put on some clothes and let's go."

Twenty minutes later, they were back at Eleanor's apartment complex. Rachel felt a chill shoot up her spine as she looked at the spot where the thugs had accosted her less than twenty-four hours ago.

"I don't like this," Jasmine said.

Rachel pulled into a parking spot. "Neither do I, Jasmine. But unless you have a better plan, I need to see what she's talking about."

"Fine."

Rachel turned off the car. "Come on." She didn't care that Eleanor had told her to come alone. She wasn't a fool.

"No, ma'am," Jasmine said, snatching the keys from her hand. "You said *you're* going to find out what she's talking about. I'm going to sit here and wait in the car." Jasmine pulled out her iPhone and began reading her messages.

Rachel didn't feel like arguing so she just shook her head and headed inside. Her heart raced as she tapped on Eleanor's door. The woman slowly opened it.

"Eleanor?" Rachel asked. The girl's eyes were wide and she looked frightened. Maybe she had some bad news about her father. "Are you okay?"

"Come on in," Eleanor said, stepping to the side. "Are you alone?"

Rachel was about to say Jasmine was in the car, but something made her say, "Yes. What's going on? Have you heard from your father?"

"I haven't," she said, looking down nervously, then slowly looking up, over Rachel's shoulder, toward her long hallway and the two men who had stopped Rachel yesterday.

"She doesn't know where he is, but we think you might," the shorter of the two said.

A flash of panic swept over her and Rachel immediately darted for the door, but she wasn't quick enough as the tall, lanky one grabbed her and flung her down on the sofa. Rachel tried to get up and found herself facing the barrel of a shiny handgun.

"Sit your five-dollar ass down before I make change!"

Eleanor gasped and Rachel froze as the gun touched the bridge of her nose. Then suddenly, the tall one burst out laughing as he moved the gun.

"I've always wanted to say that." He kept

laughing, like that was the funniest thing he'd ever said. "Nino Brown is one bad dude."

Both of the goons cracked up.

Seriously? Her life was in danger and these dudes were quoting lines from *New Jack City*?

"Look here," the first guy said, sitting on the coffee table in front of Rachel. "We don't want any trouble. We just want answers."

"But I don't have any answers," Rachel protested.

"You and your girl here know something." He motioned between the two of them.

"I told you all I don't know her," Eleanor cried. "I just met her over the phone yesterday."

"Yeah, tell us anything." The man motioned at the sofa. "Please, have a seat next to her."

Rachel blurted out, "I'm a first lady."

The tall one replied, "Then I hope you're prayed up because if you don't do what we need you to do, you're going to need your God sooner than you think."

Rachel glanced over at Eleanor. She couldn't believe she'd walked right into this trap; that this young girl had actually set her up. But the fear in her eyes told Rachel that Eleanor had only done what she'd been ordered to do.

"What do you want from me?" Rachel finally asked.

"We want to know where your boyfriend is."

Rachel frowned. "My what? I am a married woman."

"Yeah, so is my girlfriend," the tall one chimed in.

"Where is Pastor Griffith?" his friend repeated.

Both Rachel and Eleanor sat speechless.

The goon sitting in front of her exhaled in frustration. "See this?" He pointed back and forth between the two of them. "This is going to be a problem. I don't like liars. Liars piss me off."

"I'm not lying." Rachel wanted to cry. She never would've imagined a simple trip to see Oprah would lead to all of this.

"Here's the deal," the man continued. "Me and my partner here, this is Bean" — he smiled as he pointed to the tall guy — "as in pole. You see how tall and lanky he is. I'm Muscle and we're some really nice guys at the end of the day." He said it as if they really were sitting sipping coffee. "Me and Bean make a good team because we get results," he continued. "By any means necessary. So I have no doubt that we'll get results from you. By. Any. Means. Necessary."

"I don't know how I can help you." Rachel no longer wanted to cry. She did.

"Come on. We know that you're seeing Pastor Griffith."

"No, I'm not," Rachel protested, then turned to Eleanor. "Tell them I'm not your father's girlfriend!"

"That's what I've been trying to tell them," she cried.

"Tell them who the real girlfriend is," Rachel urged.

Eleanor shrugged. "I don't know," she said through her tears. "I haven't exactly been a model kid. I've been in rehab." She sniffed. "I heard him talk about her, and I talked to her once on the phone when I was trying to find him, but I've never met her." She lowered her head in shame. "I haven't been right since my mom died and, well, I didn't want to meet my dad's girlfriend."

"Yeah, this ain't therapy," the stocky thug said.

"I'm just trying to get you to see you have the wrong woman," Rachel pleaded.

The guy exhaled in frustration. "So, you said you've never met your dad's girlfriend?" he asked Eleanor.

Eleanor shook her head.

"So, this could be her and you wouldn't even know," he said, pointing at Rachel.

Eleanor glanced up at Rachel like she hadn't really thought about that.

"But —"

Muscle waved his hand to shut her up. "Look, I don't really care about your extramarital affairs. All I know is the old man is gone and the money is gone. Either you produce the old man or you produce the money. End of story. You got kids?"

The panic in her eyes answered for her.

Muscle nodded. "Yeah, you got kids." He snatched her purse, then pulled out her wallet. He picked up her license, dropped it in his pocket, then fingered a photo of her children. "Awww, they're so cute. I'd really hate to kill a kid, but all's fair in love and my boss's money."

At this point, Rachel would do whatever she needed to do to get out of there. "I don't know anything about any money," she said, reaching for her purse.

"Whoaaa," Bean raised the gun at her.

"Calm down! I just want to get my checkbook," she snapped. "I'll just write you a check for whatever is owed to you if you just let us go." He tossed the purse at her. She dug in, then pulled out her checkbook

250

and a pen. She didn't have a whole lot of money in her account, but she was sure the ABC would cover any shortage. "Who do I make it out to?"

Bean and Muscle exchanged glances, then burst out laughing.

"You hear that, Bean? She's gonna write us a check." They continued laughing for a minute, before Muscle's expression turned serious. "I'm sorry, our check machine is out of order so we're only able to accept cash at this time. Or the old man."

"I don't have anything to do with any of this. I just want you to let us go. How much cash? I can go to the bank. I have a debit card."

"And your debit card lets you withdraw ten million dollars?" Muscle asked nonchalantly.

Rachel's eyes bucked. "Excuse me?"

"My man didn't stutter," Bean interjected.

"I-I don't have that much."

"But your boyfriend did. And it belongs to my boss and he wants it back."

"He's not my boyfriend!" Rachel yelled. "What makes you think I'm involved in this?"

Rachel looked to Eleanor for some help. She hadn't stopped shaking, nor had she uttered another word.

"Eleanor," Rachel said, reaching for her hand.

"They found his car this morning," Eleanor finally said. She looked up at Muscle. "I told you. My dad is dead."

Rachel's heart dropped as she faced Eleanor.

"I just got the word, before these jerks showed up," Eleanor continued, tears streaking down her face. "They found his car in Lake Michigan. His body was inside."

"Oh, my God," Rachel said. All kinds of emotions were running through her. They'd found Pastor Griffith's body? And from the way these thugs were acting, they weren't the ones who had dumped him in the river. But if they didn't, who did? Just what kind of mess was Pastor Griffith involved in?

"Well, my condolences if he really is dead," Muscle said with a smirk. "But that just means the debt passes on to his woman, especially since we know he wouldn't trust his crackfiend kid with that kind of money." He smiled sympathetically.

Rachel wanted to tell them one last time she wasn't involved with Pastor Griffith, but it was obvious they weren't listening, so instead she said, "We don't have that kind of money."

"Then it looks to me like it'll be a triple

funeral," Bean said. "Rockabye, baby." He pointed the gun their way.

Rachel watched Eleanor shake uncontrollably. She looked like she was on the verge of a nervous breakdown. Tears were streaming down her face. As Bean pursed his lips like he was deciding who to shoot first, all Rachel could think was that she didn't want to die like this. She had four kids who needed her. She had a family that loved her. So Rachel did the only thing she could think of. She bolted off the sofa and ran as fast as she could toward the front door. The sudden movement definitely caught the two thugs off guard and both of them scrambled toward her but by that point, she was out the door. She ran across the complex's lawn like her life depended on it. Muscle and Bean were right behind her as she screamed at the top of her lungs, "Help! Help!"

Rachel had just made it to the street when she spotted Jasmine, who had jumped up in the passenger seat and was looking on in shock.

"Do something!" Rachel yelled, scurrying on top of a nearby Hummer. Muscle and Bean tried to grab her just as she pulled her feet onto the roof and out of their reach. Rachel knew they were about to shoot her in the head and she was just about to accept her fate when she heard a horn blaring. She looked over to see Jasmine bearing down on the horn, the loud sound permeating the neighborhood. People began sticking their heads out of their apartments and Rachel took her cue. "Help me! They're trying to kill me," she shouted.

They reached wildly for her, and Jasmine continued holding the horn down.

"Yo, Ma. Why you on my truck?" a young guy yelled as he raced down the sidewalk.

Muscle looked at his cohort. "Come on, man. Let's get out of here."

Muscle glared at Rachel. "This ain't over, First Lady," he hissed, before both of them took off running around the corner.

The owner of the Hummer came running up to the truck. Half his hair was braided, and he wore a wife beater and a pair of saggy jeans.

"What you doin'?" he yelled.

"They were trying to kill me," Rachel said, shaking.

"Yeah, and I'm gon' finish if you don't get the hell off my truck," he snapped, pounding the hood.

Rachel slid down the front. "What in the world happened?" Jasmine asked, running over to her.

Rachel did the only thing she could. She

wrapped her arms around Jasmine and sobbed.

"Do you need me to call the cops?" some elderly lady said.

At the mention of police, both Jasmine and Rachel froze. Finally, Jasmine spoke. "No, we're okay. We're leaving."

Rachel didn't protest as Jasmine led her back to the car. Part of her wondered if she should go back and check on Eleanor. But the other part of her wanted to get as far away from this place as possible. That's why Rachel didn't say a word as she slid into the passenger side and prayed for this nightmare to end.

CHAPTER TWENTY

"So is this man dead or alive?" Jasmine asked after Rachel finished mumbling out the story of what had gone down in Eleanor's apartment.

Rachel shook her head, her eyes still wide and wild as if she were reliving each second of her near-death experience. "At this point, all I know is that *I'm* alive."

Jasmine raised an eyebrow. "Well, I'm kinda alive, too."

Rachel's glance rose to where Jasmine paced in the living room section of their hotel room. Her eyes softened and she tilted her head. "Yeah, you're alive, though after some of the things you've done to me, I've always wondered if you had a heart."

"This coming from a woman who practically kidnapped my daughter."

"Dang! Why you always bringing up the past?" But then Rachel lowered her eyes. "You know, I've never liked you, but I

256

always wanted to apologize for that. I didn't mean to get you that upset, but did you have to cold-cock me the way you did?"

"Tell me that you wouldn't have done the same thing to me!"

A wisp of a smile crossed Rachel's face. "I would've done worse."

"I know you would've tried," Jasmine said as she sat down on the bed next to Rachel. "After all we've been through, who would've ever thought we'd be here working together like this."

"I know, it is something." Rachel paused, then added, "But don't get it twisted . . . I still don't like you," though the wider smile on her face belied her words.

Jasmine laughed. "Right back at you."

After a moment, Rachel said, "Thank you."

Jasmine frowned. "For what?"

Rachel added, "For what you just did. For getting me to think about something else for just a moment. I'm not as scared as I was when we first got back here."

"We both needed a break. But we've got to get back to work. So," she paused as if she was giving Rachel a moment to change mental lanes, "let's go over what we know."

"Well, one thing I know is that I really can't go home now. Before I just wanted to clear my name, but now," a sob rose in her throat, "I can't let those thugs get anywhere near my family. I'd die if . . ."

"That's not going to happen," Jasmine piped up, not even letting Rachel finish her thought. "We're going to figure this out. Come on, look at everything we know. We know that Pastor Griffith may be alive . . ."

"But he's dead! They found his body."

"And he owes some folks some money . . ."

"*Some* money? Ten million dollars is not *some* money."

"And they think you have something to do with it."

Rachel threw up her hands. "That's the part that's just killing me. Not only did I hardly know that old man, but I couldn't stand him and he didn't like me."

Jasmine tilted her head. "So, why do they think you're his girlfriend?"

"I don't even know, 'cause if I was to ever mess around on Lester it wouldn't be with somebody as old as Methuselah; it would be someone more like Bobby."

Jasmine arched an eyebrow. "Bobby? Who's that?"

She sucked her teeth before she said, "None of your business. And before you go jumping to conclusions, I ain't cheating on

258

Lester and never have. I was just sayin'."
Shaking her head, she added, "So I have no
idea why those gorillas think I'm Pastor
Griffith's girlfriend."

Jasmine snapped her finger. "That's it!"

"What? Gorillas?"

"No. Girlfriend. We just need to find
Pastor Griffith's *real* girlfriend."

"And how are we supposed to do that?
Even Eleanor doesn't know who she is, so
how are we supposed to find her in a city
that has, what? Almost three million
people?"

Jasmine jerked back a bit, impressed that
Rachel would know something like that. But
she didn't compliment Rachel. Instead, she
said, "Well, do you have any other ideas? I
mean, we could go back to those guys we
seem to keep running into and ask them
some questions so that we can get clarity."

The image of the men must've passed
through Rachel's mind because she said,
"So, where are we supposed to look for
her?"

"Church."

"Church?"

"Yeah, this man was the pastor of a
church. Surely someone there knew something about his life; someone knows his
girlfriend."

Rachel nodded slowly. "Okay, I'm feeling this. I like it. Do you know the name of his church?"

"I don't, but how hard can it be to find out?" she said before pulling out her iPad.

As she did, Rachel's cell rang. She groaned. "I'm sure that's Lester." But then her eyes widened when she looked at the screen. "It's Yvette," Rachel said. "Should I put her on speaker?"

"Yeah."

"Hey, Yvette," Rachel said. "Jasmine's here with me."

"Hey, I was just checking on you guys. I felt kind of bad that you came all the way over to see me yesterday and didn't even stay."

"That's okay, we saw you had company."

"Cecelia? Please, she's not company. I would've much rather been hanging out with you guys. So, is everything cool? You're still in Chicago, I take it, since the two of you are together."

"Yeah," Rachel said.

Jasmine added, "But we're getting ready to leave."

"Really?"

"Yeah," Rachel said, following Jasmine's lead. "After you said you couldn't get us back on *Oprah,* there really isn't reason for

260

us to stay."

There was a long pause. "Well . . . before, when you came over, you said that you wanted to ask me some questions."

"We asked them," Rachel said.

"Yeah," Jasmine added. "We asked about *Oprah.*"

More silence. Then, "Okay. Well, do you need a ride to the airport?"

"No," they said together, then grinned at each other.

"Okay, so I'll be in touch."

"Okay," they sang together again.

When they clicked off the phone, Rachel said, "You know, I almost asked Yvette where was Pastor Griffith's church, but when you didn't say anything . . ." She stopped as if she wanted Jasmine to fill in the blanks.

"I'm beginning to figure that the fewer people who know that we're here, the better," she said as she typed into her iPad.

"She might be able to help," Rachel said. "At least, that's what we thought before."

"She might, but let's see what we find out first at the church." Another tap on the tablet keys, then, "Got it. Here it is. Pastor Griffith was the pastor of Church of the Deliverance."

Rachel chuckled. "That man needed to be

delivered."

"It's over on Martin Luther King Boulevard." She looked up at Rachel.

"Eleanor lives right off Martin Luther King."

"Uh-huh." She clicked off her tablet. Grabbing her coat, she said, "Okay, let's go."

Rachel stayed right in place, sitting on the edge of the sofa. "Now? Today?"

Jasmine frowned. "Yeah. What were you thinking?"

"I was thinking about Sunday."

"You've got to be kidding me."

"Well, I was just thinking that there would be more people hanging around on Sunday."

"Yeah, but I'm not interested in talking to his church members," Jasmine said. "I want to talk to the people who actually work at the church. I'm sure he had a full-time staff." Jasmine headed to the door. "Let's go."

Rachel was already shaking her head. "I don't think I want to go back over there. I can't do it."

"But where else can we go? His church is the only place that makes sense. 'Cause if he had a girlfriend, the church folks would be the ones to know, and they're gonna be the ones who're gonna tell it." The look on Rachel's face made Jasmine ask, "Do you have any other ideas?"

"Yeah. Let's go on Sunday when there's lots of people and less of a chance of someone stepping up to us and pushing a gun in our faces."

"And if we wait until Sunday, what are we supposed to do in the meantime?" She didn't even let Rachel respond. "I need to get home to my family and so do you. We're going now." Jasmine paused. "Well, if you don't want to then I'll just go."

"But what about the time?" Rachel glanced at her watch. "It's almost five o'clock."

Jasmine shook her head. "Stop making excuses. Somebody will be there. Every church has something going on every night. Look, like I said, I'll go by myself."

Jasmine swung her purse onto her shoulder, then marched to the door like she was going off to war. But just as she put her hand on the knob, Rachel sighed. "All right."

Jasmine turned around and faced her with a grin.

Rachel sucked her teeth. "You knew I wasn't gonna let you go by yourself."

"Yup."

Rachel shook her head. "I just hope that this time if the thugs come, they go after you!"

"Thanks a lot," Jasmine said as she closed the hotel room door behind her.

This was a lot to handle in two days, but Jasmine wanted to get out of this James Bond saga and coming to this church was her best idea yet.

At least that's what Jasmine thought, until Rachel rolled the car to a stop in front of Church of the Deliverance. The church was one of the sturdier buildings in this neighborhood, a brick monstrosity that looked like it was constructed during the time of Abraham Lincoln's childhood.

But it wasn't the building that stood out most to Jasmine. It was the activity that was going on in front of the building. On one side, a couple of teenage boys sat on the brick wall in front with a boom box of a type that Jasmine hadn't seen in years, blasting Jay-Z's "Empire State of Mind" for everyone on the block to hear.

Concrete jungle where dreams are made of . . .

The volume made Jasmine shake her head. The words made her wish that she was back in New York.

Just a few feet away from the music maestros was another set of young men, stepping up to everyone who passed by. Jasmine couldn't hear their words, but their body language told their business — they were drug dealers.

Jasmine wondered if Rachel noticed, then Rachel said, "What is all of that?" as she took in the same scene. "That's just blasphemy, acting like that in front of a church."

"I know, right?" Jasmine said as Rachel eased the car along the curb, several doors down from the Church of the Deliverance. When she turned off the ignition, Jasmine said, "Let's do this."

But just as she put her hand on the door handle, Rachel shouted, "Wait!"

Jasmine frowned.

"Look!"

Jasmine's glance followed where Rachel pointed. To a Town Car that had stopped in front of the church. And the woman who slid out of the backseat.

Cecelia King.

Jasmine and Rachel stared as Cecelia stopped to chat with the ghetto pharmaceutical salesmen and then she pushed herself up the three stairs that led to the church's front door. The stained-glass windows on either side of the door rattled before Cecelia disappeared inside.

Jasmine and Rachel were silent for several seconds until Rachel whispered, "What do we do now?"

After a moment, Jasmine said, "We come back on Sunday."

CHAPTER TWENTY-ONE

From the moment she met her, Rachel knew that Cecelia was a low-down, dirty snake. Well, maybe not from the *moment* she met her; after all, she'd tried everything to get in the woman's good graces while Lester was running for president of the ABC. But of course, that was before Rachel found out that Cecelia had been playing Jasmine and Rachel against one another so she could ease her own name in to be president. After that, Rachel knew Cecelia King was not a woman to be trusted.

She'd figure out what Cecelia was up to, but right now, she needed to see if she could dig up anything on Pastor Griffith. Both Rachel and Jasmine had been exhausted when they'd returned to the hotel last night. They'd gone to their respective rooms and crashed. But today was a new day. They'd eaten breakfast in the suite and had spent the last several hours sitting across from each other, strategizing and searching the web for clues.

Rachel closed out the article she was reading — another positive one about Pastor Griffith's work. Her eyes caught the Angry Birds icon and for a moment, Rachel thought about playing the game that was her favorite stress reliever. *No.* She pushed that thought away. She didn't have time for Angry Birds. They had work to do and if she took time to play games, she'd have a real angry bird to deal with. Rachel immediately chastised herself for having disparaging thoughts about Jasmine. The woman had literally saved her life; they'd just had a great bonding moment, so Rachel needed to stop being mean. Besides, they were a team now and the last thing they needed was any lingering animosity.

"Are you coming up with anything?" Jasmine asked, breaking the silence that filled the suite.

Rachel looked up from her iPad. "Nothing but all this great stuff, like the man is a saint or something."

"Hmph," Jasmine snorted. "I was hoping that we could stumble across an article, a photo, something that would give us a clue as to who this girlfriend is."

"My gut tells me it's Cecelia. And if it's

268

not her, then she knows who it is. We should just ask her."

"Yeah, like she would just say, 'You got me. I'm cheating on my husband with Pastor Griffith.' "

Rachel sighed. This was all getting so frustrating. Jasmine must've felt the same way because she set her iPad down, stretched, and announced, "I'm tired. We've been at this for hours. It's almost four o'clock. Let's get out of here. I'm tired of being stuffed up in this hotel room."

"Get out and go where?" Rachel asked.

"I was thinking we could go walk The Magnificent Mile."

"I'm not trying to go walking, especially a mile."

Jasmine laughed. "The Magnificent Mile is called that because it's a mile-long popular shopping area."

"Oh." Rachel hesitated, then flashed a smile. "I knew that. I was just messing with you."

"Sure you were." Jasmine chuckled. "Go put on something comfortable. Shopping will momentarily help us forget all of our troubles."

A few minutes later, they were back in the suite. Jasmine was wearing a cute pair of jeans with a white button-down blouse and some low-heeled pumps. Rachel wore a cream velour warm-up suit with some tennis shoes. Jasmine ran her eyes up and down Rachel's body. Rachel could tell she wanted to say something, but Rachel wasn't fazed. If she was going to be walking a mile, she was going to be comfortable. Jasmine could try to be cute if she wanted, her feet would be hurting after a block.

"Should we really be shopping?" Rachel asked once they were in the elevator heading down.

Jasmine fumbled in her purse for something, then said, "We've done all we can do for now. We go out, shop, get something to eat, then tomorrow we go to church."

Rachel nodded pensively. It's not that she didn't enjoy shopping. She just felt guilty about doing it in the middle of this crisis. "Do they have a Marshalls?" she finally asked. Jasmine chuckled and Rachel raised an eyebrow. "Oh, I'm sure you only shop at Nordstrom," Rachel said with an attitude, "but I like to spend my money wisely and there's nothing wrong with Marshalls."

Jasmine hailed a cab. They'd decided not to drive to avoid the issue of parking. Once they were settled in the backseat, Jasmine said, "As a matter of fact, they do have a Marshalls and some other discount retailers, including Filene's Basement."

"What's that?"

"It's a high-end discount store where they sell last season's clothes."

"And what makes you think I wear last season's clothes?"

Jasmine's eyes roamed up and down Rachel's outfit. She smirked.

Rachel waved her off. "Whatever; you're the only one concerned about that anyway. I happen to have some cute clothes."

"If I must admit, you do," Jasmine conceded. "I've seen you in some cute stuff, even if it is last season's." She smiled, but this time neither her smile nor her tone was condescending.

"Is right here fine?" the driver asked as he pulled up at the corner of W. Grand and Michigan Avenues.

"This is fine." Jasmine handed the man a twenty. "Keep the change," she said as they climbed out of the car.

Rachel shook her head. That man hadn't said a word to them the entire time they were in the car. No way did he deserve a nine-dollar tip.

"Come on," Rachel said, stepping out of the cab. "I'm going to teach you a thing or two about bargain shopping and when I'm done, you'll be like 'I can't believe I used to spend all that money.' "

"I doubt that very seriously," Jasmine said, following her out.

Forty minutes into shopping on The Magnificent Mile and it was obvious Rachel and Jasmine were from two different worlds.

"So you seriously are going to pay fifteen hundred dollars for a pair of shoes?" Rachel asked as they browsed in yet another high-end store.

"They're Jimmy Choo," Jasmine said, like that was a crazy question.

"Unless they're Jesus Christ, that's ridiculous," Rachel said, removing the shoe from Jasmine's hand.

Jasmine shook her head pityingly.

"Don't get it twisted," Rachel said. "I have some Jimmy Choos, but guess what? I got mine at Off 5th. Just as cute, a third of the price."

"Oooh, look at this handbag," Jasmine beamed, picking up a black snakeskin hobo bag.

"Now, I'm all for purses," Rachel said, going straight for the price tag. "Oh, my God, do you know how many people you can feed with the money you'll spend on this purse that you'll probably grow tired of in two weeks?"

"Okay, now you sound like Hosea," Jasmine groaned.

Rachel shook her head. "It's true. This stuff is ridiculously priced. I believe in rewarding yourself, but how many black purses do you actually have?"

"A woman can never have too many black purses."

"She can if they're five thousand dollars. Who you think you are, NeNe?" Rachel headed toward the door. "Come on, let's go. This is the third shi-shi poo-poo shop you've dragged me in and I want to go somewhere that's more my speed."

Jasmine placed her item back on the shelf. "I don't know if there's a Walmart around here," she casually said.

"Jokes, you got jokes," Rachel said, walking out the door.

They walked for another ten minutes before Rachel finally spotted the Marshalls.

"Finally," she said, a huge smile across her face.

Jasmine stood outside the large white building, a look of disgust on her face. "You seriously want me to go in Marshalls?"

Rachel grabbed her arm and pulled her inside the store. "If you don't bring your siddity tail on."

"Oh, my God. I hope no one sees me in Marshalls," Jasmine mumbled.

"That's the problem with you nouveau riche folks," Rachel said once they were inside. "When you get a come-up, the way you stay up is by being smart with your money."

Jasmine looked around the store, clutching her purse tightly like they were in the middle of the Goodwill.

Rachel ignored her as she browsed a rack. After a few minutes, she held up a plum-color jumpsuit. "This looks like your size. Go try this on."

"Are you crazy?"

"What?"

"I don't do Baby Phat," Jasmine said, horrified.

"I don't know what you're talking about. Kimora is a top designer." Rachel held up some jeans. "What about these?"

Jasmine turned up her nose even more. "I don't wear anyone else's name on my behind."

Rachel put both items back on the rack. "Bourgie folks, I tell you."

"Please tell me you don't wear this mess," Jasmine asked.

Rachel smiled. "I'm just teasing you. Of course I don't. Anymore," she mumbled.

Jasmine's eyes bucked in horror.

"What? I'm young, remember? I like

274

trendy stuff."

"You're also a first lady."

"Hence the reason I stopped wearing it. The people at my church were trippin' about it."

"As well they should have been."

"Well, I don't wear it anymore." Rachel walked over to the next aisle and started looking at the suits. "Oh, hold up, wait a minute," Rachel announced. She picked up a suit, turned around, and flashed it at Jasmine. "Correct me if I'm wrong, but did you or did you not wear this suit to one of the ABC meetings at the conference?"

Jasmine snatched the suit. "Oh, my God, they sell Dana Buchman in Marshalls?"

"My point exactly. And if I recall, it wasn't last season when you had it on." Rachel flashed an "I told you so" look.

Jasmine looked at the price tag and gasped. "Ninety-nine dollars?"

"And let me guess, you paid twice that?"

"Try five times that."

Rachel tsked as she took the suit and placed it back on the rack. "I rest my case."

"Okay, maybe I will have to give Marshalls a chance," Jasmine acquiesced.

Just then, two little boys came barreling past them. A woman in a bright red head-scarf was chasing after them.

"Junie and Lil' Man, if y'all don't get your behinds back here, I'm gonna beat the black off you!" she screamed as the boys rounded the aisle and began racing down the other side, giggling like crazy. The woman stopped, took her shoe off, and threw it over the rack of clothes, hitting the older of the boys in the head. "I ain't playin' with y'all. Can't bring y'all bad asses nowhere!"

Jasmine looked at Rachel, lost her smile, and said, "On second thought, maybe not," and then headed toward the door.

They browsed a few more stores on The Magnificent Mile before Jasmine announced that she was starving.

"How about we go to this nice Italian restaurant on Michigan Avenue?"

"Got a better idea," Rachel said, hailing a cab. "Come on."

"Where are we going?" Jasmine said, climbing in the cab.

Rachel leaned up and whispered in the driver's ear. He nodded and pulled off.

Just five minutes later, they were pulling in front of the small brick building.

"You have lost your ever-loving mind if you think I'm about to go in there."

Rachel pulled her arm. "Stop being a prude. You only live once. Think about it. Can you go to Hooters in New York?"

"Absolutely not and wouldn't want to."

"Right. We're here where no one knows us, so let's live it up."

"I cannot go in there."

"Okay, you can wait right here then. I'm going to get some wings."

"Ugggh," Jasmine said, following her out of the cab.

Jasmine cringed as the scantily clad waitress showed them to their booth.

"Relax. It's not like you've never been around women with their boobs all out," Rachel said, unable to resist getting the dig in.

Jasmine ignored her as she slid into the booth.

"I have to go to the restroom," Rachel said before sitting down.

"They're right over there," the waitress said, pointing to the corner.

Jasmine had been right, Rachel thought as she headed to the restroom. The shopping, even this trip to Hooters had been just what she needed to get her mind off the nightmare of these last few days. And truth be told, she enjoyed the bonding time with Jasmine.

She'd just returned to the table and was about to apologize for the quip she'd made a minute ago. She needed to stop doing that and wanted to let Jasmine know that. But the look on Jasmine's face stopped her in her tracks.

"You look like you've seen a ghost," Rachel said.

Jasmine didn't say a word as she pointed at the TV directly in front of their booth. Rachel turned around to see what she was looking at and almost fainted when she saw her face plastered across the 32-inch television screen.

Rachel watched in horror as the photo of her dressed in her Sunday best, with a fuchsia wide-brimmed hat to match her fuchsia suit, filled the screen. It was the photo Rachel had taken for the ABC website.

Jasmine jumped up and raced over to the bar so she could hear better.

". . . Authorities have identified the woman wanted in connection with the death of prominent minister Earl Griffith, whose body was discovered earlier today in a car pulled from Lake Michigan," the anchor announced. "She is Rachel Jackson Adams, the wife of the current American Baptist Coalition president, Lester Adams. Police are stopping short of calling her a suspect, but for now, they are saying she was the last person with Griffith and that makes her a person of interest in his murder."

Rachel fell down onto the bar stool, her mouth open. This was an absolute and utter nightmare. All of her efforts to destroy the surveillance video and they still had ended up with her photo?

"What? How?" Rachel gasped.

Jasmine eyed Rachel, like she was wondering if this would send her over the edge.

"Oh, my God!" Rachel sobbed. "Yesterday they were just looking for someone. How did they tie me to this?"

"Calm down, Rachel," Jasmine whispered. "Don't bring attention to yourself."

"This is bad. This is so bad," Rachel cried. What did this mean? Could she be arrested? Suddenly it dawned on her. "Lester watches WGN."

Jasmine rubbed her hand over her face. The look on her face told Rachel she wished she had never agreed to help. Rachel braced herself for Jasmine to announce she was leaving. Instead, Jasmine looked around as several people had started staring at them, then said, "All I know is we need to get out of here. Let's go back to the hotel. Then we can figure out what to do next."

Dazed, Rachel followed her out, grateful that Jasmine had once again stepped in to save the day.

CHAPTER TWENTY-TWO

All Jasmine could think about was that this had all started because of Oprah.

But as she watched Rachel scramble through the room, inside her head, she took that lie back. There was no way she could blame any of this on the Queen of Daytime. This had all started because she wanted to get one up on Rachel. That's why she'd befriended Yvette, that's why she'd come to Chicago without giving Rachel any notice or any chance to come with her, and that's what had the two of them here in the middle of this mess today.

All of their fighting had led to this.

"I don't care if I have to walk to Houston," Rachel shouted as she rolled her suitcase across the bedroom and flung it onto the bed. "I'm getting out of here tonight."

"You can't go," Jasmine said.

Rachel looked at Jasmine with wide, incredulous eyes. "Watch me."

Jasmine sighed. All of the talking she'd tried to do with Rachel on the way back to the hotel had done nothing except stop her from screaming hysterically in the cab. "But you wanted to clear your name," she reminded Rachel.

"That was before they knew my name . . . and had my picture." She stopped slinging clothes from the closet long enough to look up at Jasmine. "I cannot believe this. My face is all over Chicago. I'm wanted for questioning in a murder. A *murder.*" She shook her head as if she couldn't believe it. "Pastor Griffith is really dead and now the police think I did it."

"No. That's not what the reporter said. She said you were wanted for questioning in connection with his murder."

"Well, what do you think that means?"

"Rachel, remember, you didn't do anything."

"And how many people do you think are sitting up on death row right now *remembering* that *they* didn't do anything?"

"Death row? Come on, Rachel. You have yourself arrested, tried, convicted, and sentenced before you've talked to the first person."

"Why are you making light of this?" Rachel cried, and Jasmine was surprised that

Rachel had held her tears back for this long.

"I'm not. I just know that you didn't do anything and that you're not going to jail."

With the heel of her hand, Rachel wiped the wetness from her cheeks. "I can't go to jail." Her voice sounded so small. "I can't. I have children. And Lester."

With slow steps, Jasmine moved toward Rachel, took her hand, and pulled her down onto the edge of the bed. The two sat side by side as Jasmine said, "I'm not going to let anything happen to you."

"I don't think you can stop it."

"I can."

"How?"

"By doing what we were going to do. All we have to do is find Pastor Griffith's girlfriend and she can tell the police whatever they need to know."

"But they're not looking for her. They're looking for me."

"They don't know about her, but once we find out who it is — whether it's Cecelia or not — we'll tell the police what we know and you'll be fine."

"But suppose they don't believe me."

"They'll believe *us,*" Jasmine said. "I'm not going to let you talk to the police by yourself. If they come after you, they'll have to take me."

Through her tears, Rachel tried to smile. "Really?" she asked, sounding like a ten-year-old.

Jasmine nodded. "Plus, I *can't* let you talk to the police by yourself. There's no telling what kind of nonsense you might say."

Rachel rolled her eyes, but when she turned back to Jasmine, there was nothing but gratitude in them. "So what do you think we should do?"

"Like I said, let's stick to our plan. We'll go to church tomorrow and —"

She was already shaking her head before Jasmine could even finish. "I'm not showing my face anywhere. Seriously." She stood and paced in front of Jasmine. "I'm going back to Houston and if the police want to find me, they're gonna have to get on a plane and get to looking."

"Okay, calm down," Jasmine said, holding up her hands like she was surrendering. "We'll leave Chicago."

Rachel stopped moving and exhaled.

"But first," she paused when Rachel looked at her with a sideward glance, "before we go to the airport, we'll stop at the church." Rachel opened her mouth to protest, but Jasmine intercepted her. "*And,* I'll go in. You'll stay in the car, but I'll go in and see if I can find out something from someone."

"How are you going to do that in the middle of a church service?"

"I've done it before," Jasmine said, thinking about the time she'd gone to Hogeye Creek, Georgia, to get evidence on a pastor who she'd been sure was blackmailing her. Jasmine had marched right into the Church of the Solid Rock, scanned the women in the pews, and parked next to the one she was sure would do the most talking. And she was right. Jasmine had found Mrs. Evans, the town crier who'd given Jasmine everything she needed, plus some.

If Jasmine ever needed a career beyond being first lady, she would be an investigator. She was definitely as good as any investigator out there. She had no doubt that she'd find out whatever she and Rachel needed to know — tomorrow.

"So does that sound like a plan?" Jasmine said to Rachel.

Rachel gave Jasmine a long glance before she answered, "And I don't have to go into the church?"

Jasmine shook her head.

"And after that, we'll go straight to the airport?"

This time, Jasmine nodded. "Straight to

the airport and on the way, I'll call the police with an anonymous tip — the name of Pastor Griffith's girlfriend. By the time you land in Houston, you'll be cleared."

"Sounds kind of simple."

"Usually life is. People just make it complicated."

Rachel nodded. "Okay. I'll stay here, just one more day." She glanced around the bedroom and shivered as if she was suddenly cold. "I can't wait to get home."

"Neither can I," Jasmine said as she stood up. "Okay, pack up the rest of your things, then call Lester, but don't say anything to him. If he's heard about it, play dumb and tell him you're coming home tomorrow. Don't turn on the TV unless you're gonna be watching the Cartoon Network or something. Better yet, why don't you read a book?" She paused and grinned. "The Bible, maybe."

Rachel's neck twisted with every syllable as she said, "I hope I'm not that bossy when I get to be *your age*."

"You should be so lucky."

"Do you always have to have the last word?"

"Yup." Moving toward the door, Jasmine's voice softened as she said, "Call me if you need me, okay?"

Rachel nodded. "Thank you, Jasmine. Thank you for everything."

"I have a very bad feeling about this."

Jasmine rolled her eyes. If Rachel said that to her one more time . . .

"I really do, Jasmine. I think we need to get out of Chicago. Let's just go to the airport, let's get out of here."

"And once you get home to your family, what's going to happen? You think the police are just gonna forget that there's a dead man and they're looking for you? You think those thugs are just gonna forget about their money?" Jasmine didn't wait for Rachel to answer. "Before we can get on that plane, we have to find the girlfriend and you know she'll be here in church, especially today. Now that Pastor Griffith is no longer missing, everyone is gonna be here talking about it. This is a perfect time for me to go in there." She paused. "I'll make it quick, find out what we need to know, and then we'll head straight to the airport."

Rachel nodded and stayed silent this time and Jasmine was grateful. It was a good thing that they were all packed and ready to go, because though she was growing fond of Rachel, she still couldn't say that she really liked her — especially not when she was in

286

this scared-of-everything mode. Plus, both Lester and Hosea had been caught up in church business, but it was just a matter of time before they found out what was going on and demanded that Rachel and Jasmine come home.

This time, when Rachel turned down Howard Street, it was impossible to drive to the front of the church. The street was packed with cars parked and double-parked and others still trying to pass through.

"This is a mess," Rachel whispered as she tried to swing around a van that had stopped dead in the center of the street.

"Yeah, the church is definitely packed this morning, especially now that everyone knows that Pastor Griffith is dead. There are probably a lot of looky-loos here."

"I bet you're right," Rachel said. With a bit of hope in her tone, she added, "I bet his girlfriend is here."

"Definitely." Jasmine nodded. "Look, you're gonna be backed up here for a while, so let me get out. The sooner I can get to work, the better."

"Okay," Rachel said, stopping the car completely.

"Just make sure that you wait for me right at the front. I don't care how many cars are parked there. You never know when those thugs are gonna show up again and if they do, I want to make a quick getaway."

"Okay," she repeated.

As she moved toward the church, Jasmine mingled with the crowd of latecomers who strode quickly toward the church doors. She hadn't planned on being late and she wished she could blame it all on Rachel. But she was the reason they were driving up to the church just a little after eleven. She'd overslept and hadn't awakened until Rachel was banging on her door, dressed, packed, and ready to get the hell out of Chicago.

Jasmine had pulled it together as fast as she could, and really, being ten minutes late was probably a good thing. This way, she could stand in the back of the church, scope through the crowd, and find the woman that she needed to sit next to, to get the information they needed.

Inside though, the church was already packed to the rafters and Jasmine didn't see one empty seat.

"You're gonna have to go to the standing-room-only section," one of the white-gloved ushers shouted at her, raising his voice above the praise and worship that had started.

She followed behind a double line of men and women to the far right wall.

"Stand, church, and let us give praise for the life of our founder, Pastor Earl Griffith!"

Everyone in the sanctuary was on their feet, some with their hands lifted toward the heavens, some clapping. All of them raised their voices and spoke, some in English, some in tongues. It was a mournful sound as the members grieved their pastor together.

As those around her wailed and wept, Jasmine scanned the colossal space. Even though sorrow filled the air, the church was a beautiful bouquet of color as the sun burst through the massive stained-glass windows.

But her admiration for the church was short-lived as Jasmine's eyes searched the people. This certainly wasn't going to be as easy as she'd thought. When she'd done this in Georgia, the church had been small enough for her to peruse the sanctuary in one swoop. There was a big difference, though, between a small one-hundred-member church deep in the South and this giant-size membership. There were at least four thousand people in this church.

Jasmine had no idea that Pastor Griffith had been pulling in the people this way; but then, why not? She remembered her own fascination with the pastor and she knew just about every woman who could see found the green-eyed man so sexy. Back in the day, she would have made him her boo.

But this was a new day, and she was looking for his real boo.

"I stand before you today, saints, with a heart filled with sorrow."

Jasmine's eyes shot to the altar where a man stood at the podium, dressed in a burgundy and gold robe, the type that Hosea wore when he performed weddings and funerals.

"The man who has meant so much to so many has departed from this earth."

He had to pause because of the wails that rose in the sanctuary. There was not a dry eye anywhere around Jasmine.

"Church of the Deliverance was founded by Pastor Griffith because he wanted to reach out to the forgotten in the community."

That's a lie. He needed a new place to hide his drug money after Jeremiah Wright kicked him out.

"Our pastor was never one to forget not only where he came from, but those who were less fortunate."

He remembered them, all right. He sold them drugs to keep them down.

"And it was because of his good heart that he was taken from us."

290

More wails.

"You know," the pastor at the altar continued, "when I first heard that Pastor Griffith was missing, I held out hope. Hope against hope that he would come back to us."

"Yes!"

"Amen!"

"Me, too," rose through the sanctuary.

"And even when I got the call from Pastor's beautiful daughter, Eleanor . . ."

When the pastor paused, Jasmine craned her neck to follow his glance. From where she stood, she couldn't see the front row, which is where Jasmine was sure that Pastor Griffith's daughter sat. But still, Jasmine stared, trying to take in the faces in the first few pews because surely, the pastor's girlfriend would be close to the front.

The pastor continued, "Even when I got that call that a body had been found, I didn't want to believe!" He shouted and pounded on the podium. "I didn't want to believe that our pastor was gone. I didn't want to believe that someone had taken his life. I didn't want to believe that this was the end."

More weeping.

"But you know what, saints? This is not the end. This is Pastor Earl Griffith's beginning!"

"Amen!"

"Hallelujah!"

"Glory to God!"

"This is our pastor's beginning to his everlasting life that he now has with our Lord."

"Yes!"

"So, saints, I know that while today your hearts are troubled, take joy in knowing that our pastor, the great Earl Griffith, is sitting on the right hand of God, right next to Jesus, because of all that he's done on this earth!"

Through their cries, the crowd cheered and Jasmine rolled her eyes. She wondered if this was an act or if these people really didn't know just how shady their pastor was. He had a special seat in the afterlife, all right — she could almost see him right now sitting on the left hand of the devil.

"Now, I have to announce that we will have special services this week for the pastor, though . . ." The pastor paused, lowered his eyes, and shook his head. "Though," he began again, but then stopped as if he was choked up.

"Take your time," someone yelled from the sanctuary.

After a few deep breaths, the pastor continued, "Though there will be no viewing of the body. We will still say goodbye to our pastor."

When the lady standing next to Jasmine began to sob, tears filled her own eyes. Last night, she and Rachel had heard on the news how it had taken a couple of hours for the special police team to drag Pastor Griffith's decapitated body from the river. He had been identified though, from his wallet, and all his other personal effects: his keys, his cell phone, and even a special pen he always wrote with that had been given to him by his daughter.

The image of that had made Jasmine sad, especially for Eleanor, who would always have a picture of her headless father in her mind.

"Services are set for Friday at eleven and you know as beloved as our pastor is, this place is gonna be packed for the tribute to this special man. So get here early," he said, as if he was announcing the opening of a Tyler Perry premiere.

Once again, Jasmine rolled her eyes and shifted from one leg to the other. She wasn't here to listen to all of this nonsense; she needed to find this girlfriend . . . or at least find someone who could help find her.

Then, "But before we can get to the celebration of Pastor Griffith's life, there is some business to be taken care of." The pastor's voice was louder now, harder. "There is the business of coming together as a community to help this young lady" — he pointed to Eleanor — "find peace. There is the business of coming together as a community to find the men who did this to our wonderful pastor!"

It had happened in a split second. This was no longer a Sunday church service. This sounded like a political gathering.

"We are not going to leave it to the police alone, though they know that they have to have justice for someone like Pastor Griffith. We have to step up and help. Lift our voices. No more being quiet because you're afraid of being a snitch. No more being quiet because you once had a run-in with the police. Now that it's happened to one of our own, we are going to be partners with the police. We are going to find justice for Pastor Earl Griffith!"

The organ player hit a few chords as people rose in their seats, clapping, shouting, lifting their hands to the heavens.

"Here to help us with that is someone who was very close to Pastor Griffith. Someone who is a friend to us here at Church of the Deliverance. Mrs. Cecelia King."

The membership stood to their feet. A

man held Cecelia's hand as she rose from her seat and took the three steps up to the altar. She stood next to the pastor as people cheered and Jasmine's heart pounded. With Cecelia here, it would be harder for her to ask questions, especially since Jasmine suspected that Cecelia was the girlfriend.

When the crowd quieted, Cecelia began, "My heart is so heavy as I stand here with you. You see, Earl was one of my dearest friends."

Oh, really?

"I knew him even before I met my husband, so you know we go way back."

Is that right?

Cecelia gave a little chuckle. "That is why I will not allow my friend to become another statistic. He will not be a victim twice: murdered and then forgotten because he is black."

"That's right!" someone shouted.

"Like Pastor Andrews said, we must step up and help the police, and I know how we can help." She held up a photo and Jasmine gasped. Even from back here, Jasmine could see the image.

"Pastor, you said that we must find the men who murdered our friend. But I'm here to tell you that the murderer is a woman. This is the woman who was involved in our

295

pastor's murder."

People scooted to the edge of their seats.

"I'm sure many of you saw this photo on the news last night," Cecelia said. "Don't worry if you can't see it now."

In the next second, the lights dimmed and an image of Rachel appeared on a huge screen that descended from the ceiling behind the altar. Even though the sunlight still illuminated a good part of the sanctuary, it was dark enough for Rachel's photo to be clear.

"This is the woman who was last seen with Earl," Cecelia said.

Jasmine wanted to raise her hand and tell everyone that wasn't true. No one had seen Rachel with Pastor Griffith once he left Oprah's studio. Where was that lie coming from?

"Her name is Rachel Jackson Adams," Cecelia continued, "and she is the wife of the president of the American Baptist Coalition!"

It was a united gasp that filled the room.

"The police know her identity and are looking for her right here in Chicago. Even though she lives in Houston, she came to Chicago to do this, and then returned because she had some unfinished business." She paused. "We believe that Eleanor Griffith's life is now in danger."

More cries from the sanctuary.

Cecelia held up her hand, letting the members know that she wanted to explain. "It seems that Pastor Griffith found out about some illegal activity going on in the Coalition and he was just about to expose the president and his wife when he was murdered."

Jasmine shook her head, stunned at what she was hearing.

"And now, Reverend Lester Adams and his wife believe that Earl may have confided in his daughter and so she has to go, too!"

"Oh, no!"

"That's right!" Cecelia continued. "We have to bring justice for our pastor and we have to protect his daughter. So, if you see her around Church of the Deliverance, report her immediately."

"Yes!" the people shouted.

"And she's traveling with others. We know two men have already broken into Eleanor's home."

More gasps.

"And there's a woman. Another pastor's wife who is traveling with her, who's her accomplice."

At first, Jasmine stood frozen in place, expecting Cecelia to shout out her name and then have the spotlight shining on her. But Cecelia said nothing more except "We must have justice for Pastor Earl Griffith. Help us find his killer."

A standing ovation accompanied Cecelia to her seat and Jasmine used that time to hike up the collar on her coat and push her way through the crowd. She had to get out of here and get Rachel away from the church. She doubted if anyone would seriously be able to identify her through the tinted car windows, but she didn't want to take any chances.

Maybe Rachel had been right. Maybe they should have just gotten on planes this morning and handled their business from Houston and New York. Well, whatever, it was time to go now.

Outside, Jasmine dashed down the church steps, hoping that it wouldn't be hard for her to find Rachel.

And it wasn't.

Rachel was right in front of the church, double-parked. But what made her stand out the most were the three police cars that surrounded her. And the police who stood outside their cruisers, yelling for Rachel to step out of the car, slowly and with her hands up.

"Oh, my God!" Jasmine whispered as she

ducked behind a huge ficus tree.

All kinds of questions galloped through her mind. Should she go back into the church? Hide from the police and then help Rachel from the outside? Or should she run over there now and go with Rachel to wherever they planned to take her? Because Rachel would die going through this by herself.

The seconds ticked by. Jasmine just didn't know.

What should she do? What should she do?

CHAPTER TWENTY-THREE

If she had to imagine her worst nightmare ever, concoct a situation she'd never dream of finding herself in, Rachel Jackson Adams would've never imagined this.

As she sat inside the rented Buick, cop cars facing her from every direction, she felt like Cleo in the movie *Set It Off.* All she needed was some CDs to throw out the window.

But this was no gangsta movie and she dang sure wasn't ready to die. So Rachel eased the car door open, put her arms out, and yelled, "I'm coming out. Don't shoot. I'm a mama."

The first officer that reached her grabbed her and pushed her against the car.

"Owww!" she yelled when the handle hit her in the groin. Rachel couldn't understand why, if she was just wanted for questioning, they were being so rough. Why the whole SWAT team? Why in the world was she being treated like she'd just robbed Bank of America?

"Rachel Jackson Adams?" a plainclothes detective asked as he approached her.

"Yes, that's me," she cried, standing up as the officer pulled her arms behind her back. "But why are you doing this?"

The officer leaned in, surveyed the inside of the car, and then nodded toward the other officer, who released his tight grip on her arms.

"I'm Detective Harwin Davis. Sorry about the aggressiveness," he said, "but we were told you were armed and dangerous."

"What? Told by whom?"

"That's irrelevant, but we have been looking for you."

"Yo, Davis?" another officer yelled from the back of the car. Rachel hadn't even noticed that he'd popped the trunk.

Detective Davis eyed Rachel, then looked at the first officer, who tightened his grip again like she was going to try and flee. "Whatcha got?" he asked, walking to the back of the trunk.

"Just luggage."

Davis smirked as he walked back over to Rachel. "Going somewhere?"

"Home, I'm going home," Rachel said, panicked. "So, please, let me go."

He grinned like they were discussing a new flavor of coffee at Starbucks. "Now, we're not going to be able to do that. See, we've been looking for you. We just want to ask you a couple of questions. We didn't mean to get rough." He nodded at the officer again and this time, the man released her arms altogether. "But we had to play it safe and make sure you weren't armed and dangerous. We see that you're not."

Rachel studied the smiling man. They hadn't tased her and thrown her in the back of the police car, so maybe it wasn't going to be that bad. Maybe they just wanted to ask her a few questions. She took a deep breath. She was overreacting. These men just wanted to talk to her.

"Okay," she said, trying to calm down.

Detective Davis suddenly lost his smile. "But I do have to warn you that you have the right to remain silent. You have the right to an attorney. If you cannot afford one —"

"Hold up, are you reading me my Miranda rights?" She'd watched enough cop shows to know they only did that when they were about to take someone in.

"— anything you say can and will be held against you in a court of law," he continued.

As the first officer who had grabbed her stepped closer, Rachel jerked away. "Hold up! I haven't done anything."

By this point, a growing crowd was gathering across the street. Church couldn't have let out — it wasn't that many people — but word must've spread about the drama taking place because several people were piling out.

Rachel scanned the crowd for Jasmine. She hoped Jasmine had the good sense to see something was wrong. She didn't know what Jasmine could do, but right about now, Rachel just needed her right there reassuring her that everything was going to be all right.

"What am I being arrested for?" Rachel finally said as she felt the cold handcuffs clamp down on her wrists.

"You're being detained for questioning in the death of Pastor Earl Griffith," Detective Davis said.

Rachel wanted to protest, tell these people they had the wrong person, that she was a lot of things, but a murderer she was not. She had so much she wanted to say, but the words wouldn't form.

"But I didn't do anything," she finally managed to say.

"Then you have nothing to worry about," Detective Davis said. "We just want to ask you a few questions."

"But why do I have to go to the police station? Why couldn't you just call me and ask?"

Detective Davis shrugged. "You'll have to ask the D.A. that. But you do know Pastor Griffith, right?"

"I —"

"Hey, Raquel, remember, everything you say can and will be held against you, so don't say nothin'!"

Everyone turned toward the scraggly man standing in front of them. The man wore a tattered gray sweater that looked like it was swallowing his body, and some dirty khaki pants. His salt-and-pepper beard looked like it had something living in it, and his long, stringy dreadlocks gave Rachel the creeps.

"Excuse me, sir, may we help you?" Detective Davis asked.

The man stood straight and brushed lint off his arm (like that would really help) and said with conviction, "I was just reminding Raquel to be quiet."

Who the heck *was Raquel?*

"And who would you be?" Detective Davis asked.

"Maybe he's her attorney," one of the officers said, laughing.

"For your information, I'm her . . . ummm, I'm her man," he said.

Rachel's eyebrows rose in surprise. She wanted to say something, but was stunned silent.

"Buster Brown is the name," he said, extending his hand. Nobody bothered to shake it.

"Well, Mr. Brown," Detective Davis said, "if you'll excuse us, we need to get going. If you want to see your *woman,* she'll be down at the main police station being questioned."

Buster ignored Detective Davis and stepped in front of Rachel. His stench assaulted her nostrils. If he got any closer she hoped police would taser *him.* "Honey-drop, I just wanted to tell you that everything is gonna be okay." He winked at her. "Yeah, ummm . . . ummm," he snapped his fingers like he was trying to remember something. "Oh yeah, June Europe is gonna take care of everything." He nodded like he was proud of himself for remembering.

Rachel looked at him, confused. This man was certifiably psycho. Who in the world was June Europe?

"Can we just go?" Rachel muttered to the detective. More and more people were filing out of the church and the last thing she wanted was a spectacle on the grounds of the Church of the Deliverance.

"I'm serious. Don't say nothing," Buster

reiterated. "Your friend said she is calling June Europe right now. Or is it April Germany?" He scratched his dreads and began mumbling. "Dangit, I told her I wasn't gonna remember the name. Okay, month and country, month and country," he muttered.

Rachel paused as she studied the strange man, then it dawned on her.

Her friend. Month and country. Jasmine! Jasmine was calling Mae Frances! Rachel didn't know what that old coot would be able to do, but since everyone knew she knew everyone from Al Sharpton to Al Capone, she would definitely be able to help Rachel out of this mess. She was surprised Jasmine hadn't thought to call her earlier.

Jasmine hadn't abandoned her! She'd probably given this homeless man twenty bucks to come relay that message. For a minute, Rachel questioned why Jasmine hadn't come over herself, but Rachel would've done the exact same thing. They were more alike than she ever would've admitted.

If Rachel hadn't been caught up in the middle of this nightmare, she might've actually smiled.

"Let's go," Detective Davis said, pushing her down in the backseat of his car.

"Bye, baby!" Buster waved, a huge tooth-less smile across his face.

Rachel gave him a solemn wave and just as the police car pulled away, she noticed Cecelia King standing on the corner, watching everything. Her smile was even bigger than Buster's, and satisfaction was written all over her face.

There was a reason the Good Lord had blessed Rachel to have never led a life of crime. She wasn't cut out for jail.

She'd been at the Cook County Jail for three hours and she was ready to confess to being the person who assassinated Dr. Martin Luther King, Jr. She'd stayed strong as the detectives played good cop, bad cop; hurled accusations at her; but tried to cut her a deal if she would just tell them why she did it. Rachel was so exhausted and out of tears that she'd been ready to say whatever she thought they wanted to hear. But she kept hearing Jasmine's voice telling her to "be strong." It was funny, because Rachel had never been a weak woman. Sure, she'd had a momentary pity party when she thought her husband had gotten another woman pregnant, but she was a fighter at heart. Somewhere between viewing Pastor Griffith's dead body and having her picture plastered all over the news, she'd turned into a withering wimp.

"So you're just not going to cooperate?" Detective Davis asked, obviously frustrated.

"I don't know what to tell you," Rachel said, her voice filled with weariness.

The second detective, a portly black man in a too-small, cheap suit slammed his hand on the table. "How about you start with the truth?"

Detective Davis nodded in agreement. "Yeah, because I'm not buying for a minute that Buster dude is your man. Everyone knows your man is Pastor Griffith!"

Rachel was fed up. "That is insane!" she shouted. "First of all, I'm married. Secondly, look at me!" She stood and motioned up and down her body. She wasn't looking her best, but even on her worst day, Rachel still looked good. "What would a fine woman like me want with an old decrepit man like Earl Griffith? One night in bed with me would kill that old man," she snapped.

Both of their eyes bucked and Rachel winced. Definitely a bad choice of words. This would be why lawyers advise their clients to be quiet.

Rachel sank back down in her hard wooden seat. "I didn't even like Pastor

Griffith, let alone date him. Or kill him," she threw in for good measure. *Now* she was done.

They must've known it, too, because the overweight detective tossed his notepad on the table. "This isn't getting us anywhere."

"Yes, Mrs. Adams, you are indeed fine," Detective Davis said, continuing his good-cop role. "But money can make many a woman put aside age and looks. So, why would you want Pastor Griffith? Money. Power. Money."

Rachel thought of protesting more but finally just said, "You have the wrong woman." She glanced up at the clock on the wall. She'd hoped Jasmine would've gotten Mae Frances to work her magic by now, but so far, nothing, and frankly, Rachel was tired of waiting.

"I'd like my one phone call now." She didn't know what Lester could do from home, and she dang sure didn't want to hear his mouth. But at this point, Rachel had no doubt that not only had her husband heard about the fiasco, he probably was already on the plane to Chicago to come see about her.

"Fine," Detective Davis said, exasperated. "You're just in for questioning, so you can call who you'd like." He motioned for an officer standing by the door to lead Rachel out to the phone. She stood, massaged her neck, and was at least grateful that they'd removed the handcuffs.

"Don't try anything funny," the overweight detective said.

Rachel looked at him, then at the six-foot-three-inch officer guiding her out, then back at the detective. "Seriously?" She shook her head in disgust and walked out to call her husband.

Since she had to call collect, Rachel called her house. Maybe by some miracle, no one at home knew anything. Well, if they didn't before, they would now, Rachel thought as she heard the operator say, "You have a collect call from the Cook County Jail. Press one to accept. Hang up to decline."

Rachel was grateful when she heard the button chime.

"Rachel!" Her father's voice boomed through the phone and Rachel immediately felt like a child again. The only other time she'd been to jail — some ghetto drama when she was a teen — her father had left her in jail overnight to "teach her a lesson." She couldn't endure any chastising now.

"Hey, Daddy."

"Baby girl, what in the world is going on? We have been worried sick. It's all over the news. Everyone here is talking about you've been arrested for murder! Lord Jesus, what's happening?" His voice held a mixture of relief and panic.

"Technically I wasn't arrested. I was taken in for *questioning* in a murder," she said, like that made any difference.

"But what . . . why? I mean, they said you had something to do with Pastor Griffith's murder."

"Daddy, you know I didn't kill anyone, nor did I have anything to do with it."

"Well, of course I know that," he replied. "But why do they think you did?"

"It's a long story, Daddy. Where's Lester?"

"Baby, that boy hightailed it out of here the minute he heard you were taken into custody. He should be landing any moment now, if he hasn't already."

A sense of relief filled Rachel's body. "Thank God."

"God's got this under control, you just stay strong. Lester's on his way. We called Brother Lampkin from the church and he's on his way over here. He's not licensed to practice in Illinois, but he can advise us 'til we figure this mess out."

"Okay, Daddy. How are the kids? They don't know, do they?"

"The kids are fine. You don't worry about

none of this. We already decided to keep Jordan home from school tomorrow because you know that boy's short-tempered and we don't want nobody giving him a hard time."

Rachel felt hot tears fill her eyes. Now even her kids were suffering . . . all because she wanted to be on *Oprah*.

Rachel wiped her eyes. "All right, Daddy. Hopefully, I'll be home soon."

"You will. Everybody here is praying for you." He hesitated. "Have you prayed for yourself?"

Rachel thought about it. She hadn't. Not once during this entire nightmare had she turned to God.

Her father didn't wait for a response. "Well, regardless of whether you have or haven't, we 'bout to pray again. You find comfort in Psalms 46:1, *God is our refuge and our strength, and ever-present in trouble.*"

Rachel closed her eyes, listened intently as her father began to pray. And in no time at all, she was praying right along with him.

CHAPTER TWENTY-FOUR

There weren't many times when Jasmine turned to her Bible. Even though she was a first lady, she found the Good Book filled with too many "thou arts," "ye begots," and names she could never pronounce.

But as she sat inside this Starbucks only blocks from the Cook County Jail, she'd pulled up a Bible on her iPad, hoping that reading a few scriptures would take away her fear and help her stop trembling.

It was a good thing that she'd carried her purse into the church since the police had impounded the rental car. All she had was her iPad, phone, and wallet. She didn't even have her makeup bag since she'd tucked it inside her carry-on.

By now, Jasmine was sure that the police knew Rachel wasn't traveling alone. Actually, the police had probably known that all along according to what Cecelia had said as she stood in the pulpit.

How could a woman of God stand at the altar like that and tell all of those lies? Jasmine wondered. And then she answered her own question. Clearly, Cecelia King was no woman of God.

So what did Cecelia have to do with this whole thing, anyway? Because Jasmine knew for sure Cecelia was somehow knee-deep in the middle of Pastor Griffith's murder. She just couldn't figure out Cecelia's role, no matter how many angles she looked at it from. She needed help — not only to get answers about Cecelia, but also to get Rachel out of jail.

There was only one thing to do. She had to do what she'd told Rachel she'd do, through that wino that she'd paid to give her the message.

She had to call Mae Frances.

Jasmine wasn't surprised that she hadn't heard from Mae Frances. Her friend had to be majorly pissed that Jasmine had ignored all of her warnings to stay away from Chicago. And now, here she was, needing to make this call. She'd have to tell Mae Frances that she'd been right — that was okay. She'd just suck it up if that would help Rachel.

Once again, she glanced at the scripture that she'd looked up, Psalm 27:1: *The Lord*

*is my light and my salvation — so why should
I be afraid? The Lord is my fortress, protecting me from danger, so why should I tremble?*

She'd been shocked when she'd first read
those words. It was as if God knew her fear.
But still, she trembled, especially as she
thought about Rachel. What was Rachel saying? What was she doing? Did she know that
Jasmine had her back?

With a deep breath, she picked up her
phone, scrolled to her contact list, and hit
Mae Frances's number.

Her friend answered on the first ring. As
if she'd been sitting by the phone, waiting.

"Where are you?" Mae Frances growled
without saying hello.

"Don't be mad —"

"You're still in Chicago!"

"Mae Frances, I had to come. I had to
help Rachel."

"I told you —"

"I know you did and I wish I'd listened to
you because now, everything is a mess."

"I know."

Jasmine frowned. "You know what?"

"That Rachel has been taken in for questioning regarding Earl's murder."

"Your people work fast."

"Not this time. I got my information the
old-fashioned way — it's all over the news."

Jasmine closed her eyes and pressed her fingertips against her temple to massage away the headache that she knew was coming. All over the news? If Mae Frances saw it that meant that Lester and Hosea probably had, too. Which explained why Hosea had been blowing up her phone.

But she shouldn't have been surprised. Of course, this would be big news nationally. It involved the American Baptist Coalition, it involved another Christian having a public fall. The media loved those stories.

"Cecelia King has been all over the news talking about how Rachel Jackson Adams is an embarrassment to the American Baptist Coalition."

Jasmine's eyes snapped open. "What? But Rachel was just arrested."

"Well, I don't know what she did, but Cecelia's already held a news conference that's been on every channel and she's demanding that Reverend Adams step down as the president before the Coalition suffers major damage."

"I cannot believe this."

"Believe it, because right now, I'm looking at her on WGN talking about how she tried to warn the Coalition against putting people in place who weren't ready. This is so big, they interrupted one of the football games and that hasn't happened in years."

"Oh, God!" Jasmine said. She couldn't imagine how Cecelia had pulled this off so quickly. It was like she had a press conference waiting. "Well, I can't worry about this right now. I have to get Rachel out of there," Jasmine said.

"It's not going to be that easy. They can hold her for hours just to question her."

"She'll never last for hours." Jasmine paused. "Mae Frances, I need help."

"I know you do. From what I've heard, you and that Adams chick have been making a mess of things. Do you know who you're dealing with?"

"Uh . . . yeah. I was there when the police stuffed Rachel into the back of their car."

Mae Frances laughed, surprising Jasmine. "The police are the least of your worries. It's the other folks that I'm talking about."

"Yeah," Jasmine said, scooting to the edge of her seat. "We've come up against some seriously bad guys." She shook her head. "I wish to God that I never sent Rachel that blackmail letter."

There was a long pause. Mae Frances said, "Jasmine, I never mailed your blackmail letter."

Jasmine frowned. "What? No, of course you did. Don't you remember? You had

317

someone in Chicago mail the letters and I got mine. Then Rachel told me she got one, too, and —"

"She didn't get *yours,*" Mae Frances said, interrupting her. "I don't know who sent her a letter, but I didn't mail the one that you'd put together for her."

"That doesn't make any sense. Why didn't you send it?"

"Because I found out that what was going on with Earl was really deep. Like deep in the game."

Jasmine held back the urge to say "Duh!" Of course he was deep in it. The man was dead.

"After I spoke with you," Mae Frances continued, "I checked things out. I made a few calls, found out exactly who Earl had been dealing with, and I knew you didn't need to be anywhere near these people or this situation. So, I didn't mail the letter to Rachel. Just mailed yours."

"Why did you go through all of that? Why didn't you just tell me?"

"Because you're hardheaded and I knew you wouldn't listen to me, Jasmine Larson," she snapped. "I only mailed your letter to keep you quiet."

"You still should've told me."

"Why? I told you not to go to Chicago,

but where are you right now?"

"So who sent Rachel that letter?" Jasmine whispered, more to herself than to Mae Frances. The question made her shiver some more.

"See what I'm saying, Jasmine Larson? This thing is no joke. There are people out there who want to take Rachel down."

"But why? Why her?"

"I don't know. Maybe the real killer set her up. Maybe the killer knows that the police will keep looking until they put someone away for Earl's murder. Maybe it's that simple . . . or much more complicated. I don't know which, but I know that those people in Chicago are not to be played with."

"I'm beginning to see that."

"Well this twenty-twenty vision that you suddenly have may be a little too late."

"There's nothing I can do about the past. I'm here, Rachel's in jail, and I have to do something."

"What you need to do is get on a plane and get back here to New York."

"I can't leave Rachel!"

There was a pause before, "Why not? I thought you couldn't stand the skank!"

"She's not a skank." Jasmine raised her voice as if she was protecting a dear, dear friend. When the barista glanced her way, Jasmine lowered her voice. "She's not a skank," she repeated. "Rachel's really cool."

In the pause that followed, Jasmine imagined Mae Frances with her eyebrows stretched high. "She's cool? So, what? Y'all friends now?"

"Yeah, I mean, no, not really. Look, we've been working together and Rachel really isn't that bad. Like I said, she's cool people and I'm going to stay here and do everything I can to get her out 'cause that's what she would do for me. So," Jasmine paused, "will you help me?"

Mae Frances released a long sigh. "You two really kissed and made up?"

"Yeah, well, being chased by thugs and the police will bring you closer to anyone," Jasmine said. "Plus, I kinda feel responsible for her being here," she said. "I mean, I started this whole thing with that blackmail letter . . . or at least that's what I thought."

"Well, give me fifteen minutes. I'm gonna get Buddy Clemons right on it."

"Who's that?" Jasmine asked, surprised that Mae Frances hadn't called out one of her famous friends. Wasn't there an Al Capone heir that she could get to help them?

"Buddy is Al Sharpton's godson. I'd call

Al, but he's been really busy doing that TV thing. Buddy is the next best thing. He's an attorney right there in Chicago and he knows whatever is going down in his city. If anyone can help Rachel, he can."

"Thank you," Jasmine breathed, feeling the trembling that had taken over her body subsiding.

"And after I get him on this, I'll catch the next plane out there. Not sure if I can get a flight out today since it's Sunday, but if I can, will you pick me up?"

Jasmine knew exactly why tears sprang into her eyes. She'd missed her friend. Through every adversity, Mae Frances had been by her side, helping her to wiggle out of every situation. Clearly, the way she and Rachel had been stumbling around Chicago, it would've been much different if Mae Frances had been with them. Mae Frances would've had the whole thing figured out and fixed in two minutes flat.

"Definitely," Jasmine finally said. "Whenever your plane comes in, I'll be there. And, thank you, Mae Frances."

"Don't thank me yet. Let me get there and get you two out of this mess first."

"I know exactly where we can start. Who's Pastor Griffith's girlfriend?"

A beat passed and then, "Well, I was one

of his ladies back in the day."

Jasmine's eyebrows rose, though she couldn't say that she was surprised. That had been her first thought when she'd met Pastor Griffith and saw the way he and Mae Frances interacted. In fact, when Jasmine had found out that Pastor Griffith was a crook, she wasn't too sure if she could trust Mae Frances anymore.

"I'm talking about now. Who's his girlfriend now?"

"Why?"

"Apparently you haven't heard everything," Jasmine said before she filled Mae Frances in. She spoke for almost five minutes, telling Mae Frances about everything from Rachel being accosted on the steps of Eleanor's building to her being held in Eleanor's apartment. "For some reason, they think Rachel was Pastor Griffith's girlfriend."

"Hmmm." Mae Frances hummed as if she already had some ideas.

"Do you think he could have been messing around with Cecelia?"

"Cecelia who?"

"King! Cece—"

But before she could finish, Mae Frances was laughing so loud, Jasmine had to pull the phone away from her ear.

It took Mae Frances a couple of minutes to compose herself enough to say, "Why would Earl want anything to do with Madea's twin?"

"Come on, Mae Frances. Cecelia doesn't look *that* bad."

"Have you taken a good look at her? And do you remember what Earl looked like?"

"I'm just sayin', Cecelia seems to be everywhere and —"

"Trust me, she ain't the one. We'll figure that out when I get there." She paused as if she needed a moment to get herself completely together. "That was a good one, Jasmine Larson, but we need to stop playing around and get back to business."

Huh? She wasn't the one who'd been cracking up like she was watching *Def Comedy Jam.*

Mae Frances continued, "You need to get over to wherever they're holding that girl and Buddy will meet you. He'll have Rachel out of there in no time; the police never mess with Al Sharpton's kin. Not if they don't want to see a riot in their city."

"Okay."

"I'm going to tell Buddy to make sure that you two get to a hotel," Mae Frances continued, "and just wait there 'til you hear from me."

"Okay."

"I mean it, Jasmine Larson," Mae Frances warned. "I won't be able to help if you two go off to do things on your own."

"Ohhhhkay! I promise. I won't make a move."

"And what about that ghetto Scarlett O'Hara? Make sure she doesn't do anything either."

Jasmine wanted to defend Rachel once again, but this time, she only said, "We'll both wait for you."

"You better!" Mae Frances snapped as if for good measure.

Jasmine clicked off the phone and she almost smiled. Mae Frances's mumbling and grumbling gave her a peace that she hadn't had in all the days that she'd been in Chicago. Jasmine had no doubt that help was on the way.

Now, she could get over to that jail and let Rachel know that all was going to be well. But before she could do that, there was still one more thing she had to do.

She had to call their husbands.

Jasmine didn't have her story completely straight when she dialed Hosea, but just like when she'd called Mae Frances, he answered on the first ring.

"Jasmine!"

"I know, I know, babe. I'm sorry I didn't call you back before now."

"That's okay, I just wanted to make sure that you were all right. It's all over the news — Rachel's been arrested."

"I'm not sure that she's been arrested," Jasmine said. "I think the police just might be questioning her right now."

"Well, the news said that she was arrested, right outside of Pastor Griffith's church."

"We went there this morning for the service. We had no idea that all of this was going on."

"Tell me about it! I thought you were in Chicago for interviews and now you turn up in the middle of this mess."

"Technically, I'm not in it."

"Well, what happened? How did Rachel get in it?"

Jasmine paused, not sure how much she wanted to tell Hosea. She and Rachel hadn't had any time to figure out the stories to tell their husbands and she wanted their tales to sound similar.

So Jasmine stayed as close to the truth as she could. "I really don't know how Rachel got wrapped up in this. We were waiting for Yvette to set up a few more things and we decided to go to church this morning."

"And the police just came in there? In the middle of service and arrested Rachel?"

"Something . . . like that."

"I know Rachel is probably frantic," Hosea said.

"Yeah, I'm on my way to the jail to see if there's anything I can do," Jasmine said, deciding not to mention Mae Frances just yet. Though she knew her husband loved Mae Frances as much as she did, Jasmine never knew how Hosea would react to Mae Frances and her connections. He always wanted to leave everything up to God when there were times when God just needed a little help. And Mae Frances was the right one to help Him.

"I'm glad you and Rachel worked out your . . . challenges. I'm glad you're there with her, at least until Lester gets there."

"You spoke to Lester?"

"Yeah, as soon as I saw the report on the news, I called him. He was running out the door to catch a flight right then." Hosea paused. "You know what? I wonder if I need to come to Chicago."

Jasmine closed her eyes. As much as she wanted to see Mae Frances, she was dying to see her husband. Just one hug from him and all of this trembling would stop.

"Yeah," Hosea said as if he was thinking it

through as he spoke to her. "Lester may need some support and it's not that long a flight."

"But what about Jacquie and Zaya?" Jasmine said, especially concerned about her children ever since Jacqueline had been kidnapped when she was just four.

"Mrs. Sloss is here. And I'll call Mae Frances and my father. Don't worry, darlin'. I wouldn't leave them if I didn't think they were safe."

"I know," Jasmine said, deciding to let Mae Frances tell Hosea that she was coming to Chicago, too. "I can't wait to see you, Hosea. It's all been so horrible."

"I'm on my way. I'll call you when I have my flight details."

"I love you," she told him before she hung up the phone.

Jasmine closed her eyes. The two people she loved the most were coming to rescue her, to save her. She wanted to just sit there and cry, but she had work to do.

She lifted her iPad to power it down, then glanced at the scripture again.

The Lord is my light and my salvation — so why should I be afraid? The Lord is my fortress, protecting me from danger, so why should I tremble?

Now she had to smile. Why should she tremble, indeed?

CHAPTER TWENTY-FIVE

Rachel struggled to contain her shock as her eyes roamed up and down the length of the towering, caramel-color man standing in front of her. This Walker, Texas Ranger–looking man was supposed to be her savior? This man in his cowboy hat, tan blazer, khaki pants, and alligator boots — and was that a perm? This was the best Mae Frances could do?

Rachel released a long sigh as she leaned back in her seat.

Death Row, here I come.

"Good afternoon, gentlemen," the man said, slamming his alligator skin briefcase on the table. "Buddy Clemons is the name, attorney at law. My client is done talking." He looked at Rachel, flashed a lopsided smile, then turned back to the detectives. They hadn't been too happy to hear that Rachel had an attorney here to represent her.

Buddy took out a legal-size notepad and an expensive-looking pen. "I'd like to know the charges against my client."

The detectives exchanged glances. "Well, ah, technically, she's not formally charged," Detective Davis finally said.

"Are there plans to formally charge her?" Buddy asked matter-of-factly.

"Well, we're working on that," the other detective said.

Buddy tossed his notepad back in his briefcase and stood up. "Here's my card," he said, tossing it on the table. "Call us when you get some charges." He extended his hand toward Rachel. She looked uneasy, but took it as he helped her stand, then led her toward the door.

"Are we just going to leave?" she whispered.

"We're not done questioning her," Detective Davis said.

"Yes, you are." Buddy swung the door open and walked out.

"Don't leave town, because this isn't over," the other detective called out behind them.

"Are we really leaving?" Rachel asked as she scurried behind him toward the front door.

"We sure are," he said, without breaking

his stride. He walked with an air of confidence that was empowering.

"We can do that?"

"Yep."

Rachel expected one of the officers to tackle them before they reached the door, but no one said a word as they walked out the front of the building. Buddy's confidence was overwhelming. She hadn't even thought that she could just get up and leave.

Buddy directed her to his Mercedes Benz, one of the huge models that one would expect a man like him to drive.

"So they're not going to come after us?" Rachel asked once they were both seated in the car.

"I checked before I came in. They were done with their questioning. Probably just wanted to keep you in there to scare you into confessing."

"I don't have anything to confess to."

He shrugged like that was irrelevant. "Well, unless they had some formal charges, they had no right to keep you there."

"But wasn't I under arrest?"

"Not technically."

"But they read me my Miranda rights."

"They do that just to cover their bases. But if there are no formal charges against you, there's nothing they can do once they question you."

Rachel sat back as he pulled his big-bodied Benz out of the handicapped parking spot. The whole show at the church, all the cop cars, and she wasn't even technically under arrest?

"Wow, well, uh, thank you," Rachel finally managed to say.

"Don't thank me. Thank Mae Frances." He smiled as genuine memories filled his mind. "That woman means the world to me. My godfather was crazy about some Mae Frances. And so was I."

That was hard for Rachel to imagine. Still, she asked, "Who's your godfather?"

"Al Sharpton." He didn't notice the stunned expression on Rachel's face as he shook off his nostalgia. "Enough of that. I'll get busy on your case first thing in the morning."

Rachel nodded. "Where are we going now?"

"Back to the hotel. Not much else we can do tonight."

"I want to go home."

He shook his head like that wasn't an option. "I wouldn't advise that just yet. You leaving town could make them think you're fleeing."

"I'm not fleeing. I just want to go home,"

she protested.

"And you will. As soon as we get this mess cleaned up."

She sighed in frustration. "I need to get my rental car. My purse, everything is in there."

"Got my staff working on that now," he replied. "They're going to go pick it up from the impound and have it delivered to your hotel. I've already talked to your husband. I told him to just wait for us at your hotel."

Rachel leaned back in her seat. At least this man was on top of things. And for all his over-the-top looks, Rachel definitely felt like she was in capable hands with Buddy Clemons.

Twenty minutes later, Rachel walked into the hotel suite and was greeted at the door by her husband.

"Oh, my God, Rachel," he said, throwing his arms around her neck before she could get all the way inside.

"Are you okay?" He pulled back and inspected her like she was just returning from war.

"Yeah, I'm just exhausted. It's been a crazy day. But I really am okay."

"What in the world happened?" he asked, touching her face. He looked genuinely relieved and she had never been so happy to see her husband.

"Baby, it's been a nightmare. I don't know how I got caught up in the middle of all of this, but I'm just happy to be out of that godforsaken place." She glanced back at Jasmine, who was standing behind Lester.

"Hey, you all right?" Jasmine asked.

Rachel nodded appreciatively. "Thanks to you."

Then Jasmine shocked Rachel when she reached around to hug her. Even Lester looked surprised by the exchange, although a small smile crept up on his face.

Buddy cleared his throat. Rachel had forgotten he was standing behind her.

"Well, I hate to break up this reunion," he began, "but I need to go check up on some things. Something about this whole thing isn't sitting right, and Buddy Clemons won't rest until he gets to the bottom of it."

"Thank you, Mr. Clemons. So much," Lester said. "Can I take my wife back to Houston now?"

"Well, that wouldn't be a good idea. At least not until we work all of this out and figure out what's going on."

"Are they charging her with anything? The news said she was picked up for questioning."

"We should know that in the morning. I'll meet with the D.A. first thing and we'll try to get some answers for you, but it wouldn't look good if she got on a plane going home."

"Okay," Lester said as he reached into his pocket and removed his checkbook. "What's your retainer? We want to make sure you're taken care of."

Buddy held his hand up to stop Lester. "Don't you worry about a thing. Any friend of Mae Frances's is a friend of mine."

Wow, Rachel thought. Mae Frances really was the business.

Lester smiled in appreciation, then dropped his checkbook back in his pocket. "Well, thank you. Let me walk you downstairs, because I have a few questions."

Rachel was sure her husband wanted to hear from Buddy exactly what had gone down. As much as Lester loved her, Rachel knew he didn't completely trust that she would tell him everything.

Rachel couldn't even think about that right now. She just wanted to get in that Jacuzzi tub, take a bath, find something in the minibar to help her calm her nerves, and rest for the rest of the night.

"So you're really okay?" Jasmine asked once the two men had left the room.

Rachel released a long sigh. "I am. Thank

you for having Buster come over."

"Who is Buster?"

"The wino. He said his name was Buster Brown."

Jasmine chuckled. "I told him to use a fake name. I guess that's the best he could come up with. I should've known." She paused a minute, then said, "Sorry I didn't come over myself but . . ."

Rachel held up her hand to cut her off. "No need to apologize or explain because I would've done the same thing."

They exchanged smiles, then Jasmine added, "So, you really can't leave town?"

Rachel plopped down on the plush sofa in the suite. It felt so good to sink into something soft, rather than perching on that uncomfortable chair she'd just spent the last five hours sitting in.

"Buddy said that I shouldn't. And honestly, I thought about doing it anyway. But these thugs are no joke. Even if I leave, the last thing I need is them showing up on my doorstep, messing with my family. I'm still trying to figure out why they're even after me."

Jasmine slid onto the sofa. Rachel could tell her mind was whirling.

"But why would she try to set me up?"

"Cecelia doesn't like losing and she lost

big-time. I can see her not resting until she redeemed herself."

"Well, we've got to figure this out. I just wish I had some idea of how we can figure out who the real girlfriend is. Did you find out anything inside the church?"

"Nothing except the fact that Cecelia is all up in this."

"It just seems that by now, a girlfriend would've come out of the woodwork or something. You would think there would be a girlfriend somewhere crying, something."

"I don't know," Jasmine said. "Maybe there isn't even a girlfriend."

The whole thing was making Rachel's head hurt. She wished she could turn back the hands of time. She would've let Jasmine have her moment on *Oprah* and they wouldn't be smack dab in the middle of an episode of *CSI*. "I feel like there's something I'm missing," Rachel said.

"We have been over this backward and forward and it's been a long day," Jasmine replied. She patted Rachel's knee. "You should rest. I have to go pick up Mae Frances from the airport, anyway."

Rachel smiled at the mention of Mae Frances's name. "I guess I can't give her a hard time anymore."

Jasmine stood. "I guess you can't. As you

see from Buddy Clemons, she's no joke."

"Yeah, I gotta give the old lady credit." Rachel sat straight up in her seat, snapping her fingers. "Old lady! That's it!"

Jasmine's eyes issued a stern warning. "I would advise you not to call her an old lady when she gets here."

Rachel waved her off. "No, no. I'm not talking about Mae Frances." She jumped up and became animated. "Remember when we went to Pastor Griffith's apartment and I helped that old lady put her stuff back in her purse?"

Jasmine nodded. "Yeah, what about her?"

"She said someone had run past her and knocked her over. Maybe it was the real killer. Maybe she can help identify that person."

Jasmine looked unsure before saying, "Or maybe she can pinpoint you even more by confirming that you were at the apartment when he died."

"Dangit," Rachel said. She paced back and forth for a moment. Something told her this old lady was key. "Okay, well then. You go talk to her."

"Rachel . . ."

"No, take Cecelia's picture. She said she's in the building all the time because she was sewing something for Pastor Griffith's neighbor. Ask her if she's ever seen her. Ask her what she remembers from that day."

Jasmine thought about it for a minute, then finally said, "I guess it's worth a shot. What's her name and how are we going to find her?"

"I don't remember her name. But I have her card." Rachel raced into her bedroom and tore through her bag. She searched for the teal jacket she had on that day. She found it tucked at the bottom of her suitcase and immediately, her hands began fumbling in the pockets. Rachel's heart flittered with relief when she felt the card. Thank God she hadn't thrown it away like she initially had intended.

"Okay, it says she works at some seam-stress shop on 103rd. Maybe you can go by tomorrow. If she can describe the person who bumped into her, then she can take that to the police."

Jasmine looked unsure. "I still don't know what good that'll do because she can also confirm that you were there."

"Okay, maybe it's not about clearing my name anymore," Rachel said, exasperated. "But I know the only way I'm going to get these thugs off my back is by either finding the real girlfriend and turning them on to her, or finding out who really killed Pastor

Griffith."

"Okay, in the morning, I guess we get back at it."

"I'll just have to find a way to let my husband let me keep at it because if I know Lester, he's going to want to keep me locked up in this room until the police say it's safe to go back home."

On cue, Lester walked back into the suite. He looked frazzled. "This is not good," he said, clutching his cell phone in his hand as he paced the floor.

"What is it, baby?" Rachel immediately wondered if Buddy had told him something bad about her case.

"Rev. King has called an emergency meeting of the board!" Lester announced, his eyes wide.

"Andre King, Cecelia's husband?" Jasmine asked.

"Yes." Lester ran his hands over his curly mound of hair, a nervous habit of his when he was stressed. "And in the morning, of all things! How can they just do that? I told them I couldn't make it and they still plan to move forward."

"Why are they saying they need an emergency meeting?"

He looked like he was about to lose it. "Rev. King has convinced the board that we need an emergency vote. We are up for a huge grant from the Family First Foundation, and he says the ABC can't endure the scandal of you being accused of murder."

"But I didn't do anything," Rachel protested. Andre King may have been leading the charge for an emergency meeting, but this had Cecelia King written all over it.

"Of course I know that, and I don't see how they can try to convict you without even hearing your side," Lester said. He took her hands. "Baby, I am so sorry, I have to go home. I can't let them get there tomorrow and crucify you."

Rachel hugged her husband. "Don't worry about me. You've worked too hard to let them take this away from you. Buddy said I can't leave, but you go back and fight for your title. I'll be damned if the Kings are just going to steal this presidency from you. I'm not guilty and we're not going to let them run us out. I don't care what the Kings say."

He seemed relieved to have her support. "Where is Hosea?" he asked, turning to Jasmine. "I want to ask his opinion."

Jasmine glanced at her watch. "He's probably at the airport about to board a plane here. But you can try his cell. Maybe he hasn't gotten on yet."

"Okay." Lester leaned in and kissed Rachel on the cheek before disappearing into the bedroom.

Rachel turned to Jasmine, her lips pursed. "So I guess we now know why Cecelia would want to set me up. She's probably behind this whole thing. It wouldn't surprise me if she killed Rev. Griffith herself."

"It's amazing that she would do all of that just to get a position."

"It's like you said, she doesn't like to lose." Rachel was no longer scared. Now she was downright angry. She didn't have all the answers, but she was determined to find them out. "We're going to find out how she's tied to Rev. Griffith's murder," Rachel continued, "and I want to be right there when the police slap handcuffs on her and haul her away. Whatever it takes to get to the bottom of this, I'm game."

Jasmine cracked a conspiratorial smile. "Ooooh, I like this side of you. And trust, I know you can get down and dirty."

"That's right," Rachel replied. "And if Cecelia King thinks she's big and bad, we're about to show her we're bigger and badder."

Jasmine smiled and for Rachel, all doubts were erased. They wouldn't rest until they cracked this case and when all was said and done, she and Jasmine would be bonded for life.

CHAPTER TWENTY-SIX

Jasmine didn't know what to make of this. The deal was that Mae Frances would call from the airport when she landed and since their hotel was just about fifteen minutes away, that was when Jasmine would leave to pick her up.

Mae Frances had called, but she told Jasmine to stay right in place.

"I'll get there, Jasmine Larson. Just wait at the hotel for me. Don't go anywhere. Don't go getting into any more trouble."

She'd hung up before Jasmine could protest, but Jasmine couldn't figure it out. It wasn't like Mae Frances to cab it. When Jasmine had met her all those years ago, Mae Frances had been riding around in her own limousine — at least that's what Jasmine had thought.

So she couldn't help but wonder what Mae Frances was up to now. Maybe she was meeting one of her many Chicago connections. Maybe she was bringing someone who could really help them get out of this situation.

"Yeah, that's it," Jasmine whispered.

"What did you say?"

Jasmine glanced over her shoulder and was glad to see that Rachel had finally relaxed. Her feet were curled beneath her as she was tucked in the far side of the sofa, flipping through a magazine.

"Are you talking to yourself?" Rachel asked without even looking up. "I heard" — and now she glanced at Jasmine — "that's the first sign of dementia. You know, the kind that comes with old age."

"Ha ha," Jasmine said, though there was no humor in her tone.

Rachel tossed the magazine onto the sofa table. "What's got you all worked up?"

Jasmine's eyebrows were arched high when she turned back to Rachel. "In case you haven't heard, my friend was almost arrested today, and she's being chased by thugs who want her to pay ten million dollars even though she hardly has a dime."

Rachel grinned. "Your friend, huh?"

Jasmine shrugged. "Well, she's not really a friend. But she's a good kid."

Rachel stood up and, with her hands on her hips, said, "I am so far away from being

345

a kid." Her neck twisted in her usual ghetto-fabulous way. "Just look at all of this."

Jasmine couldn't help but smile as she shook her head. "Good to see that you really are feeling better."

Rachel shrugged. "What else can I do? I mean, I could be pacing the floor with you, or back in my room crying and wondering what's going to happen to me and what's going to happen to Lester. But I've learned that worrying ain't gonna add a single hour to my life. At least, that's what it says in Matthew."

Jasmine grinned. "You? Quoting scripture?"

"How would you know? You wouldn't recognize a scripture if you heard one."

The knock stopped their banter and Jasmine rushed to the door, sure that it was her friend.

"Mae Frances," she called out before she even opened the door. But then she stood frozen, gaping.

"Well, this is a first," Hosea said. "My wife, speechless."

"Hosea!" She jumped into his arms. "What are you doing here?"

"I told you I was coming."

"But I thought you were on the last flight," Jasmine said with her arms still gripping Hosea's neck.

"Somebody didn't get to the airport on time," Mae Frances mumbled as she rolled her suitcase in behind him. "You know it was probably some black folks, thinking that United had a special CP schedule just for them. So there were two extra seats and Preacher Man got one of them."

"Mae Frances!" Playfully, Jasmine shoved her husband aside so that she could hug her best friend. She couldn't remember a time when she was happier to see two people.

"Rachel!"

It wasn't until Hosea shouted out her name that Jasmine remembered that Rachel was in her room.

"Hey, Hosea," she said, still standing off to the side as if she wasn't sure how she'd be received.

Hosea let his garment bag slip off his arm. "How are you?" he asked, giving her a hug. "I thought you were with the police."

"No." She shook her head. "They let me go." She faced Mae Frances. "The attorney that you sent over, he got me out."

Mae Frances stood there, wrapped in her mink coat, with her arms folded as if she was waiting for more, and finally Rachel added, "Thank you."

Mae Frances nodded her head slightly,

but she didn't break her stare. Rachel stood her ground, too. Looking Mae Frances up and down, up and down.

Jasmine sighed. She could feel it already. She was going to be in the middle of these two and the middle was not a good place to be.

But maybe this situation would have them on their best behavior. After all, that's what happened with her and Rachel. Being hunted down by thugs made them fast friends.

"Where's Lester?" Hosea asked.

"He was here, but had to get right back on a plane to Houston," Rachel said, and then she explained the call that Lester had received.

"What? They're gonna try to force him out over these bogus charges?"

"And I wasn't even charged with any-thing," Rachel said.

"Let me get Lester on the phone," Hosea said.

"He probably hasn't landed yet, but you can talk to my dad," Rachel said, jotting down the number on the pad on the desk. "He's at my house and probably knows a lot more about this."

Shaking his head, Hosea said, "I'll call from the bedroom."

When they were alone, Jasmine said, "Mae Frances, so much has been going on."

"I know; I told you I heard about how you two have been playing around and making a mess of things."

"A mess?" Rachel snapped. "We haven't been playing at anything. We've been working hard, trying to figure this whole thing out."

"Well, whatever you've been doing, it's *still* a mess."

"And you think you could've done any better?" Rachel rolled her eyes.

It was the way Mae Frances took slow steps toward Rachel that made Jasmine hold her breath. Mae Frances may have been older, though she'd never told Jasmine her age. She could've been fifty, sixty, or seventy. But whatever she was, she wasn't one to be played with and Jasmine was afraid Rachel was about to find that out.

"Let me tell you something, little girl. I could've done a *whole* lot better. If I'd been here, this whole thing would've been worked out already and your skeezer behind wouldn't have ever been arrested —"

"Skeezer?"

"And you wouldn't have needed the best attorney in Chicago that I got for you."

"Who you calling a skeezer?"

"So, you better remember," Mae Frances continued as if Rachel wasn't shouting, "who you're talking to."

"All I know is that I'm nobody's skeezer." Rachel's neck was twisting again. "And anyway, I'd rather be a skeezer than to have been at the parting of the Red Sea. What school did you and Moses go to, again?"

Mae Frances's eyes narrowed, so much that Jasmine wasn't sure if her friend could see anything. "Are you calling me old? Is that what you're trying to say?"

"Both of y'all need to quit," Jasmine hissed. "Come on, we're on the same side, remember? We're supposed to be working together."

They stared each other down as if they were having a standoff at the O.K. Corral. But at least she'd quieted the two down. She just had to figure out how to get them to stay that way.

It was Hosea who broke their silence when he came out of the bedroom. "I spoke to your father, Rachel. Just like you said, Reverend and Cecelia King are behind this. They're calling for Lester to step down and they want the board to vote tomorrow morning, though that's not gonna happen."

"It's not?" Rachel asked.

Hosea shook his head. "They haven't

given all the board members enough time to get to Houston. There probably won't be a quorum for them to take a vote for something this big."

"Thank God!" Rachel said, before she plopped onto the couch.

"Yeah, but I still don't like it," Hosea said. "I have no idea what tricks Reverend King and his wife have up their sleeves. It's clear they're planning to take over the Coalition and that's not gonna happen if I have anything to say about it."

It was amazing — the way this might all turn out after all. Hosea might actually end up being the president of the American Baptist Coalition. But now, Jasmine wasn't so sure that's what she wanted. Not after all of this.

Hosea said, "I think I'm gonna head down to Houston."

"Really?" Jasmine said, not trying to hide her disappointment. "But you just got here."

"I know, and if I didn't think that you were in good hands, I'd stay to make sure you and Rachel stayed out of trouble. But with Mae Frances here, I know you'll be fine."

Mae Frances gave Hosea that sweet smile that he was used to. That smile that completely had him fooled. That smile that made him believe she was just a little ole grandmother who only did good things.

Jasmine shook her head. If her husband only knew; she got into far more trouble with Mae Frances than without her.

"I'll catch the first flight in the morning. That should put me there before the meeting at noon." When Jasmine pouted, Hosea put his arms around her waist. "Don't worry, baby, we still have tonight."

When his lips brushed against her cheek, Jasmine shivered. "Uh, Rachel, don't you want to go back to your room and . . . call your kids . . . or something?"

With a grin, Rachel nodded.

"And, Mae Frances," Jasmine said, talking faster now, "you're already checked in. Buddy took care of your room when he brought us back the rental car."

"That's good. But I think I'm gonna sit here for a little while. Rest a spell."

Rachel grabbed Mae Frances's roller bag. "I'll help you get down to your room," Rachel said and then she gave her a smile that was meant to be sweet, but showed nothing but her disdain.

"Naw, that's okay," Mae Frances said, crossing her legs as she leaned back on the sofa. "I'm good."

"Mae Frances!" Jasmine and Rachel said

at the same time.

The woman looked from Jasmine to Rachel, then her eyes settled on Hosea. "Oh! Oh, yeah!" she said as she pushed herself up. She snatched her suitcase from Rachel's grasp.

Rachel said, "I told you, I got this."

"What? You sayin' that I'm old again? I can carry my own bags."

"Ladies," Hosea said, jumping in between them. "I'll take the bag and escort both of you to your rooms."

Mae Frances and Rachel stared at each other once again before they followed Hosea to the door. It was clear Jasmine and Rachel had made up, but it was just as clear that Mae Frances and Rachel were in a totally different place.

But right now, Jasmine didn't care about either one of them. All she wanted to think about was her husband and the hours they had between now and the rising sun.

As Rachel and Mae Frances stepped into the hallway, Hosea turned around and winked at his wife. "I'll be right back," he whispered.

Jasmine grinned. Oh, yeah! This was exactly what she needed. In the middle of this mess of a murder, she was about to get hers.

The moment the door closed behind them, Jasmine began stripping. There was no need to wait for Hosea to return. By the time he got back, she'd be good and naked and good and ready.

She couldn't wait!

CHAPTER TWENTY-SEVEN

Barely fifteen minutes had passed since Hosea had left for the airport before the pounding on her door began. Jasmine zipped up her jeans before she dashed to the door.

"Are you finally up, Jasmine Larson?" Mae Frances barked as she marched into the room.

"I've been up all night."

Mae Frances rolled her eyes. "Well, now that Preacher Man's gone, you need to get your mind out of all of that sex and focus on the work we have to do."

"Okay, let me call Rachel and we'll tell you our plan."

"Why we gotta work with her?" Mae Frances snarled. "I can only work with people I trust."

"First of all, Mae Frances, you can trust Rachel. I told you, we're . . . friends . . . now. And anyway, we wouldn't be doing any of this if we weren't trying to help Rachel, so she needs to be involved."

"I can move faster without a snake slithering behind me."

Jasmine sighed. "I'm gonna need you to shut all that negativity down," she said.

"Whatever!"

Less than five minutes later, Rachel sauntered into Jasmine's room, once again wearing her all-black ghetto ninja outfit, like she was once again on a spy mission.

This time, Jasmine didn't laugh. But Mae Frances did. "Who do you think you are?" Mae Frances snarled. "Catwoman?"

"Look, old lady —"

"I got your old —"

"Can you two stop it?" Jasmine shouted, wondering if this is how she and Rachel used to sound. She hoped not. They were no better than her seven-year-old daughter and her friends. "We have work to do."

They may have been silent, but that didn't stop their death stares. That would have to do for right now.

"Anyway," Jasmine said, taking the lead, "Rachel and I have a theory." She paused and waited for Mae Frances to take her eyes from Rachel. When she turned to her, Jasmine continued, "We think Cecelia King killed Pastor Griffith."

"What? Why would she kill him?"

"Well, you heard what Hosea said. Reverend King and Cecelia are trying to take over the Coalition."

"And so you think they murdered a man to do that?"

Jasmine and Rachel nodded together.

Jasmine said, "I think she killed him and then set up Rachel to take the fall."

Mae Frances chuckled and shook her head. "That doesn't make any sense, Jasmine Larson. She wouldn't have to kill anybody to do that. Remember, you were just going to —"

Jasmine shook her head wildly and Mae Frances clamped her mouth shut.

Rachel frowned. "You were going to do what?"

"Nothing," Jasmine said as Mae Frances smirked. Jasmine wanted to choke her friend. Mae Frances was too smart to let something like that just slip out. She'd done it on purpose and once they finished figuring all of this out, Jasmine was going to kill her.

"Nah, I wanna know. What was you gonna say?"

"I was just gonna remind Jasmine that when she was trying to get Hosea elected we didn't kill anyone." She paused and glared at Rachel. "Although we did think about killing you."

"Mae Frances!"

"What? We never killed her. We just set it up so that her husband would win."

"Mae Frances!" Jasmine exclaimed again. She was really going to kill her now.

"What are you talking about? Lester *won* that election. You didn't have anything to do with it."

"Exactly!" Jasmine said as she stared Mae Frances down and with a glare dared her to say anything else.

Rachel turned her scowl to Jasmine and Jasmine wondered if things would ever be the same between the two of them.

Five minutes. Mae Frances had been in Chicago for all of five minutes and already she was tearing down what the two had built together.

"Can we just get back to business?" Jasmine asked, hoping this would make Rachel forget what Mae Frances had said. "Anyway, Mae Frances, you may not believe that Cecelia killed him, but let me ask you a couple of questions. Why did Cecelia just happen to have meetings while we were here?"

"I don't know, but what —"

Jasmine interrupted, "And why is she everywhere? Cecelia seems to know things before they happen. Is she the one that turned the police on to Rachel? How did they know Rachel was at the church?"

"Well let me ask you something. If she murdered Earl just so she could frame Rachel, how did she even know Rachel was going to be in Chicago?" Mae Frances turned back to Rachel. "You weren't invited to Oprah's show, right? You just showed up. Uninvited."

Rachel frowned and paused. As if she wanted a moment to think through this thing that sounded like a trick question. "I *should've* been invited."

"So, I repeat, how did Cecelia know that Rachel was going to be here? And," Mae Frances held up her finger, "how did she know that you were going to come back?"

Jasmine paused and thought about her friend's questions. Okay, so Mae Frances had some good points and maybe her and Rachel's theory didn't make sense. But none of this did.

"You know what?" Rachel said, her mind replaying the call from Yvette once she'd made it back to Houston. "When Yvette called me in Houston, she told me about the surveillance video."

"Because she knew you'd come running back to Chicago," Jasmine said, finishing her thought.

"And she's the one who insisted I drink that bottle of water when we went back to Pastor Griffith's. She was trying to make sure my fingerprints would tie me to being there!"

"But what does that have to do with Cecelia?" Mae Frances asked.

Jasmine shook her head. "I don't have all the answers, but we may have someone that can give us the proof we need."

"Who?"

"A really old woman, about your age," Rachel said and without missing a beat, she added, "I saw her right before I went into Pastor Griffith's apartment. She was kneeling on the floor because someone had just about knocked her down as they ran down the hall."

"And you think it was Cecelia?" Mae Frances asked.

"We do," Jasmine and Rachel said at the same time.

Jasmine added, "So, we're gonna go talk to this woman, take this picture of Cecelia," Jasmine pointed to the photograph she'd pulled up on her iPad, "and once she identifies her, we're gonna tell Buddy everything that we know."

Mae Frances sighed. "You two are such

amateurs. We need to just wait to see what my connections come up with."

"I don't want to sit around and wait for anything. The longer I'm here, the longer I'm away from my kids," Rachel said as if she was the only one missing her children. "If she can identify her, I know I'll be cleared."

"Whatever," Mae Frances said, standing once again and slipping into her coat. "If this is how you two want to play it, let's go."

Rachel glanced at Jasmine and then rolled her eyes. As the two marched behind Mae Frances, Jasmine whispered to her, "Remember, she hired Buddy for you and he's good, right?"

With a sigh, Rachel nodded.

Jasmine added, "So be nice."

Another sigh, another nod. "I'll try," Rachel hissed, not sounding like she was going to try anything.

As they stood at the elevator, Rachel smiled at Mae Frances. "I really love your coat."

Jasmine groaned, not knowing what was coming, but knowing whatever it was, it wasn't going to be good.

With just the very tips of her fingers, she stroked Mae Frances's mink. She didn't get too close, though, as if she was afraid something might be growing inside those old hairs. Rachel said, "So what do you feed this thing? Cat food?" Then she laughed as she strolled onto the elevator.

Mae Frances actually growled under her breath, while Jasmine shook her head. It was gonna be a long afternoon.

This had almost been too easy — finding Windy City Custom Tailors, the shop on 103rd where Martha Miller worked.

"So what do you geniuses plan to do?" Mae Frances asked. "Just barge in there?"

"She gave me her card," Rachel began, "so that I'd come by if I ever needed anything. Well, now, I need something."

As they edged the car to the curb, Rachel glanced at the buildings. This had to be some kind of manufacturing section of town, with its nondescript gray buildings and not a sign of nature in sight. No grass, no trees. Just brick and mortar.

Jasmine jumped from the car, then Mae Frances slipped out from the back. But Rachel stayed inside, her eyes still studying her surroundings.

"What's wrong?"

Rachel shook her head. "I don't know. It doesn't seem to be safe."

"What?" Mae Frances grunted. "You think the police are gonna come 'round here looking for you? Oh, please. And even if they do, Buddy Clemons will get you out of it. So just get your silly behind out of that car."

"I'm not thinking about the police . . . at least not right now. But those other guys. Maybe I should stay out here and be the lookout."

"If you're thinking about those thugs, I'm not gonna leave you out here by yourself," Jasmine said.

"But someone should stay," Rachel insisted. "Just in case we have to make a fast getaway."

Mae Frances laughed, but Jasmine didn't. She and Rachel had been through so much, she knew Rachel had a point. Which was why she wasn't about to leave Rachel alone.

She turned to Mae Frances. If those thugs stepped to her, Jasmine knew the thugs would be the ones who'd end up sorry. "You can stay out here while Rachel and I go inside."

"Fine!" Mae Frances said, and Jasmine was glad that her friend didn't mention that there would be no quick getaway if they needed it since Mae Frances didn't know how to drive.

A bell tinkled as Jasmine and Rachel stepped inside the shop, and the four women who all sat behind sewing machines glanced up. It was the woman at the first machine who stood.

"May I help you?"

"Yes, I'd like to talk to Ms. Martha," Rachel said, pointing to the woman she recognized right away. It wasn't hard to pick her out. She was the oldest one in the shop by at least three decades.

The old woman frowned as she heard her name. Even from where they stood Jasmine could see Ms. Martha squinting, and the way she looked didn't give Jasmine a lot of hope. But according to Rachel, Ms. Martha had seen the person who was barreling down the hall up close and personal. She just prayed the woman had been wearing her glasses that day.

"Ms. Martha, remember me?" Rachel asked the moment the woman was right on top of them.

The lady squinted and leaned forward, though she couldn't get much closer. "Ahhh . . ."

"Remember we met when I helped you get your things off the floor because someone almost knocked you down in the hallway when you were leaving a customer's apartment?"

"Oh, yeah! How you doing, baby?" She grinned. "You got something you want me to make for you?"

"No, not yet. I wanted to ask you something about that day we met."

"Chile, I'll never forget it. I thought that fool had broken my hip."

"Well, Ms. Martha, this is my friend Jasmine, and we want to show you something."

Already, Jasmine was pulling her iPad from her purse. "Ms. Martha, do you recognize this woman? Is this who knocked you over?"

"Well, it can't be her," she said, before taking the tablet.

"You haven't even seen the picture," Rachel said.

"But I know it wasn't her, because it was a him that knocked me over."

Rachel and Jasmine exchanged defeated glances. They'd been so sure it was a woman.

"Well, you said you are in that building a lot. Have you ever seen this woman? Did you see her that day?"

The woman took the tablet from Jasmine and squinted even more as she brought the screen close to her face. After a moment, she said, "No, I can't say that I know that woman."

Jasmine and Rachel both sighed. "Are you sure?" Rachel asked.

Finally, Ms. Martha lowered the picture. "No, I ain't never seen her before. Who is she?"

"I was thinking that she was the lady who bumped into you that day. I thought maybe she was friends with Pastor Griffith."

Ms. Martha shook her head. "No, like I said, it was a man that knocked me over." She paused like she was thinking. "But you talking about that handsome preacher that lived in four-oh-four?"

"Yes!" Rachel said excitedly.

"Oh, I saw a woman there that morning when I first got to Lucy's — that's the lady that I sew for." She glanced at the picture again. "But this definitely isn't her."

"Well, can you tell us what she looked like?" Jasmine asked.

Ms. Martha was quiet for a moment. She leaned her head back a little as if she were thinking. "Well, she wasn't too tall, wasn't too short, brown skinned . . ." She paused. "In fact, she looked . . ." She moved closer. "A little . . ." Now she was right on top of them. "Like you," she said, pointing to Rachel. "I didn't think about it 'til right now, but she looked like you."

Rachel sighed. "That's all I need. Some-one else identifying me."

"I'm sorry if I didn't help."

"No, you helped tremendously. Thank you," Jasmine said before she dragged Ra-chel out of the shop.

"Now what are we gonna do?" Rachel asked, sounding like she was about to cry.

"Don't worry, Rachel. We're gonna figure this out. I know you don't like her, but Mae Frances will fix this. Mae Frances knows how to fix everything!"

Jasmine didn't say another word when she heard Rachel's deep sigh.

CHAPTER TWENTY-EIGHT

"Are you sure you didn't off Earl?" Mae Frances asked once they were in the rental car heading back to the hotel.

If Rachel wasn't so disheartened by Ms. Martha's declaration, she might have given Mae Frances a piece of her mind.

"Miss Daisy, can you just sit back there and let us drive you, please?" Rachel did manage to say.

"I'm just saying, since we all BFFs now, you can come clean."

Her steady tone didn't reveal whether she was being serious or sarcastic. Either way, Rachel didn't have the energy to try to deal with her. Thankfully, Jasmine stepped in.

"Come on, Mae Frances. This is trying for us all," she said as she pulled onto the freeway. They'd filled Mae Frances in on everything Ms. Martha had said and as expected, she'd reminded them that she had warned the visit would be useless.

"Us? There is no *us.* Y'all maybe, but no *us."*

Jasmine glanced up at her friend in the rearview mirror. Rachel turned and stared out the passenger window. Every road she turned down in trying to solve this disaster was a dead end, and Rachel was starting to lose hope.

"Well, I was with Rachel and I can vouch that she didn't do it," Jasmine said.

"Umph, so you're vouching for her now?"

"I sure am," Jasmine replied with confidence. That brought a small smile to Rachel's face, but it quickly dissipated when Mae Frances added, "Well, that lady we just left could only identify Rachel. One witness. That's all you need to get executed these days. Just ask Troy Davis."

Rachel suddenly sat up in her seat. "Wait, Ms. Martha said the woman looked like me."

"Exactly," Mae Frances said.

Rachel turned around in her seat. "Right. Looked *like* me. Not *was* me."

Jasmine smiled. "Of course. So that could mean Pastor Griffith's girlfriend resembles you."

"So, Earl's girl looks like a hoodrat?" Mae Frances said.

"Mae Frances!" Jasmine admonished.

Rachel waved her off. She was on to something and she wasn't about to let that old biddy get her off track.

"So that's a clue. Now we at least have a description of who we're looking for. That's probably why the thugs think I'm Pastor Griffith's girlfriend — because we look alike."

Mae Frances released an irritated sigh. "Okay, Columbo, slow down. Maybe, the man that bumped into that old lady was some person that had nothing to do with Earl. Or maybe the real killer went out the side door, or hired someone, or any number of other things," she snapped. "So what, Pastor Griffith's girlfriend was there earlier in the day? You were the last person Earl was with."

"His killer was the last person!" Rachel shouted.

"Little girl, don't raise your voice at me," Mae Frances warned.

"Sorry," Rachel muttered halfheartedly. "I'm just so frustrated with all of this."

Mae Frances groaned as she pulled out her cell phone. "Let me call Gil and see if he knows anything."

"Who is Gil?" Jasmine asked.

"Gil Kerlikowske, the U.S. Drug Czar."

"Drugs? You think this has something to

do with drugs?" Rachel asked, panicked, not even bothering to ask how Mae Frances even had the drug czar's phone number in her contacts list.

Mae Frances flashed a strange look at Jasmine, who suddenly seemed intently focused on the road.

"Hello!" Rachel said, waving her hand. "Does someone want to tell me what's going on? Drugs?" She turned back to Mae Frances. "You think Pastor Griffith is involved in drugs?"

Mae Frances continued to glare at Jasmine before finally turning to Rachel. "You said those thugs wanted ten million dollars. That kind of money can only be drug-related."

"Oh," Rachel said, slumping back in her seat.

She waited while Mae Frances pulled up a number on her phone. She paused before saying, "Hey, Gil, it's me . . . I'm fine . . . how's the job? Tell Barack and Michelle I said hi and I promise I won't come to DC again without calling . . . Uh-huh . . . Well, look, I'm trying to find out some info on a missing pastor in Chicago. It's big-time. Wondering if you know about any drug connections . . . ." Rachel stared on in fascination as she continued her call. "Oh, okay . . .

yeah, I sure would appreciate it . . . Okay, I'll wait to hear from you. By the way, tell Anna and the kids hello."

Rachel and Jasmine stared at her, stunned.

Mae Frances dropped her phone back into her purse. "Now, we wait. Hopefully, he'll find out something for us." She leaned back in the seat, closed her eyes, and rested, like her work was done.

Rachel turned back around in her seat, amazed at the seemingly insurmountable powers of Mae Frances. They rode in silence for another fifteen minutes. Rachel replayed all aspects of the case in her head, trying to come up with something new. Her thoughts then shifted to Lester. He should be wrapping up the emergency board meeting by now. She hoped that the board didn't do some underhanded stuff and vote him out. She knew that according to the bylaws, if there were any moral infractions, they could vote him out. But she'd have to ask Buddy if they had any legal recourse in case the vote didn't go in their favor, especially since the infractions involved her and not Lester.

Rachel's thoughts were interrupted by her ringing cell phone. She pressed the Talk button. "Hello."

"Rachel, it's Buddy. Where are you?"

"We're all heading back to the hotel," she replied.

"How long before you get there?"

His no-nonsense tone was making her nervous. "I guess another ten minutes. Why?"

"I'll tell you when I see you. I'm on my way there." He hung up the phone before she could say anything else.

"Who was that?" Jasmine asked.

"Buddy," Rachel said. "He's meeting us at the hotel. It sounds serious."

Jasmine gently reached over and gave her hand a squeeze. "It's gonna be okay. Everything is going to work out," she said.

"Oh, Lord, guess we're gonna start singing 'Kumbaya' next," Mae Frances said, her eyes still closed.

Rachel smiled as she leaned back and closed her eyes, too. She said a silent prayer that Buddy had some good news and was about to tell her the whole thing had been a big misunderstanding. She didn't allow herself to get wrapped up in that delusion, however. Somebody was going to have to pay for Pastor Griffith's death and right now, all evidence was pointing toward her.

Ten minutes later, they were walking back into the lobby of the Omni.

"If it isn't the most beautiful woman in

the world." Buddy stood, greeting them as they walked into the lobby.

"Well, thank you," both Jasmine and Rachel said in unison.

Mae Frances pushed them both aside. "Now, y'all know he's not talking about you." She stopped and smiled widely. "Well, if it isn't my little buddy."

He grinned like a kid on Christmas morning as he swooped Mae Frances up and spun her around.

She swatted his arm. "Boy, if you don't put me down! You know I can't do all that."

Buddy set her down, but kept his wide smile. "Whatever! You forget, I know that you taught Alvin Ailey everything he knows. Now you want to act like a little spinning around is too much."

Both Rachel and Jasmine dropped their mouths in shock. "Alvin Ailey?"

Mae Frances grinned but didn't respond.

Buddy nodded proudly. "Yeah, she taught the man everything he knows. And one of his most successful performances is dedicated to her," he said.

"Is there anything you don't do?" Rachel asked.

Mae Frances ignored them. "Hush your mouth, boy. How's your godfather?"

"Mad because he's going to miss you."

"Tell him I see him every night. He's looking good putting those folks in their place on MSNBC." She patted his cheek. "But we aren't here to reminisce. What's going on?"

His tone turned serious, but he kept his smile. "Let's go over here and sit down," he said, pointing to a small sitting area in the corner of the lobby.

They followed him and, once they were all seated at the table, waited for him to say the first word.

He stuck his chest out, like a proud peacock. "As you may or may not know, I'm the best in the business," he began. "When Buddy Clemons is on the case, you'd best believe, results are guaranteed." He sounded like one of those late-night commercials, but his confidence set Rachel's heart to racing. She just wished he would get to the point.

"What's going on?" Rachel asked.

"You're free and clear," he announced.

"What?" all three of them said together.

"Case dismissed," he said, still smiling.

"So, there won't be any charges?" Rachel asked, not wanting to believe her ears.

"Nope. At least not for now."

"What happened?" Jasmine asked. Even though she'd been proclaiming that everything would work out, the look on her face now said she hadn't really believed that it would.

"No body. No crime," Buddy said.

"What do you mean, no body?" Rachel asked.

Buddy pulled out a sheet of paper and handed it to Rachel. "It seems like the body they fished out of Lake Michigan was *not* Pastor Griffith."

Rachel and Jasmine simultaneously gasped. Mae Frances looked shocked herself.

"But the news said he had ID on him and everything," Rachel said. "It was his car, his belongings."

"Oh, someone wanted everyone to believe it was Pastor Griffith, but the Cook County folks aren't as dumb as they look. They're not just gonna say someone died without an autopsy. They're usually pretty slow about it, but I put the pressure on them and they expedited things." He pointed to the piece of paper. "The autopsy shows it's a John Doe from the morgue. The bottom line is, if it's not Pastor Griffith, they can't charge you with killing him. At least not without some concrete evidence that the man is even dead."

Tears of joy threatened to overtake her

and she leapt from her seat and threw her arms around Buddy's neck. "Thank you so much!"

He returned her hug, then stood. "Well, I just came by to let you know the good news. I gotta get going. Got to meet another client."

Rachel wiped her tears. She had never felt so relieved of anything in her life. "I am eternally grateful to you."

"My pleasure. Now, I don't know if it's over for good. But for now, you can go home and rest easy."

He said his goodbyes, promising to be in touch as soon as he had any more news. As soon as they were back in the suite, Rachel announced, "Thank God, this nightmare is over. I'm going to pack!"

"No, it's not over," Mae Frances announced, stopping her just as she reached her door.

Rachel turned to face her. "Excuse me?"

"This is far from over," Mae Frances said, as she began removing her coat.

Rachel looked confused until Jasmine interjected, "I agree, because if that wasn't Pastor Griffith in the river, where is he? And now that there's no body, it's just a matter of time before those thugs find out, and they'll be more sure than ever that he's not dead and that *you* know where he is."

Rachel fell down on the sofa. This nightmare wasn't over? She wanted to break down in tears, but at this point, she didn't think she had any tears left.

CHAPTER TWENTY-NINE

Jasmine took a long sip of the steaming coffee that had been delivered by room service. Sipping the coffee gave her time to think this through, to figure out how she was going to handle this situation.

Rachel stood in front of her with her arms crossed and her lips set in a determined line. When Jasmine remained silent, Rachel repeated what she'd been saying ever since she'd marched into Jasmine's room fifteen minutes before.

"I'm serious," Rachel said. "I don't care what Mae Frances thinks, I've got to get out of here."

Taking more time as she gently placed the cup on the tray, Jasmine tried to gather patience before she looked up at Rachel. "Have you thought about this? Really thought about this?"

"All night! I couldn't even sleep. But this is ridiculous. It's like I get out of one horrible situation and there's another one waiting for me. I can't take it anymore. So I might as well go home."

"That's not a good idea."

"So what do you think I should do? Go around Chicago looking for the thugs instead of having them look for me?"

"No," Jasmine said, trying to maintain her calm tone and volume. Last night, it had taken her hours to get Rachel settled after Mae Frances had made that grand announcement. She had wanted to slap her friend when she'd told Rachel that this wasn't over; she was sure Mae Frances knew that her words would set Rachel off.

This whole nightmare would have set Jasmine off a long time ago. Thugs and guns? Interrogation by the police? And now Mae Frances riding her all the time? This would have been all too much even for Jasmine to handle.

So with as much concern in her voice as she could muster, Jasmine said, "No, we're not looking for those guys. We're looking for the girlfriend."

Rachel threw her hands into the air. "You've got to be kidding me. We've been looking for this girlfriend and we don't have a thing to go on. We don't have a name, we don't have a telephone number, we don't have anything. Hell, I'm beginning to wonder if there really is a girlfriend."

"We do have something. We have a description. We know from Ms. Martha that she looks like you, and obviously, there's a reason those punks think you're her, too. They must have seen Pastor Griffith with her at some point. This all makes sense to me."

"None of it makes a bit of sense to me."

"For some reason, people think she's you, or you're her. I don't know. I just know that I'm right about this."

"Well, I don't care," Rachel said, shaking her head. "I've had enough. It's time for me to end this and go home."

"What makes you think that this will be over when you get back to Houston?"

"Maybe it won't be, but I'll be able to handle it better with Lester and my folks and the rest of my family. I need to be around people who love me." Jasmine's blank stare made her add, "I know you've been here for me, too, and I'm really grateful because I couldn't have gone through all of this without you. But Jasmine, I can't do it anymore."

Jasmine said nothing.

Rachel said, "I'm out. I'm sorry."

As Rachel moved away from her and

toward the door, Jasmine called out to her, but Rachel didn't turn around.

Jasmine sighed. Why was she fighting this? Maybe Rachel was right. Maybe they all needed to go home. Really, this wasn't her fight anyway and if Rachel wanted to go, then why should she stop her? She needed to get her butt on a plane and head home, too.

As she heard the hotel room door open, Jasmine stepped into the bedroom, but a second later, she heard Rachel gasp loudly.

Jasmine paused, frowned.

"Well, here you are, little lady."

It was Jasmine's turn to gasp. She eased the bedroom door closed, but kept it open enough to peek through.

"We've been looking for you," said the tall, lanky man whose arms swung long and low by his side.

But it was the short, muscular one that made Jasmine shiver. It was the man . . . and his gun that was pointed straight at Rachel's face.

Jasmine recognized the men right away since she'd seen them twice already.

"Where you been?" the short one asked as he jiggled the gun at Rachel.

"Nowhere, Mr. Muscle," Rachel cried.

Jasmine turned away from the door and

her eyes searched frantically for her purse. But she'd left it in the living room area of the suite.

Damn!

"You here by yourself?" Jasmine heard one of the men ask.

"Yeah," Rachel squeaked. "What do you want?"

"You know what we want."

Jasmine tiptoed across the carpet and grabbed the phone by the bed. Her cell would've been better — then she could've made the call from the bathroom. But she had no choice, she had to do it this way. She was sure the goons outside would hear her, but there was nothing else that she could do.

Pressing the button for the front desk, Jasmine began speaking the moment the phone was answered. "Help," she whispered.

"Yes, Mrs. Bush. How may I help you?"

"Please help. He has a gun. Please."

"A gun?"

"Yes, call the police," Jasmine said, speaking fast, so sure that the men would burst into the bedroom at any moment. She hung up and braced herself, but when she heard nothing, she tiptoed back to the door.

"That was a good trick you pulled." The one with the gun seemed to be doing all the talking now.

The two had Rachel pinned against the wall, their backs to Jasmine. Could she take them? She glanced around the room for a weapon, but saw nothing. And did she really want to hit the one with the gun upside his head? Suppose the gun, still pointed at Rachel, went off?

Rachel said, "What trick? I didn't do anything."

"Yeah, that trick where you and your boyfriend pretended that he was dead."

"How many times do I have to say this? He's not my boyfriend!"

It was the way Rachel cried, the way she trembled, that made Jasmine swing the door open. "Hey! What's going on here?" she asked, praying that hotel security would be right up and then the police would be behind them. "Who are you?"

The one without the gun said, "I'm Mike, but everybody calls me Bean."

The one with the gun swung around, but his eyes were on his friend. "Fool, why are you answering her question?" Then he aimed the gun straight at Jasmine's head. "And since I'm the one with the gun, I need you to tell me who are you?"

Jasmine crossed her arms as if she wasn't terrified. "This is my room and I'm the one asking questions."

"Uh, no, you're not," Bean told her as he grabbed her arm and pushed her against the wall next to Rachel. Then he grinned at Muscle as if he hoped that made up for what he'd said just seconds before.

"You think that little gun scares me?" Jasmine rolled her eyes, though she stayed pinned to the wall.

"Well, if it don't, then you dumber than you look," Muscle said, eyeing her up, then down. "So, who are you?"

"I'm a friend of Rachel's," Jasmine said, "and I want to know why you keep bothering her."

"Look, I'm the one with the gun," Muscle said as if Jasmine was getting on his nerves. "So I'm the one asking the questions, a'ight?"

"Fine, but why do you keep saying she's Pastor Griffith's girlfriend? 'Cause she's not."

Muscle threw his hands up in the air. "Do you hear this ho?" he said to Bean.

"Who you callin' a ho?" Jasmine said.

"You, ho! You need to keep your mouth shut 'cause I ain't playin' here." With the barrel of the gun, he pushed Jasmine back to the wall and Rachel grabbed her hand as if she was trying to calm Jasmine down.

"Don't get us killed," Rachel hissed.

"You better listen to this trick," Muscle said to Jasmine.

"Who you callin' a trick?" Rachel rolled her neck at him.

"These . . ." Muscle paused as if he was thinking about the right word to use this time, "these *ladies* just won't shut up," he said to Bean. Turning back to Jasmine and Rachel, he said, "But y'all need to listen to this." When they both stayed silent, Muscle nodded as if he felt he had control of the situation. "Now, I'm gonna say this and say this quick 'cause I don't trust you, heifer," he said, glancing at Jasmine.

When she opened her mouth as if she was going to protest, he pushed the gun barrel inside.

Rachel screamed.

"Look," Muscle said. "I ain't gonna hurt nobody. Not yet. But I'm sure you already called the police, right?"

There were tears in Jasmine's eyes as she tried to shake her head. But she didn't want to move too much. Not with the cold, hard metal of a gun in her mouth.

"We just need the money."

"We don't have your money," Rachel cried.

"Yeah, but your boyfriend does and we

know that you helped him get away."

"I don't know how many ways to say this. He's not my boyfriend, I don't have any money, I don't know where to get that kind of money, and I don't even know if Pastor Griffith is dead or alive."

"That's a whole lotta stuff that you don't know, but let me tell you what you need to know."

Rachel nodded. "All right, but please take that gun out of her mouth."

"As soon as I finish what I came to say, a'ight?"

Rachel nodded again.

Muscle said, "You need to tell your boyfriend to come back here with our boss's money or else you need to give my boss ten million dollars yourself."

"Where am I supposed to get that kind of money?" Rachel shrieked.

Muscle shrugged. "You a big-time businesswoman. Get it from one of your celebrity clients."

"Or didn't you say that your husband had a church," Bean piped in. "Ask him to give you some of that money he steals from the church every week."

When Bean and Muscle laughed, Jasmine closed her eyes. The tip of the gun was still pushed inside her mouth and the way

Muscle's shoulders shook as he laughed, Jasmine knew that with one move, her life would be over.

"You got one of 'em big churches?" Bean asked Rachel.

She shook her head. "But she does," she said, pointing at Jasmine.

Jasmine's eyes opened wide. Rachel was just gonna give her up like that?

But Jasmine didn't move. And then, Muscle removed the gun from her mouth.

Rachel sighed and Jasmine coughed, trying to get the taste of the metal off her tongue.

"You got a big church?" Bean asked Jasmine as if that was of great interest to him.

"Look, we don't have any more time," Muscle said. "I know this b—" and he stopped as if he didn't want to start another round with Jasmine and Rachel. "I know this *lady* probably done called the police or something."

"I didn't call —"

He stopped her. "I just need you to understand. You've got a week. The money or the man. Your choice." Muscle backed away. "And don't think you can run away. Wherever you go, we'll find you. Houston ain't that far away."

Then, as fast as they'd busted into Jasmine's room, they were gone.

Seconds passed, maybe even a minute before Jasmine and Rachel breathed.

"Oh, my God," Rachel said, hugging Jasmine. "I thought we were gonna die."

"Well, I thought I was gonna die when he put that gun in my mouth . . . and when you told him that I had the bigger church."

"I didn't mean to do that. I was just so scared."

"It doesn't matter now," Jasmine said, rushing to the phone.

"What are you gonna do? I don't think you should call the police."

"I already did that. At least I called the front desk when those goons first broke in. But now, I'm calling Mae Frances."

Rachel groaned. "What is she gonna do?"

Jasmine was shaking as she pressed the number to Mae Frances's room. "She's gonna help us." Turning to Rachel, she said, "I know who Pastor Griffith's girlfriend is. I know!"

Jasmine was sure that the police were going to pull them over with the way she was speeding, but she didn't care. Maybe the police could even help them, since the front desk at the hotel had never called 9-1-1. The clerk had thought Jasmine's call was a prank, just kids playing.

Jasmine shook her head just thinking about the way she'd wanted to kill the lady when she'd gone down to the lobby and found out that was why neither hotel security nor the Chicago police had come to rescue them.

"Are you sure? Are you sure?" Rachel asked, breaking through Jasmine's thoughts.

"I am," Jasmine said. She had such clarity now. It all made sense.

"I just can't believe it," Rachel said.

"Believe it," Mae Frances said from the backseat. "I've taught Jasmine Larson well and if she said it's Yvette, then it's Yvette."

Rachel shook her head. "Yvette's the girlfriend," she said, repeating what Jasmine had explained to her back at the hotel.

"Think about it," Jasmine said. "You guys are about the same age, you're the same height, you have the same coloring." She paused and glanced sideways at Rachel. "And until you got this new weave, you wore your hair almost the same way, too."

"I cannot believe anyone would get me mixed up with her," Rachel said. "I mean, I'm much cuter and I weigh at least thirty pounds less."

Jasmine held back her words and her laugh, but Mae Frances said what she'd been thinking. "In your dreams," Mae Frances cackled. "You should be flattered that someone thought you were that girl."

"What are you talking about?" Rachel said. "Have you ever seen Yvette?"

"I don't have to see her. I just know that she probably looks better than you."

Jasmine spoke before Rachel could respond. "But the biggest clue was what Muscle said." She prayed that changing the subject would keep the peace. She didn't need Rachel and Mae Frances fighting — this was a war that all three of them were going to have to fight together.

When Rachel said, "About the business," Jasmine knew that her plan had worked.

Jasmine nodded. "Who else do you know who has celebrity clients?"

"Lots of people," Rachel said. "It could be anyone in Chicago."

"Well, I just believe it's Yvette. Think about it, you said it was almost as if she wanted you to come back to Chicago, so she could've set you up."

"I was just sure that it was Cecelia." Rachel sighed.

"Me, too," Jasmine said. "But it's not, it's Yvette. They might be working together, but I'm sure the girlfriend is Yvette. Remember, she kept slipping and calling him Earl. Have you ever been compelled to call him by his first name?"

Rachel shook her head.

"Because you're not sleeping with him."

Rachel shivered in disgust like the mere thought repulsed her.

"It's all starting to add up," Jasmine said as she pulled the car to the curb a few yards away from the front door of Yvette's apartment building.

Jasmine and Rachel jumped out of the car and Mae Frances slid out of the back. As they dashed to the door, Mae Frances took her time.

"What's the rush?" she asked when she finally caught up to the other two. "Yvette will be here," she said, pulling her mink tighter.

But Jasmine wasn't paying any attention to her friend and she released a long breath when she saw Sherry, the concierge whom she and Rachel had met the last time they were here.

"Hey." Jasmine could hear Sherry's greeting through the front door before the concierge buzzed them in.

Her heart was pounding. This time, she had to get Sherry to let them go up to Yvette's apartment without being announced. She didn't want Yvette to have any time to prepare; she needed that element of surprise.

"How you ladies doing?" Sherry grinned at them.

"We're fine," Jasmine said, wishing that she'd discussed what she should say with at least Mae Frances. But she'd been so excited, so determined. And now . . .

"I hope you're not here to see your friend," Sherry volunteered before Jasmine could ask the first question.

"Why?" Jasmine, Rachel, and Mae Frances sang together.

"She's not here."

This time, the three released a long sigh together.

"Well, we'll just wait for her," Rachel said.

Sherry chuckled. "It's gonna be a long wait. She moved."

"Moved?" Now, the three sounded like a singing trio.

"Yeah, she moved to . . ." Sherry paused as she thought, "to the islands."

Jasmine groaned. "Which island?"

"The Virgin Islands."

"There are six islands," Mae Frances snapped as if the woman should know this. "Is it the U.S. or British Virgin Islands?"

Sherry looked stumped. "All I know is the Virgin Islands."

Jasmine said, "Well, she must have left a forwarding address."

"Yeah, she did. With the post office."

"Oh, my God!" Rachel exclaimed. "This is just a freakin' nightmare."

"I'm sorry," Sherry said. "And what's so bad, you just missed her mother . . ." She paused. "No, no, her godmother. She was just here cleaning out the apartment. She finished up about five minutes ago."

Dang! Jasmine thought. Five minutes. Of course, she didn't know Yvette's godmother, but she was sure she could've talked to her, found out much more than what Sherry knew.

"Are you sure you don't have any information about where Yvette moved to?" Jasmine asked.

"Yeah, this is really urgent," Rachel said. "It's a matter of life and death. Mine."

Sherry frowned.

"I mean," Rachel began to explain, "it feels that way."

Sherry shook her head. "I'm sorry."

"That's okay," Mae Frances said to Sherry, "you've been really helpful." To Jasmine and Rachel, she said, "Come on."

Jasmine shook her head. "I'm trying to think of something else . . ."

"Let's go," Mae Frances said quickly,

making Jasmine pause. Her friend knew something.

"Thanks again, Sherry," Jasmine said, as she pulled Rachel away from the desk.

"What?" Jasmine whispered to Mae Frances as they rushed out of the lobby. "What?"

"Let's just go to the car." Mae Frances spoke through lips that hardly moved.

Inside the car, Mae Frances said, "We're taking a trip."

Jasmine rolled her eyes. "Where? To the Virgin Islands? And what are we gonna do when we get there? Go around the islands looking for Yvette?"

"And you said yourself, there're six of them," Rachel said, sounding as frustrated as Jasmine.

"Are you two finished?"

Jasmine and Rachel said nothing.

Mae Frances said, "Now . . . we're going to the Virgin Islands."

Jasmine and Rachel groaned together.

"But we're not looking for just Yvette. I think Earl is there, too."

"What?" Jasmine and Rachel turned around in the car to face Mae Frances.

"I told you that back in the day Earl and I kicked it."

"*Kicked it?*" Rachel said. "Ewwww," she added as she turned around in her seat as if she could no longer stand to look at Mae Frances.

"Anyway, we're gonna check out the Virgin Islands, but not St. Thomas. No one would hide there. Especially not Earl. St. Thomas has too many people. It's too commercial. Someone on vacation might recognize him. We're going to St. John. Where he took me all those years ago."

The look in Mae Frances's eyes made Jasmine turn back around to the front of the car, too.

"So do you want to go and solve this, or should we all just go home?" Mae Frances asked.

Jasmine and Rachel glanced at each other and shrugged.

Mae Frances said, "I hope you got your credit cards because one of you is going to buy my ticket!"

CHAPTER THIRTY

Rachel stared out the window at the clear blue water as the plane touched down on the runway.

She still couldn't believe that within a matter of twenty-four hours, she'd been cleared of murder, accosted by thugs, and was now in a whole other country. Well, it might as well have been another country, even though Jasmine made sure to remind her that technically, the Virgin Islands wasn't "another country."

Lester had called to let her know that the board had narrowly voted to wait on the outcome of this whole mess before making any decisions, so that was good news. She stopped short of telling him that her name had been cleared because she knew the only thing he would want to hear after that was when she would be home, so she'd let him believe she still couldn't leave Chicago. That's why she'd prayed the entire way that the plane didn't crash. The last thing she needed was Lester getting a call that she died bound for the Virgin Islands. Luckily, the man sitting next to her had made small talk, putting her at ease. She'd groaned when he'd gotten on the plane just before the doors closed because she'd hoped to have the entire row to herself. But he'd turned out to be a welcome distraction as he talked about his excitement of seeing his family in the Virgin Islands.

Rachel glanced over at Mae Frances, who was leaning back in her first-class seat. Not only had she demanded a ticket in first class, she'd demanded two seats so no one could sit next to her because she was tired and "didn't feel like being bothered." That, in and of itself, was ludicrous to Rachel. She already thought first class was a complete and utter waste of money. First class got you to the same destination as coach for double the price. But Jasmine had paid for Mae Frances's tickets, then gotten one for herself without blinking. So naturally, Rachel had felt compelled to get one as well. Lester was going to have a conniption when the bill came. But he would just have to get over it.

The jolt of the plane touching down snapped her out of her thoughts. It also woke up both Mae Frances and Jasmine. How they could relax was beyond Rachel. But then again, it wasn't their life on the line.

"Whew, it's hot," Mae Frances said as she stepped off the plane and onto the tarmac.

"That grizzly bear you're wearing might have something to do with it," Rachel mumbled. Mae Frances cut her eyes and Rachel flashed an apologetic look.

"Where to now?" Rachel said once they were in the cab.

"We go get checked in at the hotel. Then we go by Earl's."

"That sounds like a plan." Rachel had no idea what they would do when they got there, but she knew she'd drag that man kicking and screaming back to Chicago if she had to. She not only wanted to prove he wasn't dead so the D.A. couldn't accuse her of having anything to do with his disappearance, but she also was going to demand he give the drug dealers back their money or she'd tell them where to find him. That is, if they could even find him.

They got checked into their five-star hotel, and it was a good thing Jasmine had a black American Express card because Mae Frances had insisted on a top-of-the-line room — at their expense. Rachel was about to protest when Jasmine shook her head. "I got it," Jasmine said, handing the clerk the card. "Let's just meet back down in the lobby in fifteen minutes."

In the room, Rachel dropped her bag, used the restroom, and headed right back downstairs. She didn't want to waste any more time. She still ended up waiting another twenty minutes, but finally Mae Frances and Jasmine made their way back downstairs. They hailed a cab and headed to the secluded address Mae Frances had recited to the driver.

As they pulled up to the bungalow nestled in the back of a wooded area, Rachel had to once again give Mae Frances her props. No way would they have ever found this place on their own.

Rachel's heart raced as she beat on the front door. What if this was a wild-goose chase? What if Pastor Griffith really was dead? Rachel didn't know what she would do if all of this turned out to be for nothing.

"What now?" Rachel said, after no one answered the door. Defeat registered all over her face.

Mae Frances turned and marched back toward the cab. "I'm going to eat."

"We don't have time to eat," Rachel said,

following after her.

Mae Frances didn't break her stride. "Is Earl here?"

"Well, no, but we can go look for them," Rachel said.

"You can go look all you want. I'm not about to go traipsing all around this island looking for them. Jasmine Larson, you know I get grumpy when I don't eat."

"Fine, let's make sure we feed the animal," Rachel muttered.

Mae Frances stopped and spun toward her. "Look, little girl," she said, waving a finger in Rachel's face. "I'm doing *you* a favor. There's no one after me. There's no one waiting to blow my brains out on the steps of my church. So unless you want me to march right back to that airport and get back on the plane —"

"Okay, okay," Rachel interrupted. "I'm sorry. I'm just stressed out."

"Well, I don't care how stressed you are, you need to learn a little respect for people that are trying to help you out."

"You're right," Rachel admitted. As much as she couldn't stand this old lady, they wouldn't be here if it wasn't for Mae Frances, so she needed to show the woman her respect. "I'm sorry."

Mae Frances looked taken aback, but she

forced a tight smile. "Well, thank you. Maybe there's hope for you yet." She spun and walked off. "Of course, I doubt it," she mumbled.

Jasmine flashed an apologetic expression, but Rachel just shrugged as they both followed Mae Frances back out to the taxi.

At the restaurant, Mae Frances insisted that they sit in a shaded, secluded area in the back of the restaurant. Then it took her almost three hours to eat. She feasted like she was at the Last Supper, slowly nibbling her food, sipping tea, and acting like they were on a nice, leisurely vacation. Even Jasmine was getting irritated.

"Can we go now?" Rachel said, no longer able to hold in her frustration.

Mae Frances sipped the last of her hot tea, set the cup down, then asked, "Tell me something, Raquel."

"Mae Frances, you know her name is Rachel," Jasmine chided.

Mae Frances feigned an apologetic look, and continued. "Tell me something, Rachel. You and Jasmine all buddy-buddy now, right?"

Rachel looked to Jasmine for confirmation and Jasmine nodded. "We are," Rachel said.

"Well, I think you should know Jasmine let you win the election."

"Mae Frances!" Jasmine gasped, sitting straight up in her seat. Mae Frances leaned back and sipped some more tea.

Rachel lost her smile as she turned to Jasmine. Mae Frances was crazy, but Rachel had quickly learned that everything she did was calculated — and usually right on the money. "I won the election fair and square." She narrowed her eyes at Jasmine. "Right, Jasmine?"

Jasmine shot Mae Frances the evil eye. "I can't believe you."

"Jasmine, what is she talking about?" At one point, Jasmine had alluded to her being the reason Lester won, but Rachel had thought she was just blowing smoke.

"Tell her," Mae Frances demanded. "BFFs shouldn't keep secrets."

Jasmine rolled her eyes. "Why are you doing this?"

Mae Frances shook her head in disgust. "Because, whether you two want to admit it or not — and it pains me to say this — you work well together. And if you're going to be hanging around each other from now on, I think you need to start on a clean and truthful slate."

"Since when did you become the bearer of truth?" Jasmine snapped.

"Since," Mae Frances glanced at her gold

watch, "about thirteen seconds ago. Now tell the girl the truth."

"Yes, Jasmine, tell me the truth," Rachel said with an icy stare.

Jasmine released a heavy sigh and began the story of how she'd found out about Pastor Griffith being involved in drugs and wanting to funnel drug money through the ABC, so she'd sabotaged the race to make sure Hosea had lost.

Rachel was dumbfounded by the time Jasmine had finished her story. "Are you freakin' kidding me?" She looked back over to Mae Frances. The look on her face told Rachel that Jasmine was being one hundred percent truthful. "So you set Lester up?"

"Huh? What?" Jasmine said, shocked. "I didn't set anyone up. I just wanted to make sure Hosea wasn't caught up in that mess."

"Who cares about *my* husband? You were just gonna let the drug lords use him!" Rachel stood and balled her fist up. Her blood was starting to boil. She was ready to cold-cock Jasmine in the eye, regardless of how far they'd come.

"Calm down, Laila Ali," Mae Frances said.

Jasmine and Rachel faced each other in a stare-off as Mae Frances continued. "Now, Rachel, would you really have believed Jasmine if she had come to you back then and said, 'Hey, Pastor Griffith is involved in some shady stuff so you might want to get Lester to drop out of the race'?"

Rachel paused. Of course, she wouldn't have. She would've sworn it was just one of Jasmine's low-down dirty tricks.

"Jasmine was just scared for the safety of her own husband and back then, she didn't give a flying flip about you."

Rachel poked her lips out in a tight frown.

"And you didn't give a flying flip about her," Mae Frances added.

"But —"

"But nothing," Mae Frances snapped. "You would've done the exact same thing."

"No . . ." Rachel stopped when Jasmine cut her eyes Rachel's way. Rachel slunk back in her chair. "Okay, maybe I would have."

"Exactly."

Jasmine finally spoke up. "Rachel, I never wanted to put Lester in harm's way. I just didn't want Hosea involved in any way. And honestly, I had no idea that Pastor Griffith was in as deep as he is."

Rachel just stared at her.

"Rachel, I'm really sorry."

Rachel wanted to be mad, to go off, but Mae Frances was right. She would've done the exact same thing. If she had found out

Lester was in danger, she wouldn't have wanted him involved, either. Suddenly, so much made sense. Why Pastor Griffith was always up in ABC business. Why he had demanded a slot on the board. Why he'd been insistent that Marcus Brewer keep his post as treasurer. Since Marcus was Pastor Griffith's right-hand man, that would allow him to stay close so he could keep funneling drug money.

"So, you good?" Mae Frances asked, breaking the uncomfortable silence.

Rachel shrugged nonchalantly. "I'm cool."

"Are you sure?" Jasmine asked.

Rachel nodded. "But let's be clear, we would've won regardless."

Jasmine looked like she wanted to say something sarcastic, but she held her tongue. "Anything's possible," she managed to say.

"Well, just don't let that mess happen again," Rachel said, finally breaking a small smile.

Jasmine nodded. She seemed relieved that Rachel wasn't upset. "You're my girl now, so I got your back."

"Yeah, you do," Rachel admitted.

Rachel didn't know what came over her, but she actually reached over and squeezed Jasmine's hands.

"Are we done?" Mae Frances interjected. They both said, "We're fine."

"Good," Mae Frances said casually, "because Earl is a creature of habit. And I knew it was just a matter of time." She motioned toward a corner table and Rachel almost fell over when she saw a hostess seating Pastor Griffith at a table. Well, it looked like Pastor Griffith. Rachel had to lean in closer because this man was completely bald and actually looked twenty pounds heavier than Pastor Griffith. But when Rachel saw the woman next to him, all doubt was erased. She had on a long, jet-black wig, but that was definitely Yvette Holloway. She had on a blue-and-white maxi dress and a big floppy designer hat. Pastor Griffith wore a tan button-down shirt and some Bermuda shorts. They looked relaxed — like a loving couple on vacation.

"Oh, my God!" Rachel gasped. She couldn't believe her life was near ruins over this man and he was chillin' in the Virgin Islands! "What do we do?" she whispered, raising her menu to hide her face.

Mae Frances pushed the menu down. "You stop looking suspicious for starters. I had them sit us over in this corner for a reason," she snapped.

"So what are we going to do?" Jasmine

repeated.

Mae Frances shrugged. "I did my part." She leaned back and sipped her tea some more.

"Anything I can get you ladies?" the waitress asked, approaching the table.

Suddenly, Rachel had an idea.

"I'd like a refill on my tea," Mae Frances said.

Rachel reached in her purse and grabbed two twenty-dollar bills. "Actually, I do need something." She slid the money toward the waitress.

Ten minutes later, Rachel stood over Pastor Griffith and Yvette, an apron covering her body and a menu shielding her face. "Hello, dere," she said in the best Caribbean accent she could muster. "You want to see de drink menu?"

Pastor Griffith chuckled as he took Yvette's hand. "Nah, we know what we want. Margarita for me and Sex on the Beach for my wife."

"Wife!" Rachel said, losing her accent and dropping the menu.

Both Pastor Griffith and Yvette looked up at Rachel, the smiles immediately leaving their faces when they recognized her.

"Rachel!" Yvette said. "Wh-what are you doing here?"

Out of nowhere, Jasmine appeared by Rachel's side.

"Jasmine?"

"I think the question is what are *you* doing here?" Jasmine spat.

"You bastard," Rachel hissed. "You tried to set me up for your murder." She pointed at Yvette. "And you helped him! And all along, you were plotting some grand getaway?"

"It-it's not what it seems," Pastor Griffith stammered.

"Oh, it's exactly what it seems!" Rachel said. "I'm calling the cops." She was so furious, she wasn't even going to try to reason with him to come home. She just wanted him *under* the jail. Pastor Griffith jumped up to stop Rachel just as she turned to stomp away.

"Wait!" he pleaded. "Rachel, it's not like that. We never intended to set you up. We just needed to get out of town. I was in with some bad people. They were the ones that hit me over the head that day. They weren't trying to kill me then, but it was just a matter of time."

"So you decided to make it seem like you were dead anyway and try to frame me for it," Rachel spat.

"It wasn't me," he said. "It was Cecelia

who wanted to lay the blame on you."

"Earl!" Yvette snapped.

He turned toward her. Nervousness blanketed his face. "Shut up, Yvette! I told you having your godmother involved was just going to create problems!" He turned back to Rachel, a pleading expression across his face. "Rachel, I got involved in some really bad stuff and the only way I could come out alive was to pretend to be dead. I had nothing to do with you getting involved. That was all Cecelia, who saw an opportunity to pin something on you when you showed up at the *Oprah* show."

Rachel was floored. "Cecelia really wanted to pin a murder on her?"

"Cecelia sent the blackmail letter to scare you, turned the cops on to you, all of that was her doing. She was behind all of this, trying to get your husband voted out," he said frantically.

"Earl, I can't believe you!" Yvette cried.

He ignored her and continued pleading. "Rachel, I just wanted out. I didn't want you involved. They were trying to kill me and I just needed to get out." He reached in his pocket, then lowered his voice. "Now I'm not even going to question how you found me. I just want to know how much it's gonna take to get you ladies to just turn around, get on a plane, and forget you ever saw us." He actually pulled out a wad of cash and extended it toward Rachel.

"We don't want your dirty money!" Jasmine said.

Rachel's eyes bulged at the sight of the cash. Man, she could do a whole lot with that money. Of course, she'd give her ten percent to the church, but she could finally buy her a new wardrobe, add on that private office she wanted, get that new Benz . . .

"Ummm, Rachel," Jasmine said, nudging her, "tell him we don't want his dirty money."

"We don't?" Rachel whispered to Jasmine, then quickly shook off her daze. "I mean, we don't!"

"Come on," Pastor Griffith said, pulling another stack of money out of his pocket. "Everyone has a price."

"Not us," Jasmine said defiantly.

Rachel hesitated, but then said, "Yeah, not us."

Yvette finally stood. "Ladies, I am so sorry. I never meant for things to escalate out of control, but I'm begging you. They will kill us if they find us."

Rachel was just about to say something when she heard a raspy voice say, "You are definitely right about that." Rachel turned around to see the man she'd sat next to on the plane.

It was obvious from the horror on both Yvette's and Earl's faces that this was the kingpin, or at least he was high on the totem pole.

"Hector, ummm, I, ummm," Earl began, his eyes filled with fear.

Hector immediately held up a hand to stop him. "Ummm, no. If I were you, I wouldn't talk right now."

Earl immediately shut up. Hector turned to Rachel and Jasmine. "You two super sleuths did well." He took Rachel's hand and kissed it. "I must apologize to you, beautiful lady, as I thought you were her." He pointed to Yvette. "And while you bear a striking resemblance, you are so much more beautiful."

Something about this man now gave her the creeps. He was short, but his demeanor was powerful. While he'd seemed nice on the plane, he now had the eyes of a killer. And for all the charm he was exhibiting right now, Rachel couldn't help but feel the coldness that flowed through his body as he held her hand.

"But your services are no longer needed," Hector continued, motioning toward the entrance to the restaurant. "My associates and I can take it from here."

Rachel looked back to see Muscle and Bean posted up at the door. How had they followed her and she hadn't seen them? At this point, it was an answer she no longer cared to know. She only wanted to know one thing.

"So am I good? You won't be bothering me or my family?" she asked.

Hector flashed a smile. The smile of a killer. "You're good, my lady. As long as you don't mention us to anyone, we won't be bothering you again. My debt is about to be settled."

Rachel couldn't be sure but she thought she heard Pastor Griffith gulp. "Mention who?" Rachel said quickly. "I don't know you."

"Yeah," Jasmine chimed in. "We don't know nothin' about nothin'."

Hector's grin widened. "Good. Let's keep it that way. Well, have a safe trip home, unless you plan to stay and enjoy this beautiful island."

"Oh no, we're going home," Rachel quickly said.

"Please don't leave us," Yvette whispered, her voice shaky.

"Shhhh," Hector said, putting his finger to his lips. "You make this easy and come with us, or we just end this here and now, then go back to Chicago and take care of that crackhead daughter of yours," he said, looking at Pastor Griffith, "and I'm sure it wouldn't be difficult to find your family," he said to Yvette.

That silenced the both of them and Rachel and Jasmine took their cues.

"I'll pray for you," Rachel said to Yvette, then darted toward the door.

"Try the Twenty-Third Psalm. That might come in handy," Jasmine added as she quickly followed Rachel out.

Rachel had never been so glad to be headed home, and that airplane couldn't come fast enough. She was anxious to get back home to the serenity of her house and her life. She was thankful that she'd had the opportunity to bond with Jasmine, but the next time she saw Jasmine, she hoped it was over lunch at a church business meeting. And the next time she found out Jasmine was getting anything she wasn't, she was just going to let Jasmine have it!

"Well, we're all set," Jasmine said, walking back over to Rachel's seat. "Our plane is about to board, so we just made it."

Rachel smiled when she saw Mae Frances with her fur draped across her arm. The old woman had finally taken that thing off. "I still can't believe you left us at that restaurant," Rachel said.

"Shoot, it looked like there was about to be trouble," Mae Frances said unapologetically. "And I gave up trouble for Lent."

Jasmine and Rachel giggled.

"Besides, I knew Cagney and Lacey were on the case, so you didn't need me. I just thought I'd go wait in a cab outside."

"Well, I have a question," Rachel said. "How did you know Pastor Griffith was going to be at that restaurant?"

"Gil called me back, finally," she answered. "He said they were actually on to Earl, Hector, and that whole drug cartel. Seems Earl had turned state's witness and when he found out Hector was on to him, he decided to skip town — with Hector's money. Then when that lady at Yvette's said she'd gone to the Virgin Islands, I knew exactly where he was. Earl has had a secret place here for years. And I knew it was just a matter of time before he showed up at his favorite restaurant."

"Well, why didn't you fill us in?" Rachel asked.

"Because you, Rachel Jackson, are just as hardheaded as this one over here," she said, motioning toward Jasmine. "You would've been worrying me to death until he showed up and I wanted to enjoy my dinner in peace."

Rachel couldn't even be mad at the old woman. "Well, I can't thank you enough," she said.

"Don't. I helped you, but I still don't like you," Mae Frances said. But Rachel could see the corner of her mouth fighting off a smile.

"Unh-huh, that's because you don't know me," Rachel said.

"I know you. And I won't ever trust you as far as I can see you."

"Don't pay her any attention," Jasmine said. "I trust you, and that's all that matters."

They hugged as Mae Frances rolled her eyes.

"The sinners trying to act like saints." She shook her head. "All this mushy stuff is getting on my nerves. Jasmine Larson, can we go please before I miss this flight? I —"

Before she could finish, Rachel stole a quick peck on the cheek. Mae Frances looked shocked, like no one had ever kissed her. She touched her face, then frowned. "Oh, Lord, now I got to go get a tetanus shot." She turned and marched toward the airplane.

Jasmine and Rachel stood in an awkward silence. Finally, Rachel said, "Well, I'd like to say it's been great . . ."

"But it hasn't," Jasmine said, finishing her sentence for her.

"At least something did come out of it," Rachel said, smiling. "We make a helluva team."

"That we do," Jasmine said, returning her smile.

"Maybe Mae Frances is right. Maybe we should go into business, some type of detective agency."

Jasmine looked at her like she was crazy. "And on that note . . ."

"You're right," Rachel said, "maybe we should stick to being first ladies."

"Yeah . . . at least for now," Jasmine added. "But don't worry, if I know you, drama is never too far behind."

Rachel put her hand on her hip and cocked her head to the side. Jasmine grinned. "Okay, if I know *us,* drama is never too far behind."

"Thank you," Rachel said.

"So until the next big adventure, be good."

They were about to embrace again when a voice boomed over the PA system, "Jasmine Larson, this plane is leaving with or without you! So bring your butt on!"

They both glanced over to see Mae Frances at the counter, with the speaker in her hand.

"How — ?"

"Don't even ask," Jasmine said, holding up a hand.

Rachel stopped herself. Mae Frances had managed to take over the PA system just like she managed everything else in life — by ways no one would ever be able to explain.

"I'll be in touch," Rachel called after her.

Jasmine waved as she boarded her plane and Rachel felt a twinge in her heart as she was hit with a revelation she never in a million years ever would've believed — she already missed Jasmine Cox Larson Bush and couldn't wait until the two of them met again.

READERS GROUP GUIDE
FRIENDS & FOES

RESHONDA TATE BILLINGSLEY AND VICTORIA CHRISTOPHER MURRAY

Introduction

First ladies — and first enemies — Jasmine Bush and Rachel Adams are together again in the sequel to *Sinners & Saints* by ReShonda Tate Billingsley and Victoria Christopher Murray. Spurred by jealousy, Rachel sets out for Chicago with the seemingly simple motive of preventing Jasmine from appearing on *Oprah.* However, Rachel's scheming quickly lands her in a whole lot more trouble than she bargained for. As a plot full of twists, turns, and even murder unfolds, Jasmine and Rachel are forced to rely on and trust each other in order to save their lives. With a healthy dose of humor, Jasmine and Rachel discover they not only make a surprisingly good team, but good friends as well.

QUESTIONS AND TOPICS
FOR DISCUSSION

1. Jasmine and Rachel go head-to-head with their schemes throughout *Friends & Foes.* Who do you think is the better schemer? Why?

2. Rachel and Jasmine seem to contradict at times with what one expects from a pastor's wife. How are their actions reconciled with their beliefs?

3. What role do you think spirituality plays in each character's life? What would you say is the difference between Rachel's and Jasmine's beliefs? What about Pastor Griffith's?

4. In what ways are Rachel and Jasmine similar and in what ways are they different? Which of the two do you identify with most?

5. When exactly do you think Jasmine and Rachel started to feel that they could trust each other? When do you think they started becoming friends?

6. Do you think Rachel and Jasmine will remain friends, or will their old feelings toward each other take center stage again?

7. Why do you think Mae Frances had such a difficult time accepting Rachel?

8. Jasmine seems to look up to Mae Frances as a sort of godmother. In what way is Jasmine like Rachel's godmother?

9. What do you think happened to Pastor Griffith and Yvette in the end? Should Jasmine and Rachel have left them in the Virgin Islands?

10. What other adventures would you like to see Rachel and Jasmine embark on together?

11. Humans are imperfect beings and possess natural flaws. What are Rachel's and Jasmine's flaws, and how do they play into the story?

12. Which friend would you trust in an adventure like the one Rachel and Jasmine have in *Friends & Foes*? Do you have a frenemy you think would make a good partner to go through this sort of ordeal with?

ENHANCE YOUR BOOK CLUB

1. Interested in the backstory of how Jasmine and Rachel became sworn rivals? Read the first book in the series, *Sinners & Saints,* for your next meeting. Discuss how the characters have evolved in *Friends & Foes.*

2. Have your book club over for an Oprah Winfrey–inspired pajama party. You can reminisce about your favorite shows and watch the OWN network while you celebrate your own "favorite things."

3. For all the levity throughout the book, drugs provide a sobering backdrop for *Friends & Foes.* Organize a few hours for your book club to volunteer at a local church that has community outreach activities, such as working at a soup kitchen or helping out at a shelter.